"I have to go.

She edged out of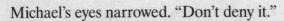

"Shanna."

"No," she said firm... ...that have happened."

Michael's eyes narrowed. "Don't deny it."

"I'm not denying anything. I'm saying we are not doing this again. Ever."

"Why?"

"Because we don't fit, jive, dance, you name it."

"Dance?"

"Compatibility, Mike. Admit it. We seldom agree. We live at opposite ends of the social scale. You're my employer, and—" her voice rose on the last reason "—we don't even like each other."

"You don't like me?"

"I like you," she said, her heart sore. "Very much." *Too much.*

Available in May 2006 from Silhouette Special Edition

A Forever Family

MARY J FORBES

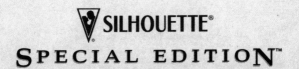

SILHOUETTE®

SPECIAL EDITION™

First published in Great Britain 2006
Silhouette Books, Eton House, 18-24 Paradise Road,
Richmond, Surrey TW9 1SR

© Mary J Forbes 2004

ISBN 0 373 24625 0

23-0506

Printed and bound in Spain
by Litografia Rosés S.A., Barcelona

MARY J FORBES

grew up on a farm in Alberta amidst horses, cattle (Holsteins included), crisp hay and broad blue skies. As a child, she drew and wrote about her surroundings and in sixth grade composed her first story about a lame little pony. Since those days, she has worked as a reporter and photographer on a small-town newspaper and has written and published short fiction.

Today, Mary—a teacher by profession—lives in beautiful British Columbia with her husband and two children. A romantic by nature, she loves working along the ocean shoreline, sitting by the firs on snowy or rainy evenings and two-stepping around the dance floor to a good country song—all with her own real-life hero, of course.

To Gary:
You taught me to not only dream,
but to *believe*.
To Kristie and Ryan:
Your faith in me is astounding.
I love you all beyond comprehension.

ACKNOWLEDGEMENTS:

Thank you to Dr Franky Mah
for his expertise in emergency and medical
care. Any errors are purely mine, not his.
Also, a huge thank-you to Cindy Procter-King
for hauling me up each time I fell and
scraped my writing fingers.

Chapter One

He looked the way a man would, catching a woman's scent.

Except he wasn't a man, but a horse. A red stallion. One that had caught *her* scent. He raised his angular chin a notch, dark eyes skeptical, as she approached the long, narrow paddock.

His muscled quarter-horse haunches quivered. In arrogant defiance, he tossed his head.

Shanna McKay took another step toward him. *Flee or charge, big fella?*

She wasn't afraid. And knew he sensed that.

Whatever it took, she wanted the horse's owner to see she loved big, domestic animals. When her hand caressed the stallion's coat, she wanted the owner to recognize her skill and knowledge.

Her steps slowed.

Manure, dust and cut clover tracked through the late June

air. A fly whirred past her face. The stallion's lips tightened, its ears flattened. He stood transfixed.

She held out a hand. "Hey, big boy."

Nose lifting higher, his eyes widened.

"What the hell are you doing?"

At the thundering voice the stallion galloped away, its elegant sorrel head swinging side to side, its tail glinting in the westerly sun like a sheaf of prairie grain.

Shanna darted a look over her shoulder and considered high-tailing it across the pasture to join her equine partner. The man standing opposite the gate was not who she'd expected. All six-feet-plus of him in tailored dark trousers and linen shirt, he stared at her as if she'd called his mother a foul name.

"Oh." She purged the instinct to set a hand to her throat the way Jane Eyre might have done with Mr. Rochester. "I didn't hear you."

"Obviously." He opened the gate and stalked toward her. "What're you doing rubbing noses with an animal you don't know?"

"I was—" If the animal she'd surveyed moments ago had taken on a human persona, it would have been this man—from his dense, saddle-burnished hair to his spit-and-shine loafers. "I was introducing myself to him."

"He bites."

"It's all right, I know horses." This man couldn't be the foreman, not dressed like that. Was he the M. Nelson from the newspaper ad?

"You know horses. Huh." His chilled gray eyes cut to the stallion watching them from the middle of the small pasture, red-gold on jade-green. "You're out of your league with him, miss."

"Shanna. Shanna McKay. For what it's worth, I've lived around horses most of my life." She looked at him pointedly, considered her options and, as usual, tossed them aside. "I know to approach with caution and a soft voice the first time."

The man's eyes cut back to her. A small pock to the right of his upper lip whitened. "Are you saying I didn't? For *what it's worth*, Ms. McKay, I'm not completely ignorant when it comes to approaching stallions, or any horse for that matter."

"Know what, I was about to leave. It was nice meeting you." *This* particular job she did not need. There were others. Dammit, there *had* to be. Jobs where people were less abrasive and the money-men more congenial.

She stepped past him.

"Just a minute." He blocked her path. "Why are you here?"

Ignoring his knife-edged cheekbones and grim jaw, she looked square into the steel of his eyes. "I came about the job advertised in the paper."

The man blinked once, clear shock on his face. "*You* want to milk *cows?*"

If it meant keeping a roof over her brother's head and money in his college fund. She hiked her chin. "I have experience."

He scanned her body. "A little slip like you? Shoving around thousand-pound cows?" A soft chuckle. "I don't think so."

"I'm not a slip. I'm five eight and weigh—"

"One-twenty."

Her turn to blink.

"I'm a doctor. I know the human body."

He was…*Michael Rowan?* Top surgeon at Blue Springs General? Well, no doubt he knew the female body best of all, then. With that face, he probably had a different girlfriend every weekend.

"You need to eat more," he continued, jerking her rumination off balance. "You're at least fifteen pounds underweight."

"Excuse me?" So she didn't eat properly half the time. He didn't know her life. Didn't know she slogged every night at her accounting courses. Of her need for a career, a stable source of income. Dr. Michael Rowan knew nothing about her.

His eyes softened abruptly. "I apologize. Bad habit I have, giving unwanted medical advice. Need to curb that." A tiny smile altered the line at the edge of his mouth.

She nodded. "Just tell me where I can find M. Nelson." In minutes she'd be out of his hair, out of his life.

"She's out of town."

"Your foreman's a woman?"

"No foreman. My grandmother." In a placid state his eyes were dull silver. "A combination of family names as well as ownership. I didn't want the clinic staff hounded with a bunch of calls." He tilted his head, a pleat between his black brows. "You were to answer the ad through *The Blue Sentinel*."

Her face warmed. She had wanted to impact with charm, wit and intelligence. Face-to-face. Michael Rowan, she saw, was not a man easily impacted. "Well," she said. "I'm probably late, anyway." The ad had run in three issues of the biweekly paper.

He studied the horse in the distance. "How'd you know it was Rowan Dairy?"

"Word gets around."

Weariness marked his eyes as he studied her. Scraping his hands down stubbled cheeks, he released pent-up air. "Again, my apologies." He held out a hand. "Michael Rowan." His fingers wrapped around hers, warm and firm. His look wrapped around her heart, cool and steady. She let go.

"I know. We went to the same high school." The way

his eyebrows took flight had her lips twitching. "I was beginning middle school when you graduated."

"McKay... The name's familiar. Have you been to the clinic?"

"I don't get sick."

"Live around here, then?"

"In Blue Springs."

"I see." He tucked his hands into the pockets of his black dress pants and looked at her as if he could see beyond her skin, into her body. Into *her*.

She turned toward the knapsack sitting in the dirt by the gate. Hoisting the bag to her shoulder, she said, "I need this job, Doctor Rowan. Are you hiring?"

"That depends."

"On?"

His hands came free of their pockets. Dust scuffed his shoes as he walked toward her. "On your expertise."

"Four years, three months."

He opened the gate, held it. She passed through. An efficient tug, a thunk of the wooden bar and it closed behind them. "Come up to the house," he said. "Might as well get this over with, right now."

"Over with?"

A sigh. "When you're applying for a job, Ms. McKay, the employer—me—needs to ask some questions. But, I'm not doing it with horse dung on my shoes."

A tobacco-brown smudge clung to the side of his left loafer. Rolling her lips inward, she looked to the pasture where the stallion grazed, picture-perfect in the distance. *I'm not afraid of you. Or your famous owner.*

"Ms. McKay. If it's all the same to you, I'd like to eat tonight before I go to bed. I've had a long day."

"Sorry," she said. "I have a habit of—"

With a crisp turn, he strode off.

Daydreaming.

So much for conversation. She watched him go. Each cant of his succinct hips plied tiny creases into the fine, white shirt at his belt. He had those streamlined Tiger Woods buttocks. And long, long legs—which, at the moment, wolfed up ground.

The job, Shanna. You need the job. Remember that.

She hurried after him.

The trail wound through a hundred yards of spruce, cedar and birch. The trees blocked the barnyard from a two-story yellow farmhouse. Why hadn't she noticed it before, this century-old Colonial—its tall windows and ample verandah strung with boxes of red and white geraniums overlooking paddock and pasture? No front lawn. Instead, a cornucopia of lush, leafy produce—beans, peas, onions, carrots, potatoes, squash and corn—fanned toward the pastures. Behind the house, the forested hill rose rapidly. She imagined its warm, emerald quilt of Douglas fir offered cozy vistas in bleaker seasons.

They crossed the driveway where the final rays of the day's sun glossed a black Jeep Cherokee. Her dented two-toned silver pickup remained down at the barn where she'd parked it, drawn first to the farm's animals instead of to its people.

The doctor walked down a flagstone path along the side of the house, to the rear door. There, from a cement stoop, he tossed his shoes to the grass. He held open the door. "Come in."

Leaving her pack, she toed off her sandals and followed. The mudroom was neat and compact while the adjoining large, bright kitchen supported a greenhouse window she inherently loved.

The living section…

Oh, my.

A wood-beamed ceiling spanned a sunken room. Ebbing daylight spilled from wide, tall windows and warmed a bouquet of lemon oil. At the base of an oak staircase, hung a woman's painted portrait. Her resolved, dark beauty emanated power.

"Ms. McKay?"

She jerked around. He stood in a small study, watching her. How long had he been waiting?

"Your home is lovely," she told him, meaning it.

"Thank you." He gestured to the den's single leather chair. "Please. Sit down."

From the rolltop desk he picked up a pen and a black notebook, then settled on the window seat, ankle on knee. Scribbling in the booklet, he waited until she eased onto the dough-soft seat where she kept her back straight, her feet planted, and her fingers loosely laced in her lap. She curbed the urge to touch the three staggered dream catchers swinging from her ears.

Confidence, Shanna.

"Where did you gain your dairy experience?"

"Lasser Farm."

He nodded. "I know it."

She imagined he did. The childless Lassers had called Washington's Whatcom County home for twenty years. "I started working for Caleb and Estelle when I was fifteen."

"You didn't finish school?" He sounded a bit horrified.

She smiled. "Of course I graduated. My brother Jason and I boarded with the Lassers while my dad—"

She wanted to observe the doctor's face. She knew why he'd offered her the chair. Shadows and light. He sat in the former, she sat in the latter.

"Yes?" he prompted.

"My dad was a saddle bronc rider. He followed the rodeo circuit." *Still does, like an old hound chasing rabbits in his sleep.*

For a moment Michael Rowan remained silent, then he

smiled, small and quick. It tempered the line of his jaw. Soothed his eyes. Doctor-to-patient kind, those eyes.

"Ah," he said. "McKay. Of course. Your father assaulted an orderly a while back for making him go through a difficult therapeutic maneuver."

No pity, Doctor. My father's conduct no longer matters. Liar.

She said, "Brent—my dad—cracked four ribs at the Cloverdale Rodeo up in British Columbia. The doctors ordered him not to ride that summer. He…he didn't take it well." True to form, he'd raved and cussed. Didn't they know he'd lose six months of winnings? He was a cowboy, for Pete's sake, a man tough as nails. A couple beat-up bones wouldn't stop him, no sirree.

But in the end they had. At least for those six months.

She continued, "He, um, took a job with the Lassers." Manna from heaven, when compared to the days—weeks— she and Jase had lived on stale cheese, chips and Krispy Kreme doughnuts. "Caleb developed angina that year and needed help." Turned out the couple had helped her and Jase far more. Loving them on sight. Opening their home and hearts with grace and compassion. Raising them as Brent had not.

Dr. Rowan jotted notes. "How many cows were they milking?"

"Forty. Some years forty-five."

"We have ninety-two. A small outfit compared to some, but…" He studied her face.

She squared her shoulders. "I can handle it."

Again, he gave her a slow, visual once-over. A small burn flickered in her belly. She wanted to leave the chair, tell him to move the interview to the living room where she could read his dark, enigmatic eyes. Equal ground. Person to person. Aspirant to interviewer. Not this…this man-woman thing.

"How strong are you?"

"Beg pardon?"

"Can you lift a five-gallon bucket of oats?"

"Yes."

When he made a point of studying her arms, her skin flashed with heat. She should have worn a long-sleeved blouse. Or a sweatshirt. What had she been thinking to pull on this silky white tank top and this flowery skirt? Hurry, that's what. Hurry to look good. To impress the employer. To look professional.

Well, no amount of hurrying would get her wiry muscles or, for that matter, pretty feminine limbs. *Sorry, Doctor. You're stuck with these long, skinny ones.*

Annoyed at her self-criticism and his scrutiny, she asked, "Do you think because I'm a woman I'm not suited for the job?"

His eyes whipped to hers. "It has nothing to do with you being a woman."

Then why the fitness quiz? "I assure you, Doctor Rowan, I can handle a bucket of grain. *And* a few cud-chewers."

Silence hung like a weight.

She stood. "Perhaps you should consider someone else." *A man. With gym muscles.* "I'm sure you'll be flooded with applicants before long." There had to be other jobs. She'd spread her search city-wise. Out Bellingham way, if necessary.

"Please, sit down."

"It's all right. I understand your concern."

"Please."

A tight moment passed. With his face lifted, the window light refined the lines around his mouth. Within his beard shadow a tiny scar shot to focus. She wondered when he'd received it. She sat.

"Thank you," he said.

Their eyes caught. In her womb she felt a little zing.

Thirty-one years, and no man had ever touched her deep-est, secret refuge—a soft, vulnerable, misty-eyed place. Not her father, not her ex-husband Wade, not even Jase, her sweet-faced brother. Then along comes the good doctor—and he rattles its door on the first meeting. She looked away. "Who's your milker now?"

"A fellow from Maple Falls. Think you might know him?"

She shook her head. "But cows are sensitive to their milker. If the person has a calm touch, they'll produce their best. About eighty pounds a day per cow is a good stan-dard."

Dr. Rowan rubbed the back of his neck as though he'd dealt with myriad crises since dawn and job interviews were an annoying side note. "Ms. McKay, just for the record, I'm not interested in whether these animals produce. The man I hired after my sis—" He broke off, pulled in air. His hand trembled on the page. "The guy gave notice two weeks ago. Saturday's his last day. You're the first applicant with any decent experience."

The first? She'd heard of the ad from Jason, who'd been scanning the Help Wanted section for mechanic work. After the ad's third run, he'd read the blurb aloud. *"Go for it, Shan. What've you got to lose?"* What indeed?

"It's been a while since I worked around livestock," she explained now. "But you won't get anyone more dedi-cated."

"I'm sure. However, let's get one thing straight. I don't want you making demands on me about the cattle, or any-thing else. I don't need you telling me how to handle them, coddle them, or…whatever. The place is for sale, which means before summer's out I'm hoping to have the papers signed, sealed and delivered to another owner. In the mean-time, all you need to do is milk those Holsteins. Clear?"

"Like spring water."

Again, their eyes held. Again, the zing.

"Do you know gardening?" he asked.

"As in hoeing and weeding?"

"As in canning and freezing. You saw our vegetable patch. In five weeks or so it'll need harvesting."

August, the hottest time of the year. She'd be sure to buy a big-brimmed, straw hat. "Consider it done."

"Thank you. There'll be a bonus for the extra work."

He pulled open a drawer near her knee and took out a checkbook. With his sleeves rolled to the elbow, she saw that his arms were solid, bread-brown, and stippled with hair. Like a farmer's, not like those of a man feeling for lumps and tying off arteries.

With a flurry of slashes he wrote out a check. "You'll need an advance to tide you over until payday which is bimonthly. Sunday will be your day off."

She gaped at the amount. Far more than what she'd earned in a month as a bookkeeper for R/D Concrete before the layoffs. And in Blue Springs, R/D had been *the* company if one wanted sound work. The doctor must be desperate.

"It won't bounce, if that's what you're wondering," he said when she continued to stare at the money.

"I—" She swallowed, sat straighter. "I know that."

"Good. There's a retired farmer, Oliver Lloyd, who lives a couple miles down the road. He comes daily to clean the barns and tend to the cows and the land. We have roughly four hundred tillable acres in corn, oats, barley and alfalfa. He'll assist you and milk on Sundays. When can you start?"

"Monday."

"Fine. We begin at 4:30 a.m. Same time in the afternoon. Milking should take you no more than two hours tops. Any questions?"

With the salary he'd laid out? Unable to think, much less speak, she managed a "No."

Without pause, he scribbled in the notebook. Thirty seconds passed. Forty.

Had she been dismissed? She read the check again. She should feel elated. She'd gotten the job. With a lucrative wage. For a few more months, Jason's college fund and her night school accounting courses would stay intact.

So what was the problem?

Michael Rowan.

He intrigued, confused, and beguiled her into silly daydreams.

Get real, Shanna. The man wouldn't look twice at you.

Staring at his bent head she unloosed a mental sigh. The logistics were as elemental as the points of a triangle. Point A: Their lifestyles—right down to his pen—were macrocosms apart. She observed the gold stylus flying across the page. Hardly a Bic special. Point B: Their natures didn't concur. His reflected the Grinch while she, fool that she was, would give her right arm to safeguard and *coddle* the powerless, the tender-footed and the ugly. She shook her head.

Why couldn't his grandmother be the one hiring?

Why couldn't his face be broad and flat-boned?

His hair sparse and colorless?

He slapped shut the book, tossed it on the desk, and strode from the den. "That pickup down by the barn yours, Ms. McKay?"

She leapt after him. "Yes, I—"

A shrill bleep arrested his progress. She almost bumped into his back. He checked his pager. "I need to make a call. Wait here." Back in the study, he closed the door with a quiet snick.

In the silence, the room lay at her feet: the tall windows, the tea set, the portrait of the woman.

What had she been thinking, Shanna wondered, envisioning herself in this house? It wasn't her. Houses like this...

A glance at the closed study. Men like that...

Like Wade. Charming in face, honed in body. Women drooling with one look of his sinful eyes and one flash of his sexy smile.

Still, standing where she was, a sense of homecoming seeped into her blood, warm and favorable. She thought of Caleb and Estelle's farmhouse where she'd spent most of her adolescence. Where she'd come to realize Brent—her father—would forever be a rodeo hound. Loving her and Jase, in his own skewed way, from miles down the road.

What she felt here couldn't compare to those days.

Why this strange house?

She saw herself curled on one of the two love seats bracketing the octagon coffee table. Browsing one of the magazines scattered there. Dreamily admiring the big African violet. Touching the child's tea set...

Her heart sank into its battered furrows. Had fate been kinder, had life taken a different route, toy trucks and trains might have covered *her* coffee table....

Oh, Timmy, my sweet little baby.

Fool. You've got to stop dreaming.

Ah, but she'd always been a dreamer. Marriage, kids, a house with a garden... But not in *this* house. Still, she couldn't shake the feeling of rightness.

An illusion, that's all. A lovely, horrible illusion.

She had to get away before the fantasies overwhelmed her. She could not work here. Not for Michael Rowan, who muddled her common sense. And not in a place that had *home* written everywhere she looked. No matter how, she'd find an office job—or wash dishes, scrub floors, flip burgers—anything but milk cows for a man who had the capability of holding her elusive hopes in the palm of his hand.

Shouldering regret, she walked into the kitchen and set the check on the corner of the oak table. Seconds later she stood outside, shoving her feet into her wearied sandals.

Already, she could feel the jerk of the old Chevy's tires rumbling off Rowan land.

She jogged down the stoop.

His leather loafers waited in the grass.

She walked past them.

Halfway down the flagstone walk, she stopped, looked back, sighed.

Ah, shoot.

She'd always been a mark for brooding men.

Michael dialed Cliff Barnette's number. Prayed his Realtor had what he wanted. He wasn't crazy about Cliff handling the sale of the estate, but the man was Blue Springs' best.

Barnette picked up on the first ring.

"It's Michael Rowan."

"Hey there, Doctor Michael," the Realtor crooned—as if he and Michael were beer-chugging buddies. "We got some bad news. That fellow who was ready to sign the deal this morning backed out a half hour ago. Couldn't get the loan, apparently. Sorry, guy, but it looks like we're back to the drawing board. Don't be disgruntled, though, it's only been a few months. Big place like yours takes a little doing."

"Yeah." Michael rested an elbow on the desk and massaged his forehead. Just what he needed. Another dose of the long haul. He was so tired of this selling business.

Oh, Leigh. Why'd you have to go and die?

He jerked upright. It wasn't his sister's fault that rig had lost its brakes on a corner and catapulted into her husband's rattletrap pickup. It had been *Michael's* inadequacy that didn't save her.

And the limitations of a small-town hospital.

"You there, pal?" the voice in his ear boomed.

"Yeah." He scrubbed a hand down his face. "Do what

you can, Cliff. Maybe something will come up in the next week or so.''

''I plan on zipping a couple ads into the southern regions. Los Angeles and the like.'' He chuckled. ''See if we can draw some interest from those rich gentlemen around Tinseltown who think farming is a hobby or a lark.''

''Fine. Let me know if anything looks favorable.''

''Will do.''

Michael set the receiver back in its cradle. What if it took years to sell the place? He wasn't cut out to milk cows, plow fields, or ride fence lines. That had been his twin's niche, *her* dream. Like a point of proof, she'd chosen to live on the land where they'd been raised by their grandparents. When their grandmother retired, Leigh had gone after her second goal and married Bob, a local man. She'd settled in this very house and had attained a stalwart status in the dairy industry.

They had been a threesome of heirs to the land, with Michael as the silent partner.

He wanted to laugh at the appalling irony. Now, Leigh and Bob were the silent ones. Eternally.

And Jenni. God, what to do about their six-year-old daughter? How to resume his career, run this place, and raise her? He knew nothing of kids. Hell, he could barely *face* the tyke most days. When her whimpers came in the night…

He set a thumb and forefinger against his tired eyes. He had to get rid of Rowan Dairy. Get rid of the memories. Take Jen away—away from the only home she knew.

Forget about easing her into her loss. He wanted to simply move them both back to his town house in Blue Springs— like he'd done right after Leigh's death.

''Why can't we live at the farm, Uncle M.? Why do we have to stay in your town house?''

Okay, so he'd keep them here. But, dammit, the longer

they stayed in this house, the harder it would be to leave later.

Still, Jenni required adjustment time. Before he removed her from the community—a hundred miles south—to Seattle. Where he had a chance as partner in a flourishing clinic, and where, God help him, first-class E.R.s could handle the worst possible cases. *Like Leigh's.*

He would not chance Jenni's future to the strictures of Blue Springs General.

He kneaded the kink at his nape.

He owed the tyke a few more weeks.

Here.

Until he found the courage to explain his plans.

If the farm fell into a non-productive state in the meantime, so be it. Jen needed this place. And someone holding her in the night when the scary dreams invaded. She needed coddling.

Mothering.

Michael opened the door and looked through the archway. The house was empty. She was gone, the woman. Wearily, he stood. Could he blame her if she ran off with his money, never to return? He'd been rude, blunt and downright miserable.

Walking through the house, he snorted softly. He could well imagine her manipulating those "cud-chewers," and her about as big around as his thumb. A little scrawny, but...pretty, in an artsy, folksy sort of style. Pretty legs, pretty lips.

On the kitchen table he found his check. *Damn.* She *had* run out, but not with his money. Sighing, he tucked the paper in a pocket. In the mudroom, he pulled on a pair of fatigued Apaches. Might as well check the barnyard before he headed back into town.

The screen door squawked when he pushed it open. He stepped onto the stoop and stared straight down at her squatted form a few feet away—cleaning his loafers with a tissue. Near her elbow, the garden hose leaked into the grass.

"Don't get used to this, Doc," she said without looking up. "I had nothing to do at the moment."

Michael came down the steps. Her ridiculously long earrings swayed with each stroke of her fine-fingered hands.

"Great footwear," she said, checking out his boots. "Next time you're down around the barns I'd suggest you wear them instead. They're more suited to what's left behind."

He combated a grin. He had to admit she was a delightful little thing. "Behind what?"

"Cows. Horses. Any critter on four legs."

This time he gruffed a chuckle.

"Oops, that's not a sense of humor I hear, is it?" She gave him a scamplike look, reached for the hose, and washed her hands. Done, she climbed to her feet.

"Now," she said, shaking wet hands like a cat with dripping paws. "You asked me to wait. Why?"

Her eyes were blue. A remarkable blue. "I wanted to let you know the employee quarters will be vacant after tomorrow."

"Where are they?"

He inclined his head toward a tiny whitewashed cabin— once the old homestead place—huddled among the trees.

She examined the dwelling. Something akin to guilt moved through him. The place was cramped, run-down. He hadn't been inside it since college. Who knew what lurked within its walls?

"Well," she said after what felt like a full minute. "My moving should make my little brother happy."

"Oh?" Michael couldn't hide his interest.

She eyed the cabin with a mixture of sadness and longing. "He's dying to live on his own. This'll put him in his glory."

Her lashes were as long as pine needles. And black…like her eyebrows.

He couldn't describe the color of her cropped hair; it oscillated between brown and blond. At times, the pale gold streaks in it seemed absurd. He wondered if she was a regular at some beauty salon. Unlikely, considering her surprise at his pay.

"What's your brother do?" he asked, just to keep her within arm's reach. *That* shook him. Women were usually a gamble he avoided.

"He works at Video Stop in town, but he's attending the University of Washington in the fall." Proud grin. Eyes lighting. Face like a candle in the dark. "He won't like having to do his own cooking and cleaning, if you know what I mean."

He knew exactly what she meant. She might have summed up his own solitary existence. It set his stomach on a low-tide roll. Eating another meal alone tonight, he would remember days he might have sat with Leigh and Bob and Jenni, laughing, joking, sharing conversation— sharing family…God, would the guilt for the should haves never stop?

She regarded him for a moment. "You okay, Doctor?"

"I'm fine." He dug the check from his shirt pocket. "I think you forgot this."

"Guess I did." She smiled sheepishly and looked at the cabin. "If it's okay with you, I'll move in on Sunday."

"I'll make sure it's ready." He'd hire a cleaning woman tomorrow. "Well, then." He shifted his feet, unwilling to let her go. Unsure why he couldn't. "That's it."

"Great." She smoothed the check. "I'll see you in a couple days."

"It's secluded out here," he blurted. "You'll be alone most of the time. Will that be a problem?"

"My brother is—"

"Yes, I know, but what of others in your family?"

She stiffened. "There's only my brother."

"No children? Husband?" *None of your concern, Rowan.* He saw it in her expression, her posture. She stood as rigid as the trees behind them.

"No." Her tone cooled. "Does *that* pose a problem?"

"None. I thought maybe…" *Your husband got fired and you were forced to take the first thing that came along.*

"I got laid off, Doctor. I didn't quit or get fired, if that's what you're wondering."

"Not at all," he said, unnerved she'd nailed his suspicions. "I'm surprised this is the only job available." *Terrific. Not just nosy, but a pompous jerk to boot. A genuine winner, Rowan.*

"Good jobs are at an all-time low around town," she replied. The tautness in her words warned him to back off.

He didn't. "But this—"

"It pays." She fluttered the check. "That's what counts."

He let it go. Here he was, offering a woman of her apparent intelligence and, okay, looks, the tugboat instead of the cruise ship. Yes, he knew three thousand inhabitants populated Blue Springs—with dairies, fruit growers, farms and a couple of small ranches shaping the community at large. He simply didn't like the way the odds fell out of her favor.

"Sorry," he said, uneasy because she made him feel…*something* when he'd rather keep his heart walled up.

Her Pacific-colored eyes staked him. "I can do the job."

"I've no doubt whatsoever that you can." He estimated that the top of her head barely skimmed his Adam's apple. A little dip and his chin could rest on her hair. "I simply want to know," he said, irked by the sudden heated pool in his nether quarters, "who I've got wandering around this establishment. It's an expensive operation and I wouldn't want anything adverse happening because of incompetence.''

She snatched up her knapsack. ''I'm not a liar.''

''I didn't say you were.''

''You were implying it.''

The fire deserted him. ''Ms. McKay—''

''Shanna.''

''Shanna, then. Please, understand. I'm a surgeon. My hours are bizarre most days. That's why who I hire for this job must be someone I can trust. Implicitly.''

Her expression gentled. Sunshine silvered the danglers in her ears. ''Well, Doctor,'' she said softly. ''You can trust me. Implicitly.''

She turned and walked to her truck, leaving him to vie with his memories—and worries about his future—once more.

Chapter Two

"Dangit," she muttered, clunking her head a second time under the kitchen sink. She'd tried to tighten the drainpipe for a good half hour and still it leaked like a sieve.

At least the cabin was spotless. The kitchen appliances gleamed, and the bathroom fixtures smelled of Lysol. Even the aged planked floor had a coat of wax. And the mattress in the main bedroom was new—a crucial detail when her mornings began at four.

All she required was for *him* to buy an elbow seal.

Clambering to her feet, she stretched a twinge from the small of her back. Ten-fifteen. The day nearly half gone and the boxes she'd piled into the Chevy's bed some seven hours ago with a grousing Jason at her heels remained unpacked.

She swiped her stinging eyes. Her baby bro. Nineteen years they had shared. She'd changed his diapers, sent him to first grade, watched him walk across the stage at his high-school graduation. *Ah, Jase. You'll go places, dear heart.*

Through a grove of fir, she caught sight of the sorrel stallion. Soldat D'Anton—Soldier of Old—according to Oliver, the barn cleaner, whom she'd met this morning. The name suited the animal.

For a moment, he stood still, chin held high, pin ears erect, tail winging the breeze. Then he pawed the earth and shook his big head.

"Me-o mi-o, but you are some piece of work, buddy."

Like his owner. Arrogant, strong-headed and extravagantly stunning.

Movement on the cabin's path caught her eye. A calico cat, its tail flagpole-straight, strutted in front of a little girl. Five or six, the child clutched her yellow daisy-dotted skirt, swishing it side to side as she walked. Dark curls framed rosy cheeks and bounced on tanned shoulders. Shanna smiled. Lost to her own will-o'-the-wisps, this little one.

Shanna's smile faded. Where was the girl's mother?

The doctor's Cherokee sat parked in the driveway next to the farmhouse. Had he brought the child with him?

She was outside in seconds, walking down the path toward the pair. "Hey, kitty." Shanna hunkered down, offering a hand to the feline. The animal sniffed her fingertips daintily.

Dropping her skirt, the girl pressed her knuckles together and approached Shanna one cautious step at a time. Through the evergreen boughs above, sunlight sifted gold sugar onto the girl's curls.

The cat butted its sleek mottled head against Shanna's knee and purred.

"Her name is Silly."

As if surprised to see someone else, Shanna looked up. "Silly, hm?"

"Uh-huh." A small giggle escaped. "It was s'pposed to be Sally. But when I was little I couldn't say Sally. Isn't that silly?'' More giggles escaped. ''Ooh.'' She clamped a hand over her mouth.

Shanna's throat pinched. Her arms ached for the snuggle of a small cuddly body.

''Oh, stop it,'' she muttered.

''Are you talking to yourself?'' The child edged closer. Her fingers worried her skirt. Silly, purring like a tiny fine-tuned motor, plopped to the grass.

''Actually, I was telling Silly to stop being so noisy because she'll scare the chickadees off.''

''Chick-a…?''

''Chickadees.'' Shanna pointed up to the trees. ''See those little birds with black caps on their heads?''

''Nooo…uh-hm.''

''They fly real fast. See, there goes one.''

A breathless little gasp. ''Oh!'' Round hazel eyes centered on Shanna, then back up to the trees. ''Oh…oh, lookit! There's another!''

''Cute, aren't they?'' Shanna watched the child. An adorable half-toothed grin plumped her freckled cheeks.

''Mmm-hmm.'' Curls swung as she nodded and sidled closer. Their knees bumped. Elfin face serious, the child looked at the cat, which stared upward with its tail twitching. ''Will Silly catch one?''

''I don't think so. They're too quick and smart. They know she's here.''

Relief swept into the girl's eyes. ''Good. I don't want the little birdies to die. My mommy and daddy died an' it wasn't nice.''

Shanna's heart stumbled.

Of course. The accident. She'd read about it killing the doctor's sister and her husband. When had it happened? April? No, March. Mid-March. Over three months ago. A freak accident that had left a child the lone survivor. This child.

The girl's eyes filled.

"Aw, sweetie." Shanna tucked the child to her side. Her cheek found soft warm curls smelling of sunshine and lemon shampoo. "Hey," she said, swallowing back the lump behind her tongue. "I bet your name is Sally. That's why you got Silly's name mixed up."

Another round of giggles. "Nuh-uh. My name's Jenni."

Shanna offered a palm. "Well, hello, Jenni. I'm Shanna."

Little fingers skimmed bigger ones. "You're pretty." The half-toothed grin. "Know what?"

"Nope."

"I'm six."

Shanna whistled mock surprise. "Whoa, that's getting old." Had the birthday been with her parents? Shanna prayed it had.

"Nuh-uh, it's not." Jenni hunched a shoulder to her ear, smiling shyly. "Grammy is old. She's got white hair an' lots and lots of wrinkles…right here." Two fingers bracketed her eyes.

Shanna laughed. It felt good. "Is she here with you?"

"No, just Uncle M. He looks after me most. Grammy looks after me when he has to work at the clinic."

Shanna envisioned Estelle. Kind heart. Soft, plump arms. A nurturer, the way Meredith, Shanna's mother, had never been.

"Sometimes," the child went on, "like when Grammy's in California, I go to the day care."

"Where's Uncle M. now?"

Jenni pointed to the house. "Home. It's Sunday. Sometimes he doesn't work Sunday. Right now he's doing 'portant stuff upstairs."

What *stuff* kept the doctor too busy to keep an eye on his niece? Shanna looked to where the stallion grazed in the paddock.

He bites.

A shudder chased up her spine. Had the cat headed toward the barnyard, where would that have left Jenni? Crawling through the fence? Walking up to a twelve-hundred-pound beast who gouged out a strip of earth with one slash of his hoof?

Shanna pushed to her feet. "Let's see if your uncle needs any help." *Or a wake-up call.*

"C'mon, Silly," Jenni sang to the calico. "I'm going back to the house now."

Curling her little palm around two of Shanna's fingers, she walked up the path, cat in tow.

"Uncle Michael doesn't like me bothering him," Jenni volunteered.

"Did he say so?"

"No." She took a little skip. "But I know."

"How?"

"He looks at me a lot."

"Maybe he thinks you're cute."

Jenni shook her head, jiggling her sun-dappled curls. "Uh-uh. He never smiles. And sometimes—" she touched the bridge of her button-nose "—he gets two splits here."

Shanna understood. Grief accounted for the pain in those gray eyes and that unsmiling mouth. But it didn't explain Michael Rowan's apparent disregard for his niece. Not for a second would she have left Jason unattended at this age. Or her darling Timmy, had he lived. Jenni ran ahead and squatted in front of a confusion of marigolds growing along the stone walkway. Someone obviously loved the sunny-faced plants. "This one's the prettiest," she said, plucking a fat bloom. "Do you like it?"

"Very much. Want to put it in some water?"

The child shook her head shyly. "In your hair."

"My hair?" With a self-conscious hand, Shanna pushed a thick chin-length clump behind her ear. "Why?"

"'Cause Octavia wears flowers in her hair. They make

her happy.'' Jenni tugged Shanna's hand. "Bend down."
Little fingers whispered like leaves in a breeze at her temple.
"Mommy told me Octavia means eight."

"Yes, it does."

"Octavia's my dolly. Her hair's the same as
yours...kinda messy and all over the place. Tavia—that's
what I call her when she's good—has a bad time combing
it. Do you?"

Shanna kept a sober expression. "Sometimes. Especially
in the morning after I wake up."

The little girl stepped back to survey her handiwork.
"Tavia doesn't like getting up."

Tavia or Jenni? Reverse role playing was common among
children experiencing severe trauma. After her mother left,
Shanna had done it herself—heaping daily problems on a
fictional friend. Hers had been Anne Frank. At school, she'd
read the girl's diary and followed Anne's resigned, coura-
geous year concealed in a narrow back annex of the now
famous house on Amsterdam's *Prinsengracht*. Shanna had
been Anne's age when Meredith left.

Anne, Shanna's partner in austerity in a small notebook.

The calico purred around their ankles. "See, even Silly
thinks it's nice."

There on the stone walkway, with the smell of a sun-
warmed child saturating her senses, Shanna leaned forward
and pressed a kiss to Jenni's brow. "*You're* nice."

The child stiffened.

"What is it, sweetie?"

Jenni's button lip quivered. "I want to go in now."
Whirling, she scrambled up the steps and fled into the house.

Shanna stared at the door. She should have kept her heart
wrapped completely in its cool detached cocoon—the one
self-preservation had driven her to create nine years ago.
The one she never allowed to chip or splinter for fear of
what could happen.

Like now.

Ten minutes and she'd formed a sweet covenant with a sad little girl. One kiss and she'd ruined it. The child hadn't been ready—and Shanna too anxious. "It'll serve you right if she never comes near you again," she muttered.

Heart heavy, she rose. She had to set things right.

But how did one go about trying to explain to a six-year-old that a peck on the head meant nothing more than thank you? That it didn't mean a stranger wanted to replace her mother?

Michael flung a second stack of Leigh's jeans into a large cardboard box sitting outside the door of the walk-in closet. A month after the accident, he had removed his brother-in-law's wardrobe from this same closet, heaped the clothes into his truck and driven to the Lady of Lourdes church.

Easy street compared to this.

This was ugly.

A sacrilege.

And the reason nearly three months had elapsed before he'd dared enter the bedroom a second time.

He hadn't been able to touch her things. Hadn't been able to look at them without the ache in his gut doubling him over.

She wasn't supposed to be dead, his only sibling, his *twin*. *Here* is where she belonged. Laughing, her rich voice invading the rooms. Giving Bob those foxy looks—

"But *why*, Uncle Michael?"

And answering her daughter's questions about this horrible after-death ritual.

"Uncle Michael?" His niece's tiny voice quivered.

"I've already told you, Jen. She won't need them any more."

"Mommy's never coming back, is she?"

"No. She's not."

He glanced out of the walk-in closet. Leigh's daughter stood near the packing box, clutching her shabby doll to her chest. The large L-shaped bedroom with its pine furniture and its queen bed spanned out behind her. In the toe of the L was a vanity and chair. Soon, he'd eradicate all of it. Brushes, makeup—

"Ever?"

One word, filled with confusion, trepidation and disbelief. In his twelve years at the hospital he'd heard those emotions often, but he recalled the first time best. When he was ten and they'd brought his parents home from Canada, broken and burned and no longer alive. Leigh had asked the same question of their grandmother, in this very room. He'd stood next to his sister, their hands clasped tight, and Katherine had shaken her head and walked out. Leigh had started crying. In his brain, the sound shattered him once more. And once more he felt the cool welcome of loathing what he could not change.

Jenni stared at the box. Leigh's silver, pearl-buttoned shirt draped over a flap, in a beam of sunlight.

"No," he said brutally, grief molding his anger into an invisible defensive sword.

The child sniffed and buried her face in the doll's drab hair. He wanted to go to her, apologize for his tone, try and—

"Jenni?" A woman's voice. *Her* voice.

In the dim closet interior, Michael's hands froze on a cluster of hangers. What was she doing here? He watched his niece pivot, eyes swimming with hurt and fear.

"Uncle Michael's taking away Mommy's clothes, Shanna. He says she's never, ever, *ever* coming home."

"Aw, peachkins…"

Jenni's mouth trembled. She darted a look his way, then dropped her doll and ran from his line of view. An instant later he heard her muffled whimper: "I hate him."

"Jenni—"

"Please, make him stop. Please, Shanna. *Please*."

Michael closed his eyes and released a sigh. When would life be normal again? *Never,* he thought and stepped out of the closet.

His lanky-limbed employee stood five feet inside the doorway with Jenni wrapped around her thighs like a tiny tenacious wood nymph. Tears crept down the little girl's uplifted face and rolled into the curls smoothed by mothering hands.

Shanna raised her eyes. He hadn't anticipated the fury in them. Or the pain.

"So," he said, ignoring a snip of guilt—and jealousy. "Three days ago you introduce yourself to my horse. Today, my niece."

"She was wandering around outside. By herself." The last two words hung like stone pendulums.

He stepped around the box and picked up the doll. "Jen, take…" *What did she call it?* "Take your doll downstairs and feed her some of your favorite tea."

The child gave him a teary, pouty look. "Don't want to."

"Jenni." Ms. McKay pushed Leigh's daughter away gently. She knelt and cupped Jenni's small shoulders. "It's okay. Do what Uncle Michael asks. He's…" She threw him a quick, cool look. "He's worried Tavia might be hungry. It's nearly lunchtime, you know."

Rubbing a palm up the side of her nose, the child shot him another look. "'Kay."

"That's a sweetie." Without so much as a glimpse his way, Shanna McKay reached for the doll. When he laid it in her hand, she straightened its frilly dress and delivered it to Jen. "I'll be down soon," she whispered.

She watched the girl head out of the room. Annoyed that he studied his employee with her sun-gilded thighs and patched denim shorts, rather than his niece, Michael said, "What's with the aloha look?"

Her head slowly turned. The wistfulness he'd seen in her face evaporated. Coldness settled in. Ah, but her wide, feminine mouth stayed soft as a ripe peach. He drew closer.

She pushed to her feet. Her eyes were severe. He fancied his battered boots, tired Wranglers and wrinkled T-shirt scored a thumbs down. Her chin elevated. "Are you talking about this?" She pointed to the flower.

He nodded, unable to look away. The foolish thing reminded him of a sultry night dancer. Sultry and night was a combination he wanted—no, *needed*—to avoid, especially around her. Purposely, to regain his balance, he glanced at the box draped in Leigh's clothes, and was jolted back to reality. "Looks all wrong," he muttered, mind back on his task.

Her laugh was soft and husky. "Well, Doc, your opinion isn't worth a hoot. But your niece is another story. She's smart, sensitive and has this charming idea that flowers make people happy. I happen to agree with her."

Michael turned again to the woman standing pole-straight in front of him. Her lean, tanned arms were folded under small, round breasts. Below his navel he felt a rush of blood.

He took in the blossom above her ear and the jumble of her hair. *Silky,* he thought, and itched to take up a fistful.

His eyes found hers. Wide, wary.

Boldly, he stepped into her space. "Happy, huh?" He watched air affect her nostrils as he touched her cheek. "Are you happy, Ms. McKay?"

"Doesn't matter if I am or not." She caught his wrist and plucked the marigold from her hair. "Question is," she said softly, placing the flower in his palm, "Are *you?*"

His skin throbbed where their fingers curled together and the knot of petals pressed. "Happiness isn't the issue here."

"Wrong. It's the only issue when it concerns your

niece." Her eyes gentled. "Don't trash her mother's clothes."

He backed away. "I'm not trashing them. I'm taking them to the Lady of Lourdes church." Defeat enveloped him. He pushed out a long breath. "I didn't expect Jenni to come up here, okay? She was to stay downstairs."

"Well, she didn't. She went outside. Luckily, she wandered toward the cabin instead of the barns. Do you have any idea what she might have run into down there?"

Guilt gnashed his gut. "Look, Ms. McKay—"

"No, you look. Your niece needs you. At the moment, she's got one person to fill those vacant spots her parents left. You. Give her some attention. Show a little concern. Heck, a pat on the head would do the trick fine."

"Playing shrink now?"

She ignored the insult. "Jenni told me you don't like being bothered. In my books that means she's in your way. No child should ever be *in the way*."

Michael stared at her. Bothering him? Was that how Jenni saw herself? *Why not? You barely see her.*

The woman before him scraped back her uneven bangs. "Fire me for pointing it out. I don't care. The well-being of a child is more important than a job."

He could see she didn't give one spit if he did fire her. To her, Jenni was at risk in his custody. He didn't know whether to feel humbled, guilty, angry or all three.

Bending to her level, he said softly, "Who do you think you are, *Ms. McKay?* Mother Theresa? You don't know flip from flap about raising kids, or how it feels to live without parents. But you're right about one thing. If you want to retain this job, keep your opinions to yourself."

Her pupils dilated. She clamped her lower lip. Retreated a step. "I think…" Another step. "I think it's…best I go."

Regret spiked his belly. "Ms. McKay—"

"Shanna," she corrected, shaking her head. "My name is Shanna," she whispered. "Just like yours is…is Mike."

"Mike? No one calls me Mike." But he liked it. Across her lips it was an intimate, seductive little breath. Yeah, he liked Mike—a lot.

A quavery laugh escaped her lips. "I'll try and remember that next time we meet."

She left the room, and he stood alone with silence and a delayed whiff of her scent closing in on him.

Jenni sat on the floor between the couch and the coffee table. She wished Shanna would come downstairs. She knew Uncle Michael and her new friend were talking about what happened.

The tears she had wiped away started plopping on Tavia's jumper again. It was getting really spotty. Octavia was so upset, and Jenni didn't know how to calm her.

"It's okay, Tavia," she whispered against the doll's hair. "I'll look after you. I won't let Uncle M. yell at you no more."

But Tavia just kept crying, wishing for Mommy and Daddy to come down from heaven instead of staying up there and helping God all the time.

She didn't like them being angels. She wanted them to be people like Shanna and Grammy. Even like Uncle M.

Jenni wouldn't let Tavia tell her to say mean things to Uncle Michael, either. That wasn't nice. She really didn't hate him. She just didn't want him to throw Mommy's things away.

"'Cause," Jenni whispered. "If he throws Mommy's clothes away, he might throw mine away. Maybe he'll even throw me away."

She bit her lower lip and palmed her nose. If Uncle M. threw her away, then she and Tavia would just go and live with Shanna or Grammy. Sniffing, she swiped her eyes with the back of her hand. Yeah, that's what they'd do. They'd live with Shanna. Shanna was fun and showed her things like the chick'bees.

Stroking Tavia's hair, Jenni rocked back and forth, singing softly. She and Tavia felt better.

He'd been a jackass.

Again.

If she called him worse names when she opened her door, he'd bow his head and take them in stride.

All day he'd kept watch on the white log house through the trees. The battered two-toned pickup, parked in the narrow driveway, meant she hadn't left as he'd feared during the hour he'd been to Blue Springs. Shortly after lunch his grandmother had called to announce her return from her six-week visit to her brother in Anaheim, and she'd demanded to see her great-granddaughter. Grateful for an excuse to get out of the house, he took the tyke into town. After this morning, he had no delusions about Jenni's eagerness to leave him for a few hours.

Damn. They should be drawing closer. Bonding, not pulling apart. They shared a loss. As the adult, and a doctor, he knew how to lessen the trauma for Jen and for himself.

Except, he couldn't.

Shanna's right, he thought, walking the pathway toward the employee quarters. As a stand-in parent he was a bozo.

Shanna. The name hummed through his blood. He didn't understand the attraction. She wasn't his type. Tall, slim to the point of being gangly. He preferred women with hourglass figures. Soft. Yet, a glimpse of her had his jeans in an uncomfortable fit.

He regarded the cabin, then the ridiculous marigold in his hand, and scowled. Seven months without so much as a dinner date was more than any normal red-blooded American man should endure. The last, with a divorced radiologist, had evolved into a date of ear tonguing and crotch palming—from her—that he would rather forget.

Not Shanna. *He'd* be the one tonguing and palming. Lean limbs, that skin slick and damp...

Booting a pinecone off her stoop, he raised a hand to knock. No use denying it. The sight of her spun something between them.

The door flung open.

Her sapphire eyes were cool. Cool as the jewel they emulated. "Hey, Doc. Come to see if I've cut and run?"

Michael shoved off a flicker of displeasure. So she held grudges. He understood. Grudges held off pain. Thumbs catching his jeans pockets, he asked, "May I come in?"

"Why? As you see, I'm not going anywhere. I realized I do need this job."

"I'd like to talk."

"About what?" Her tone dipped below ice-blue, like the blouse she wore. "We said it all this morning. I stay out of your hair, you stay out of mine. When it's over we'll say *adios* and that'll be that."

"Dammit, Miss—"

"Drop the formalities, Michael. I'm just the hired help not one of your associates at the clinic, not a patient."

He'd have preferred Mike—and the way it seared the air from her lips. Shifting, he stared down the hill at the barns. "I shouldn't be taking my problems out on you."

"Better me than your niece."

He looked at her. She had such pretty eyes. "You don't mince words, do you?"

"Seldom."

Again he observed the barns and fields. "I never used to be like this."

"Tragedy changes us in ways we don't expect."

And the tragedy I've seen in your eyes? "You're different."

"From who?"

"Most people."

"Is that good or bad?" Her tone gentled.

He studied her soft mouth. "Good. Very good."

"Well, that's a first. Come in. I'll put on a pot of tea." She gestured to his hand. "That poor marigold needs water."

She headed for the kitchen, leaving him to close the door—and to watch her backside in cropped denim pants. Baked chicken and a medley of spices hailed him. She could cook.

"Supper at three in the afternoon?"

"I skip lunch." She pulled down the oven door and checked the meal. "So I try to eat early."

He wandered around the tiny living room. "Next to breakfast, lunch is the most important meal of the day. There's a saying that goes: king, prince, pauper. It's how you should treat daily meals."

This time her laughter was rich and a little smoky and floated into his belly. "I hate to put a crimp in your diet plans, Doc, but I eat when the growlies arrive. For me that happens twice a day."

"You're too thin."

"Well," she huffed. "Sorry if that offends you."

"It doesn't." He liked her frame just fine. In fact, inordinately so. But he couldn't snub his observations—from a medical viewpoint.

He looked around. It was the first time he'd been in the cabin since long before Leigh died. What he saw shamed him. The place was old. The walls needed painting.

"Would you like some chicken?" She tossed oven mitts on the Formica and readjusted one of the two barrettes holding back her hair. Her arms were graceful as a figure skater's. He imagined them around his rib cage, his neck.

"You can't live here."

"Beg pardon?"

"The place is a dump. My sister—" How to tell her the cabin had been Leigh's responsibility and that since her death he'd neglected it. Just as he neglected the animals, the books…Jenni.

"It's not so bad."

Not bad? One of the curtains hosted a foot-long tear. He hated to think of what lurked behind the doors of the bathroom and two bedrooms. Even *after* the maid's cleaning.

Shanna took a brimming bucket from under the sink.

Striding into the narrow kitchen, he tossed the flower on the counter. "The sink's leaking?"

"Good one, Doc. You get the prize." She handed him the bucket. "Would you empty it in the toilet, please, while I put on the kettle?"

Just like her not to mention the condition of the house. He headed for the bathroom and dumped the water. About to leave, he stopped and looked. This was her space. Her secret space. Female essentials mussed the narrow, beige Formica around the antiquated sink and lined the chipped tub. Two blue-and-yellow combs, a big tube of hand lotion, glycerine soaps stuffed in a woven basket, a wooden tree strung with those ear danglers, Scooby-Doo lip balm— He did a double take. *Scooby-Doo?* Snorting softly, he shook his head. She was a rare something, this Shanna. *And you're in trouble, Rowan.*

"Toilet working okay?"

He whipped around, the bucket clanging against a drawer. Arms crossed, she leaned in the doorway, one bare ankle slung over the other. Behind him the tiny round window let in the day's light, tipping her cheekbones with rose.

"Yes," he said, voice gruff. "It works."

She smiled, glanced at the counter where he'd tarried. "Find anything interesting?"

He stepped toward the doorway. Her smile faded. A bouquet of meadows in summer caressed him. Oh, yeah. All woman. Easy angles, sweet-eyed. "Maybe I have."

Her nostrils flared. "And it would be…?"

Today, three filigree chains swung like wind chimes from each of her tiny lobes. He tapped a trio. "Just…" *You.* "Little things."

"Is there one in particular you favor?" Those blue eyes ringed in black swallowed him.

He perused the edge of her jaw, the line of her throat. "There is."

A snippet of air against his knuckles. Hers.

Once, twice, his thumb grazed the satin of her neck. He tilted her chin. Her sweet mouth. Waiting for him. God, decades down the road he'd look at her features and be captivated. Still.

Paralyzed, he stared. Giving one woman, *this* woman the rest of his life? Out of the question. He wasn't about to chance fate. Fate could involve kids. Fate had taken his parents' plane into a mountainside. Left him and Leigh orphaned.

Like Jen.

Settling down was not in his Tarot cards. Neither was waking up beside the same woman until he was ninety-plus. Trouble was, within the space of two days his ethics had taken a lopsided turn out to left field. Because of her. *Shanna.*

Caught in her eyes, finger crooked under her chin, he wanted to wrap her up like a Valentine's gift, kiss her till the cows came home, lead her through the open door of the bedroom five feet away, fly her to the stars.

But not forever.

"Mike?" she whispered.

He dropped his hand and stepped back.

"What's wrong?"

"I have to go." Two strides and he was down the hall. "I'll find a guy in town to paint this joint."

In a flash she was on his heels. "My brother can do it."

He stopped. "Your brother."

"Why not? He could use the money."

"Fine." She was close again. Too close.

The kettle whistled. He headed for the door, yanked it open.

"Where do I buy the supplies?" she called.

"Spot O' Color. It's on Riverside and—"

"I know where it is."

"Great. Tell your brother to get on it ASAP. I want the dairy sold before fall."

He slammed out of the cabin before she answered. Before he changed his mind, stormed back inside and kissed her like...hell, like a crazy man.

Chapter Three

She washed the bag of the last big-bellied black-and-white Holstein with Santex disinfectant. "Almost done, Rosebud."

In the metal stanchion, the cow chewed her cud peaceably. Shanna hung the Westfalia Surge milking unit on a hook and affixed the suction cups to the animal's sanitized teats. *Hiss-click-hiss-click.* The machine streamed milk to the sixteen-hundred-gallon stainless steel tank in the milk house.

Dressed in green overalls and rubber boots, Shanna knew a contentment she hadn't felt since growing up on the Lassers' farm. She liked the cows' broad, docile faces, their big, dark eyes, their gentle natures. She fancied the classic bovine odor within the big flatbarn: a fusion of hay and manure and sweaty hide. And, physical as it was, she liked the work.

She'd like it more if she could stop thinking about the

doctor and those moments in her washroom. When she thought—*knew*—he'd wanted to kiss her.

For the past two days, since striding from the cabin, he'd kept himself and Jenni hidden. Late at night the Jeep's headlights would come down the lane and stop at the farmhouse. The next morning, after milking was finished, the car was gone again. She wondered if the child came and went with him.

Ah, why worry? she thought, releasing Rosebud from her milking apparatus. *He made it clear you weren't to interfere.*

Prickles ran up her nape.

He stood five feet away, hands shoved deep into the pockets of black trousers. The sleeves of his gray dress shirt were flipped back on his forearms, the collar liberated of its tie.

Her breath quickened.

Ignoring the broody expression on her employer's face, she pressed a wall button and, on a clang of metal, relinquished the last group of ten cows of their stalls.

"Checking to make sure I'm doing my job, Doctor?"

"Nope."

"Good."

Down at the far end of the parlor, old Oliver Lloyd, whistling to Tim McGraw's "Where the Green Grass Grows," hosed manure and urine from the step-dam gutter. On Tuesday, the slurry man would haul away the two-week store. The animals clopped down the alleyway toward the open double doors at the rear of the long barn. Shanna tagged behind them with Michael at her shoulder.

Approaching the paddock where the cows fed at extended troughs filled with a silage of corn and alfalfa, she scanned the doctor's dress slacks—with creases down those long runner's legs—and his black buckled shoes. "Fresh patties ahead. Sure you want to walk through here in those?"

His lips moved. "Where you going?"

Away. Far away. "To check the water system."

He surveyed the galvanized vat near the opposite gate. "What's wrong with it?"

"Nothing, but I check it regularly."

He stared out over herd and land. A cluster of sparrows chirped in the eaves. From the western hills, the sun slanted long, spindly shadows beside the cattle as they found their places at the feed stanchions, tails lazily swishing flies.

"You're an amazing woman, Shanna McKay." He spoke without looking at her. "You come here out of the blue, answer my ad personally, befriend my niece who's barely talked to a soul in three months, and milk ninety head of cows twice daily as if it's the most natural thing for a woman to do."

"It is," she said and meant it.

He turned, his gray eyes searching hers. "No," he replied. "It's not. It's damned hard work."

In the natural light, he looked exhausted. Beneath the shirt, his big shoulders slumped a little. Shadows, like the prints of inked thumbs, lay under his eyes.

"And doctoring isn't difficult?" she asked, beating back the urge to lay a cool hand to his cheek. She didn't want to feel sorry for him.

A rueful smile. "At times."

"There you go. All jobs have their rough moments."

As if he hadn't heard her, he said, "I don't know how you do it. But then you're unique."

"That's not what you said in the cabin."

His eyes returned to hers. "What did I say in the cabin?"

"That I was different."

He flicked one of the three-inch gold dream-catchers she'd slipped into her ears at dawn. "Unique," he repeated softly. A corner of his lips curved. "And possibly a little atypical."

She felt the look he gave the ball cap controlling her messy hair clean to her toes. She wished she wasn't in hot, heavy barn gear, but in some light, airy thing. Ah, who was she kidding? She wasn't the light, airy type.

He looked back at the land. He did that a lot, she noticed. Gazed off as if taking a detour from what was on his mind.

A slight bump rode high on his long, thin nose. An austere, masculine mold cast his lips. Was he a timid kisser? She doubted it; she'd bet he was an openmouthed, migrant sort of guy. A tongue dancer. *How many of those cute nurses have you kissed?*

More than I want to know.

She headed for the metal vat. Plunging her bare arm into the cold water, she felt along the bottom for the outflow. Good, free of blockage. Stepping back, she shook her arm and swiped at the water droplets.

"Here." Michael rolled down a sleeve. For a dime's value of seconds she stood beguiled as he dried her hand and forearm with a strip of gray that matched his eyes.

His hands were large, the knuckles heavy with a light dusting of hair. She envisioned those hands holding a scalpel. Or maybe pressing a tummy searching for abnormalities and ailments. She envisioned his hands on *her* tummy.

She looked up and found his eyes dark with wonder, his mouth tight, the tiny scar pale. He had thick, spiky lashes. Black as pitch. How would they feel tickling her lips, her fingers?

Get real, Shanna.

Her hands reeked of cows; his had been washed with Ivory. Her hair was jammed under a Seahawks cap. His lay in a short, crisp style.

No matter how she viewed it, he was the princely physician and she the mere milkmaid.

His thumbpad, gentle and strong, brushed the veins of her wrist and, for a heartbeat, rested in her palm. An unfamiliar touch. One, if she were honest, she'd never experienced.

Certainly not with Wade. She shivered. This dreadful magnetism was wrong.

"You're chilled."

Mercy. That bass voice. She looked to where his fingers cupped her wrist, where her flesh goose-bumped. How discordant, the magnitude of his hand to her bones. Argh! Absurd, fantasizing about a man whose knuckles and flipped sleeves had her insides on a wave drill. In social circles they were as comparable as a Lamborghini and a farm pickup. She was tailored to guys like Wade with his Tony Lama boots, black Stetsons, pearl-buttoned shirts—and smelling of saddles and horse sweat. Michael was…a *surgeon.*

Carefully, she stepped back and folded her arms over her chest. Hiding. "Nothing wrong with the valve. Truth is, the entire dairy's in great shape."

"So's your kitchen drainpipe."

"It's fixed?"

"Put in a new seal when I got home from work."

"You?"

A pleased little-boy smile. "I wasn't always a doctor, Shanna. I learned to use a wrench before a stethoscope."

Heat moved up her neck. "Sorry, I wasn't being sarcastic."

"I know." They looked at each other for a long moment. He said, "I also bought a couple tins of paint. They're on the doormat. Oliver can help. I should have thought of it before." He rubbed his forehead. "I'm not used to this selling business."

Her smile faded. She had no business telling him what to do. No business *feeling* the way she did. About him or the child. But telling and feeling were two traits she'd never governed with discretion.

"You know, Doc," she said, heading for the barn doors. "You really should reconsider and keep this place for yourself and your niece. The second you sign on that dotted line, it's over. And that," she speared him with a glance, "will be a flipping shame."

Together they entered the warm, musky interior of the milking parlor.

A flipping shame? Michael thought, striding beside her. *Dammit, woman, where do you come off with your assessments?*

She knew nothing about the pain and fear he endured living in this place, in this community. What did she know about medical facilities short of resources, funding and expertise? What did she know about a life cut off in its prime?

"It's like that Amy Grant song," she continued. "'You don't know what you've got till it's gone.' This place has all the amenities you'd ever want for raising a child. Fresh air, peace, quiet. Once you sell, it'll—"

He stopped. "Did you not understand what I said the other day? I don't need your advice on what's best for this place or—"

She swung around. "Or what, Doctor? You'll fire me? We've been there, done it, framed the picture." She lifted the Seahawks cap and raked back the jungle of her hair. "Look. All I'm suggesting is don't rush into something you may regret a month from now."

They were at the midpoint of the long corridor. Light filtered through the doors and caught in the hollows of her cheeks. If he closed his eyes, he'd recall each fine detail.

Five days ago the woman hadn't existed. Now, she never left his mind. He didn't want to feel anything for her. Starting with the first of those rudimentary aspects like...lust.

Not that he didn't enjoy the *body* side of the lure. He did. He appreciated the sight of a pretty woman. Mostly, he praised his stoic heart, thumping behind his ribs, for its neutrality in spite of any attraction or spark.

Except, around this woman his heart did crazy, unorthodox things. He didn't understand it. Barring her eyes, she

was neither traditionally beautiful nor alluring. Her body
was curveless, her short hair a persistent tangle. Never mind
that she poked her slim, shapely nose in his business.

"What do you want from me?" he asked wearily.

A direct look. "Nothing. But Jenni does. Ask her."

"Oh, for pity's sake, she's six, not twenty-six."

"She's a person, Michael. She has feelings, which, at the
moment, she doesn't understand."

Anger tight in his chest, he jammed his hands into his
pockets. "You think I don't know that?"

"Then talk about her parents. She needs to know how
you feel about their loss. Most of all, that you're not angry
with her."

"I'm *not* angry with her!" *Damn.* She'd pinned him to
the wall and pared off layers he'd stapled down. He wasn't
ready to talk about Leigh. Still, fresh, the wounds tore easily.

With a heavy sigh, he massaged his nape. "Look, she
was in the wrong place at the wrong time the other day and
for that I'm sorry, but I *am* selling this farm."

Shanna hesitated, then shrugged. "Your decision."

"Yes," he said, dropping his hand. "It is."

She turned to go then stopped. "Where is Jenni, by the
way?"

He refused to feel guilty. "At my grandmother's. I'm
picking her up in a few minutes." *I wanted to come home
first. See you.*

"Does she know you'll be moving her to a new home?"

"Jen's been to my town house before."

She nodded, acquiescing.

The gesture irked him. "What I do or don't do in respect
to my niece," he said, pushing past her and striding down
the aisle, "is not your concern. Do the job you were hired
for, Ms. McKay, and we'll get along fine."

"As in stick to the barn and cows, Doc? Know my place?"

He stopped, parked his hands at his waist, and took a deep, pacifying breath. "If that's what it takes. Just leave my niece alone." *Leave me alone.* "I don't want you pumping her head full of idiotic ideas that'll only confuse her." *And me.*

He recognized the damage instantly. The distress he saw in her eyes two days ago in Leigh's bedroom was there once more. "I would never do that," she whispered.

"Dammit. You know what I'm trying to say."

She poked out her chin. "Message received." The hurt vanished in a wake of quiet dignity. "Excuse me, but I have cows to see, barns to roam, manure to clear." She walked away and disappeared into another section of the building.

Michael stood in the hushed milking parlor, in the musk of animal and hay, and thought, *You expect more than I can give.*

That was the crux of it, wasn't it? He could not give Jenni what she needed any more than he could grant life to Leigh. Would he ever master this feeling of helplessness? This terror of knowing how inadequate he was?

Ah, Leigh. You knew, didn't you?

Just as he'd known, the minute they'd unloaded her off the ambulance, that she was critical. He'd known with one glance she wouldn't make it, known as he'd jogged beside the trauma bed speeding through the electronic doors of the limited twenty-bed hospital. Her raspy voice still tore at him....

"Michael...promise me."

"Shh. Don't talk, sis. I'm here."

"Promise." She touched weak fingers to his wrist. *Internal damage, he knew, drained strength.*

Tears stung his eyes. "Sis, you're okay. Hear me?" Even to his own ears the statement rang false. Another night and *he wouldn't have been the doctor on call. Another night and it would have been his associate's turn.*

Rushing down the tiled corridor, the paramedic at the helm of the long board said, "She was a passenger in an MVA, Doc."

"Air bag?"

"No. A '91 pickup, horse trailer in tow."

Michael knew the vehicle. Old and banged up from too many haulings. Why hadn't they taken the Ford F350 to that auction?

"Get me two large bore IVs," he barked as they spun into emergency and a nurse dashed off. "Vitals?"

"Pulse rate 140—"

"BP's eighty over fifty—dropping!"

The IVs were suddenly in his hands. "Run warm ringer's lactate wide open, both IVs!" The nurse on his left disappeared. "And get X ray and lab down here! I want a C.B.C., lytes, B.U.N., creatinine, glucose, type and cross-match six units—now!"

In the end none of it, not one thing he'd given her, had helped. He looked around the cement and tiled alleyway of the barn where he still stood. Turning, he strode out into the heavy evening air. *Damn memories.*

"So, you're the one." A scratchy female voice spoke through the open doorway.

Shanna looked up from the last of the canned goods she was storing in the pantry. After milking, she'd run into Blue Springs for groceries. Now, a tiny, white-haired woman in tan cowboy boots, jeans and a poet's blouse stood leaning on a cane on the threshold of the door Shanna had propped wide for a breeze of cool evening air.

Michael Rowan's grandmother.

Same high-boned cheeks, resolute jaw and hawk nose.

Beside her on the stoop, Jenni, dressed in a pink jumpsuit, clutched Octavia and a miniature red-and-blue knapsack.

The matriarch stepped inside. Behind brown-rimmed glasses, she judged the room from corner to ceiling to floor.

"Well," the old lady said, her eyes as intense as her grandson's. "You've certainly made a mark."

You haven't seen nothing yet. "Why don't you come in, ma'am. Hey, Jenni. Want a cookie?"

The little girl nodded with a shy smile.

The old lady spied the coffeemaker. "That brew fresh?"

"As tomorrow's dawn." Shanna took out two mugs and filled them.

"You're quick. Got a wit, too. Well-shaped legs. Good qualities. Skirt's a mite short, but then this isn't my era."

Shanna choked back a laugh. Granny or not, she was like an auctioneer citing the record of an animal in the ring.

"I'm Katherine Rowan, by the way. Michael's grandmother." She didn't offer a hand. "Friends call me Kate."

"Shanna McKay. Cream, sugar?"

"Black."

Kate settled at the kitchen table with her cane across her knees. Jenni sat on the couch with Octavia and began plucking the little tea set Shanna had seen in the main house from the knapsack.

Kate pursed her lips. Her gray eyes pinned Shanna. "You're not afraid, are you?"

"Of what?"

"Me."

Shanna set two mugs on the table and gave the child a large chocolate chip cookie and a glass of milk. She stroked Jenni's hair, then slipped into a chair. "*Should* I be afraid of you?"

"I've put the run on a few hired hands in my day."

"Maybe you had grounds to do so. But, if I leave it won't be because I've sloughed up on the job."

"I like you, Shanna McKay. I believe you and I will get along very well."

"I agree."

They grinned at each other.

"Grammy?" Jenni came to stand by the woman's knee.

"What, child? Bored already?"

"No, but can I play on the step? I want to see the chick'bees again."

"Chick-a-dees. All right. But don't wander off."

Several treks later, the child had transported doll, milk, tea set and cookie outside. Within moments, she was humming and explaining to Tavia about black-hatted birdies.

Shanna watched the child play in freckled sunshine. *Nine years and still mending. I'll never forget you, Timmy.*

Kate said, "My great-granddaughter is very taken with you."

"She's a sweet child."

The old woman sipped noisily at her coffee. "Her mother, my granddaughter—God rest her soul—didn't know the first thing about raising kids. She wasn't the maternal kind." Another slurpy sip. "Bob did most of the mothering."

"Mrs. Rowan—"

"But you know about mothering, don't you?"

"I don't think—"

"I can see it in your face when you look at that child." The old lady sized up the open doorway where Jenni hummed tunelessly. "She's told me a few things about your first meeting."

"I hardly know the girl."

"Yes, you do. You knew exactly what she needed from the minute you told her about those birds out there."

Shanna looked down at her coffee. "Mrs. Rowan, I don't think we should discuss Jenni or how her mother treated her. I'm…I'm only an employee and in a few weeks I'll be gone."

Kate shot her a look. "Did you know she's barely spoken more than a handful of sentences since her parents died?"

"Michael—Doctor Rowan mentioned it the other day." *When he was giving me hot looks and touching my earrings.*

"Did he also mention she has nightmares?"

"No."

"She wakes up and thinks she sees Leigh in the doorway."

Shanna's eyes sought out the tiny form sitting twenty feet away, chatting to Octavia.

"He doesn't know how to deal with it," Kate went on. "He's had a lot of…trouble getting over—" her lips tightened "—Leigh's death. They were attached at the hip. Jen is the spitting image of Leigh as a child, you know. Though, God forgive me for saying it, she doesn't have Leigh's personality. My granddaughter was excessively driven and obsessed with the land. Anything else was a side note. Including her daughter. Shocked us all when she got pregnant. She wasn't prone to wanting children. Bob was, though. So they had Jenni. To soften the marriage, I suspect." She blew a gusty breath. "It worked."

"Mrs. Rowan…"

"Kate."

"Kate. Why are you telling me this? You don't even know who I am."

The elder woman harumphed. "For some reason unbeknownst to any of us, you've become the light at the end of a very dark tunnel for my great-granddaughter. Since she met you, your name comes into every second sentence she speaks." Again, Kate looked toward Jenni. "She's been a quiet child all her life. When her parents died…well." She looked at Shanna. "Jen's never taken to anyone so, not even me."

"I—"

"Oh, don't fuss. That wasn't meant to be nasty. I've got

more than enough of Leigh in me not to be jealous. Though, in my old age I've realized something she hadn't yet learned.'' She stirred a spoon in her unadorned coffee and gave Shanna a stern look. "Happiness counts above all else."

Shanna remained silent. Jenni sang in the sunshine. *How could you not have been happy with your baby, Leigh?*

Kate lifted her mug to her lips and rested the rim there, her wintry eyes direct. "You'd be a fine match for my grandson. Oh, now, don't worry," she said when Shanna almost choked on her coffee. "It's just an observation."

Shanna dabbed her mouth with a napkin. "Is this what you meant by putting the run on your employees?"

Kate threw back her head and laughed. "Honey, you are definitely a delight. No, all my other employees were men and as far as I know not one was prone to wearing a skirt."

"Well, that's a relief to hear."

Kate sobered. "I never say anything I don't mean. And, I've never told another soul what I'm about to tell you. The women my grandson dates are as deep as a bale of hay."

I don't want to know this. Really, I do not.

"All right," Kate said, acknowledging Shanna's discomfort. "Forget Michael. By the way, you make a decent cup of coffee." She slanted a look over her shoulder. "And keep a clean house."

"I'm having my brother paint the walls."

The old woman examined the kitchen and muttered, "Leigh could've taken a lesson from you. If it wasn't for Bob, they would've lived like pigs in mud."

Pigs in mud? "Kate—"

But Michael's grandmother went on, as if she sat in the room alone. "He was always finding dust bunnies under the furniture. It's a wonder little Jenni made it through the crawling stage without gagging on one."

Shanna's jaw dropped. *Michael's sister had raised her*

baby in filth? "But the house is impeccable, the barn spotless."

An impatient wave. "Michael. After Leigh died he spent every spare hour scrubbing, polishing, waxing. He couldn't handle Jenni living in that kind of dirt any more. As for the barn—that was Leigh's love. The outdoors, the animals, the farm. Down there everything was in its place."

Had Leigh loved her daughter at all? Been concerned about whether or not the child felt safe, warm, cared for?

Kate said, "Don't get me wrong. She loved Jenni. She just wasn't domestically inclined or the mothering type. Bob did most of the parenting. He was crazy about the child."

Shanna mulled over the information. When she met Jenni, the child had been...

Clean? Michael's doing.

Afraid of affection? Shanna's gratitude kiss proved that.

Bob had loved his daughter. Hugs and kisses came from the man in Jenni's life. No wonder the poor elf was lost.

"You see where I'm coming from now?" the old lady asked.

Yes, she did. "It's hard not to love her," Shanna murmured.

Restless, she rose and refilled their mugs. Jenni, Jason and herself, a trio with mothers who would have benefitted from Love-Your-Children 101. *And your childhood, Michael?*

"Were they close, Doctor Rowan and his sister?" she asked before she could stop herself.

Kate grunted. "They were twins." As if that explained it all. "For the most part they were inseparable, as twins are wont to be, but especially so when Davey, my son, and his wife went on their...adventures. The kids would sleep in the same room the nights their parents weren't here. Leigh was scared of the dark."

"Adventures?"

The old woman batted the air. "Another story." She picked up her coffee, blew on it then drank.

Shanna's turned cold.

The sweet sound of Jenni's singing warmed the room.

Kate pushed her mug aside. "About a year after Davey and his wife died, the twins took to different interests. Leigh got caught up in the farm and the animals and Michael…" She patted the cane in her lap. "We really didn't know what was on his mind. It wasn't until he went to college that we found out he wanted to go into medicine. He…he was the first in our family to get a degree, you know."

"Kate, I think—"

"Think I'm a gossip, don't you, girl?" Behind lenses, her eyes—Michael's eyes—were magnified.

"Not at all." *I think you're lonely for your children.*

Kate stared out the window at the serene pastures and the majesty of Mount Baker. "I'm telling you so you'll understand him better. He's a good man."

"I don't doubt it."

"Just has trouble connecting with family folk. Leigh went off on a tangent with this place. I think it scared Michael, the way she loved it. Worsened when she got pregnant. Truth be known, he didn't think much of her mothering skills. 'Course he's not much better. He's had a dickens of a time connecting with Jenni." She brightened. "But he's a wonderful doctor."

Jenni's voice tinkled from somewhere beyond the stoop, coaxing Silly to lie in Tavia's lap.

Kate looked at Shanna. "I'm glad you're the one who gave my great-grandchild back her smile. And," she went on, "as ornery and irascible as he can be, I suspect you've sparked a smile from my grandson. Both have been a long time coming."

Near the cool shadowed doorway, a bee droned before it decided to forego curiosity for the hive and flitted away.

Losing herself in beauty and peace, Shanna murmured, "He doesn't realize how much this place can heal him. Too bad it's up for sale."

For a long moment all was still. Kate set her palms flat on the table and rose. Avid eyes bore into Shanna. "What do you mean Rowan Dairy is up for sale?"

Shanna frowned. "You didn't know?"

Chapter Four

Michael stood in the cabin doorway. His grandmother picked up her mug, then clunked it down. "If my grandson thinks he's going to—"

"What, Gran?" he said, crossing over the threshold into the cool interior of the employee quarters.

Cane tapping the linoleum, Katherine stalked toward him, a miniature warrior. "You planning to get rid of Rowan Dairy, young man?"

"Grandma." He forced composure into his voice. "Let's discuss this up at the house, okay?" Over her head, his eyes locked on Shanna. She wore a skirt. A white midthigh-length skirt.

"What needs to be told can be said right here, boy. What difference does it make when she knows it all anyhow?"

"A helluva difference," he groused. Hand to her elbow, he tried to steer the old woman out the door.

One liver-spotted fist found her hip. "Don't treat me like

some old senile fool. And don't swear. I didn't raise you to speak like a hillbilly, nor do I want Jenni's ears seared.''

Michael looked at his niece with her tea set and doll. She stared back, silently. He took a controlling breath. ''Grandma, if you want to address this matter, meet me at the house.'' Not waiting a second more, he strode out the door and down the path. *Dammit.* If the old woman had been around instead of on her six-week annual trek to California, he would have consulted her.

He let himself into the main house, chucked his suit jacket on a kitchen chair and headed for the cabinet in the living room. He needed a drink. Something to burn a trail straight to his toes. Brandy. He poured a shot, downed it. Poured another.

He shouldn't have hired her.

She was an irritant, a pest, a busybody.

Who had his niece's best interests at heart.

And had his own heart beating a staccato ninety percent of the day.

He loosened his tie. *Okay, admit it. She's good for Jenni. There's a glint in the tyke's eyes again, and she giggles.*

She hadn't giggled in months. When Leigh was alive—

''Boosting for bravado, Michael?''

He turned. His grandmother stood under the archway. ''Say what's on your mind, Gran. Let's be done with it.''

Hand on the balustrade, she took the two steps into the sunken living room. ''You should have warned me, boy.'' Carefully, she eased to the sofa's arm. ''Going behind my back isn't right.''

''Leigh's death wasn't right, either.''

''I agree. But, I doubt she'd've been as eager to sell your portion were you laying under the sod,'' she said bluntly.

Glass in hand, Michael wandered to the bay window. Faded orange streamers ebbed in the face of the fast approaching night. Already above the black hills, Venus glim-

mered like the beacon of a lighthouse. As kids, he and his
sister had wished on it a thousand times. On the knoll behind the house, they'd wished for great report cards, a Chi-
cago Bulls jersey, a dirt bike, winning the 4-H calf cham-
pionship. The year their parents died, he'd stopped wishing.

"Selling wouldn't have been an issue for Leigh," he said.
"She was in love with this place."

"And you aren't."

He sighed. "I didn't say that." Setting a hand along the
window frame, he stared down toward the shadowed barnyard. In the distant pasture, the white-spotted cattle grazed
under the peace of evening. "I do love it," he murmured.
He and Leigh *were* alike; both had loved the farm. It had
been part of them, an extension, a limb. But no more. *No
more.*

He faced the woman who had raised him. "I don't have
time to look after its operation."

"Three months is hardly time to gauge success or failure,
Michael."

"It is for me," he snapped. "I can't live both here and
in town, work the clinic, the hospital, care for Jenni, and on
the sidelines pencil in a farm."

"No one's asking you to," Katherine said reasonably.
"For one thing, you could market the town house. Move
here permanently. For another—"

"Sell my town house?" He frowned. "Why should I give
up a place that suits my needs perfectly?"

With the aid of the coffee table, Katherine pushed to her
feet. "Is that what this is all about? What suits the lifestyle
you're trying to fit into?"

"I'm not *fitting* into anything. I happen to like my life."

"Do you? You've been doctoring this town for over a
decade. I haven't seen a spark in your eyes for years except
when you talk to your patients. Are you happy, Michael?"

"What kind of asinine question is that? Seeing people get well and knowing you've done it—hell, it's profound."

"And when they don't heal?"

Too deep. She scratched too deep. He turned away. "It's a fact of life."

"Was Leigh a fact of life?"

This is none of your affair, Gran. Let it go. Let me *go.*

She leaned heavily on her cane. "What's the real reason you want to sell, Michael?"

"I don't want to discuss it."

Cane tapping the hardwood, eyes as acute as when he was a boy, Katherine walked toward him. "I'll just bet you don't," she said. "But you amaze me at times." He lifted a brow. "Your arrogance whips your intelligence. You, of all people, should know that being human means flaws. Inadequacies. Limitations."

"I'm very aware of my limitations." *Every day I remember how I couldn't save my sister.*

"Leigh is not one of them, child."

Anger. It shot up his chest. He sliced the air with a hand. "Leave it alone, okay?"

"Some people can't be helped, honey. Leigh was one."

Slamming his glass on the table, he grabbed his jacket. "I'm going out. Take Jen home, will you? I won't be back till late."

"Running away is not the answer, boy. Face it."

He spun on his heel. "I'm selling this place, Gran, and moving Jen away from it." *All the way to Seattle.* "The sooner you adjust to that, the better off we'll be."

With a deep breath she tucked in her chin. "Fine. Then I want to buy it."

"What?"

"You heard me. I'll give you whatever the going rate is for a business this size."

"Don't be absurd."

"I won't have it going to some stranger, Michael. Your grandpa and I worked many long, hard years on this land. And when we passed it on to you and Leigh, we did so with the hope it would remain in the family."

The tip of her chin quivered, and he reached out, his hand touching her arm. It dropped away when she flinched. "Grandma. If there was any other way, you know I'd do it."

She removed her glasses and cleaned them needlessly. The gesture pierced his heart. Stoic as always, his grandmother.

Never crying.

Not for her only child, his father.

Not for her husband of nearly half a century.

Not for her granddaughter.

Only for the land. The thought made his stomach tilt.

He stared at her bowed face. In the twenty-seven years since his parents had died, her features had altered little. *The way Leigh, at seventy-plus, might have looked.*

Gently, he said, "You don't have the capital to invest."

"I'll get a loan. I've known Merv Giles down at First National for forty-three years. Diapered his bottom once. He'll grant me the finances. And if he can't there's always—"

"You're serious."

"Very."

"Gran, you're seventy-seven." Forty years his senior.

Something flashed in her eyes. She shoved on her glasses. "I may be old but I'm a long way from being a corpse yet, son. I'll hire Shanna. She and Oliver can keep tending the operation while I do the admin work."

"Shanna." Her name shouldn't jolt his pulse.

"Yes. Clever lady that one. Strong but with a soft side. Stows it away—for one reason or another. She'd be a superb match for you. Not afraid to get her hands dirty."

Shanna, cleaning his shoes. A flush crept up his throat. "Seems you've got it all figured out. You oversee the books, Shanna works the farm and somewhere along the line we give you a passel of kids to inherit it all." Shanna, carrying his child. "Sorry to disappoint you, but she isn't my style."

"Style? Is that what they call it these days? Check below the surface, Michael. You may find a surprise or two." With a pat to his cheek, she limped from the house.

Three minutes later, he backed the Cherokee from the garage. If he found solace tonight, it would be in his own bed. In town.

Where he couldn't smell the forest. Or hear the night creatures. Or the wind soughing in the trees.

Where reminders of *Shanna* were nonexistent.

Shanna watched Kate stalk up the path after her grandson.

"You like peanut-butter cookies, Jen?" she asked.

The child looked up from her spot on the stoop. The cat, eyes shut, dozed in a last sunny ray on the first step.

"Uh-huh, yeah!" Jenni bobbed her head. "Can Tavia and Silly have one, too?"

"You bet. Bring them in and we'll make a fresh batch while your Gram and Uncle Michael talk."

From the refrigerator, Shanna dug out a ready-made cookie mix. The child's face appeared at her elbow. "Go wash up, peachkins. Bathroom's at the end of the hallway."

"'Kay." Jenni skipped away, dark curls bouncing.

Sweet child. You could be mine.

You're dreaming again, Shan.

Down the hall, she heard splashing and high-pitched humming.

Surely a tiny dream wasn't much. Was it?

The counselor had said she'd tacked undue hope and

dreams on her baby. Especially after Wade walked out of their marriage.

"Look to the future, but without those infamous rosy lenses," the woman had said.

Shanna kept her mind off Michael.

"I'm ready!" Jenni ran back into the room, wiping wet hands on the bib of her pink jumpsuit.

Shanna patted the stool next to her. "Climb on up, peach, and we'll get started." They made twenty cookies in all. Rolling batter into small, round balls. Arranging them on the cookie sheet. Pressing them down in criss-cross patterns with forks.

"Yum." Jenni mouthed around sticky fingers. "This is *good!* Can I have one now?"

"Let's wait till they're baked. You like singing, right?"

"Uh-huh! My teacher says I can sing real good. Melody Graham thinks she's the bestest singer in the whole school." Jenni rolled her eyes. Shanna laughed. "That's so dumb cuz she's only in first grade. Like me. Miss Larkins says we'll all be bestest singers if we practice *lots.*"

Wise teacher. "Come, we'll be best today while those cookies are baking." Shanna walked to her bedroom and fetched her left-handed twelve-string Alvarez propped against the night table.

Jenni's eyes rounded. "You can play a *guitar?*"

"Yep. How about we liven up those cookies?"

"Sha-*nnaa.* Cookies can't get alive."

"Sure they can. Just watch."

Back in the tiny living area, they settled on the couch. She plucked out an easy, light tune, the sound rich and delicate along the six paired strings. Jenni snuggled against her right arm. "Okay, here goes. You are my cookie," she sang. "My only cookie. You make me happy when skies are gray."

Jenni laughed. "That's not a song!"

"Sure it is. I just changed the words a bit. It really goes like this…" Three songs later, she said, "Want to see if those cookies have some life yet?"

Jenni dashed to the oven, peered through its rectangular window. "They're getting really fat!"

"See. Told you they're livening up."

The child scrambled up on the couch again, little body nestling close. Soft, sweet. "Shanna?"

"Hmm?"

"I sure like you lots. Better'n any of my friends."

What would you say to that, Doc? "And I like you better than my friends, sweetie."

"Sing your favorite."

Her favorite. She plucked an octave. "This one's a bit sad."

"Why? Do you feel sad?"

"Sometimes," she said, thrumming quietly. *Would you have chattered like a chipmunk at this age, Timmy?*

Shifting to her knees, Jenni slid her arms around Shanna's neck. She whispered, "I feel sad thinking about Mommy and Daddy."

"I know, peach."

"Sometimes it hurts and I cry. Do you think Uncle Michael and Grammy cry? I never see them cry."

"Sadness is different for adults, Jen. Some hide it."

"Why?"

"Because they think it'll upset people they love."

The child's lower lip trembled. "I'm going to hide it, too," she said. "Maybe then Uncle M. will smile at me."

Outside the office window the late afternoon lay under dark, wet skies. Water streamed from eaves and dripped between branches.

How did she take to milking in a cold, rainy dawn? Michael wondered. *Doesn't matter. She doesn't matter.*

He reviewed his notes. *Keep your brain directed. The people who enter the clinic come first.* He zeroed in on the elevated blood pressure and the cholesterol numbers on the page before him. Would the woman he'd just examined follow the prescribed diet and do the advised regular exercise? Probably not. Four years, and her habits remained constant.

Some people can't be helped.

Okay, so Katherine was right.

And Leigh was still dead.

He stared at his hands. Big, blunt-tipped, slightly callused. Good construction hands—were he in construction. A craftsman's creative tools. But not ingenious enough to repair the damage or stop the seeping blood inside Leigh's body.

What would Shanna say if she knew you'd stood useless at your sister's side?

Tell you to get over it. Get on with life.

God, he wished it were that easy. Leigh was blood. They'd shared a *womb,* for God's sake!

He pushed back from his desk and scraped his palms down his cheeks. Two women stealing his mind. One dead, and one so alive that not driving half the night to his town house, or seeing patients, or rain could erase her.

Collecting the papers, he shoved them into the file.

He wanted Shanna as he had no other woman. She, who could short-fuse his temper in less time than it took to scrawl his initials on a prescription slip.

The phone rang.

"Doctor Rowan," he growled into the receiver.

"It's Cliff Barnette, Michael. Sorry to bother you, but there's a fellow from California who's coming into town next week. He's on the hunt for a place exactly like yours. Any chance we can arrange a meet, say, Monday evening? Seems he's a little anxious, which, if we play it right, could work to our advantage."

At his Realtor's words Michael rubbed his temple. "Let me get back to you, Cliff. I don't have my calendar in front of me." What was the matter with him? His desk calendar was right under his nose. Selling the dairy was a priority. Right?

You really should reconsider…keep this place for yourself and your niece.

And, *if* he kept it?

"—you're busy," Barnette cut in. "I'll present the place alone. It's not crucial for you to be there."

"No. I want to be there."

"Good, good. The guy's only here for three days."

"I understand. Give me an hour and we'll arrange a time."

The call ended. What was he doing? In less than a dozen words he'd nearly cancelled a decision he'd deliberated over for weeks after putting Leigh in the ground.

In less than ten days his normal twelve-year routine—waking, working, sleeping—had gone off a high board.

Because of her.

A quick two knocks and his door flung open. Rochelle Garland, his associate, breezed into the room.

"Michael." Without preamble, she flipped open the folder she carried. "I need you to give me an opinion. As far as I've determined it's low iron but—something wrong?"

He ran a hand through his hair. "I almost told Cliff to take the dairy off the market." He snorted. "I never should have listened to her."

"Who?"

Shanna, he thought. Long, lanky Shanna. With whom he was obsessed.

Rochelle touched his arm. "Michael?"

"I'm fine. Let's have a look at your patient."

He reviewed the symptoms, gave his opinion, and proceeded with an in-depth outline for treatment. It wasn't the first time their observations and conclusions had matched. He closed the folder and handed it back. He said, "We're a good team."

"Damn straight." She shoved the file under an arm. "Listen, I've got this pot of stew I'd love to get rid of. Why don't you come by the house after work? We'll have a few drinks, a couple laughs and eat till our bellies burst."

He felt hard pressed not to grin. "You hustlin' me, Roche?"

"'Course. A big, bad hunk like you, I'd be a fool not to."

He cast a half smile. "Geoff might get the wrong idea."

She winged back a skein of black hair. "Oh, who cares what that old lug has to say? Come on, you deserve a night out."

Yeah, he did. He deserved to unwind with friends who shared the same interests. He missed honing his wits on world events, missed a woman's simple meal. Easy laughter. He needed to escape the hellhounds chasing him around every bend. Besides, who waited for him at the farm?

A scrawny-limbed, sassy-mouthed female with blue eyes. Yeah right, Rowan.

Roche gave him a light jab in ribs. "See you at seven, sailor." Dashing out the door with a flap of her lab coat, she said, "Oh, and bring Jenni. It's time she met Amy."

Amy. Roche and Geoff's daughter.

One whole family coming up.

He'd gone because Roche undermined his mood.

In the end, he realized, it had been for Jen.

Something foreign tugged his heart as he glanced at the sleeping child in the rear of the Jeep. She hadn't been eager to play with Amy, but Amy's vivacious character had won out.

Easing off the gas, Michael entered the farm's lane. The main house loomed dark and unwelcome under a drape of rain. Through the trees, the cabin wavered like a ghost. Was she in bed, curled under the covers? Listening for the sound of his vehicle?

Had she made more cookies tonight? According to Jenni, she'd baked a stack the night before. Baked and sang Old MacDonald's Farm. While he drove off his frustration because of Katherine. And *her*.

Light arrowed into rainy shadows from the calving barn. Sam Dunham's veterinarian van, rear doors open, was parked in front.

Michael climbed from the truck and unbuckled Jenni. Moaning, she rubbed a fist in one eye. Cherry juice blended with sleepy child. He tucked her into his coat and set his mouth against her hair. *Aw, Leigh, I don't want to be on the fringe of Jenni's life like you were. But I'm afraid. What if something happens to me?*

He traveled through the house and up the stairs to Jenni's bedroom. In sleep, her mouth formed an O. Mercy, she was tiny. Tiny, vulnerable, innocent.

The well-being of a child is more important than a job.

"You win," he whispered to another bit of Shanna-wisdom. He'd give Jenni all the attention and care she needed.

He'd just have to keep his heart distanced.

With a physician's skill, he removed the child's clothing, pulled on her pajamas, and rolled her under the covers. He retrieved Brown Bear, fur wearied from a thousand hugs, and tucked the nightly guardian into the crook of one small arm. Silly, purr rumbling like faraway thunder, leapt to the quilt and settled against Jenni's spine.

Michael set her half of their walkie-talkies to standby and placed it on the night table. He looked down at the bundle that was his niece. He wanted to breathe in the lemon scent of her hair again and reaffirm her weighty warmth in his arms. Kiss her cheek.

Instead, he left the room.

Through the rain-scented night her soft laughter reached him. What were they up to, she and Dunham?

The radio was tuned to a country station. Some guy grieved about leaving lights on in a house. Well, she sure wasn't grieving, not with the barn lit like city center on New Year's.

Michael quickened his pace, boots pounding into moist earth.

He found them in a rear free-stall. A Holstein lay unconscious on a bed of fresh straw. Heads bent together, Shanna and Dunham stood in quiet discussion. She was dressed in her usual green coveralls with yellow T-shirt beneath its bib. Suddenly her mouth bowed and her eyes laughed. Easy, affable.

"What's going on here?" Michael demanded.

Shanna jerked around. One hand fluttered to her throat, then fell to her side. In the next instant her eyes sparked. "When are you going to stop creeping up on the animals, Doc?"

"Take it easy, Shanna." Dunham patted her shoulder. "The cow's still out of it. Hey, Michael, glad you're here."

"Sam." Michael nodded. Jealousy leapt in him like a coiled spring. He entered the stall, hunkered beside the animal and surveyed the vet's sutures. Clean, tidy. Superior. But he couldn't ignore the damage. Gashes zigzagged down the shank, mapped the cow's belly, and cut across her milk bag. Left udders, gone. *Barbed wire.*

He checked the beast's ear tag. A top producer. "How?"

Dunham shoved a bloody towel into a plastic bag. "A pack of stray dogs. Split her from the herd like wolves."

Michael looked up at the vet and Shanna standing near the Dutch door. His jaw muscles tightened. "Dogs?"

Shanna nodded. Her eyes glistened in the hazy light.

He rose slowly. "Where were you at the time, Ms. Mc-Kay?"

"In the field." Soft words. Pointed words. "Trying to scare them away. Considering the cow was a little *tied up*—" her sarcasm wasn't lost on him "—and there were five of them, I'd say her odds weren't great."

"Five dogs?"

"Unless my math skills have—"

"Good God, woman," he exploded. His fingers danced at his sides. The little twit. Was she clueless? A mongrel pack on the prowl? Excited, spurred by a chase? "Are you crazy? A bunch of vicious dogs tasting blood? They could have turned on you."

"So I should've left her to them? Take a look, Michael. Two guesses how it would've ended."

"They could have turned on *you*," he repeated. *Breathe deep*.

"I had my thirty-thirty Winchester." Their eyes caught. Held. "I know how to use a gun, Doc," she said quietly. "It's the one skill my father taught us. He didn't like big bad wolves."

Like him.

"How many?"

"Three. The other two ran off. Sam's taking the carcasses to have them checked for rabies."

Three. Incredible. "Where was Oliver?"

"Gone home. This happened around eight tonight."

Michael swore softly. She'd been alone, while he'd been relaxing back with Geoff and Roche. Talking, laughing.

The cow stirred. Its head moved, eyes fluttering. Its legs folded into a laying position.

Shanna stepped forward. Her summer-meadows scent

competed with hay and cow. "Rosebud's okay. Sam's done a terrific job." She eyed the stall's empty doorway. "Where's Jenni?"

Rosebud? "Sleeping in her bed."

"Up at the house? Alone?"

"I have the walkie-talkie in my pocket."

"What if she has a nightmare? Kate told me—"

"Kate should learn to keep her mouth shut. Jenni hasn't had one in two weeks." *Not since you arrived.* "But if she does, she'll watch TV and be asleep in five minutes."

"How comforting."

He dragged a hand over his scalp. "This is a farm. Jenni knows emergencies happen. Cows don't always wait till morning to freshen, and calves sometimes have to be fed through the night."

Dunham cleared his throat. "If it's all the same to you folks, I still have another call." To Michael he said, "I've given the cow an antibiotic shot, so she should be okay. Her production days are finished, though. My advice would be to sell her soon as the wounds heal or keep her as a breeder." He turned into the corridor. "I'll be back Friday morning for a checkup. Nice meeting you, Shanna."

"Same here, Sam. Thanks for coming."

Michael followed the veterinarian out of the barn. He'd deal with G.I. Jane later.

Shanna closed her eyes. Safer to remain with the cow than to be in Michael's presence.

Except for the money, she had no reason to persist with this job. As an employer he was rude and critical; as a man he was hostile and arrogant. All of it she'd encountered with Wade. But where Wade swaggered, Michael brooded. Where Wade exacted self-importance, Michael conveyed a skepticism born of tragedy.

Her heart forgave the latter.

Entering the corridor, she hurried upstairs to the loft. In a tiny cluttered room serving as office, pharmacy and storage, she deposited Dunham's prescribed medication in a small corner refrigerator and stripped off her coveralls. Grabbing her worn fatigue jacket from a hook behind the door, she flicked off the light and headed out of the barn.

Maybe he'd gone. Maybe his disgust with her had taken him straight to the house, out of sight. Maybe, this minute, he was writing her final paycheck.

He stood at the gate of the horse paddock.

A dark shape moved several feet beyond the fence. Soldat. Seconds later, she saw only Michael's head and the sheen of the navy nylon windbreaker on his broad shoulders. Eventually, the balance of his tall, ungiving frame evolved. Alone with the horse.

A small shiver ran through her. *Go, explain to him.* But what? That she had done what she believed was right? That she was sorry a strong producer was lost?

A sigh of lassitude and his head fell back. Rain patted his face. Flipping up her collar against the wet night, she shelved her own hands and walked to where he stood. "Cooling off, Doc?"

He remained motionless. "Rain helps me think."

She studied the drizzle sifting in the amber cone of light from the yard lamp beyond where they stood. Damp horse and moist earth scented the dark. "Mm. Makes me sleepy."

Shifting, he studied her. "Does it? You looked far from sleepy in there."

The low dip of his voice sluiced into her pelvis. She took a side step. Distance was what she needed. Maybe as far away as Montana.

"In *there*," she said, "an animal was hurting."

"I seem to lose control when I'm around you."

"Not good enough, Michael. You embarrassed me."

"That, too." He offered a crooked smile. "Would it help if I sutured my mouth shut?"

She wouldn't let his attempt at humor move her. Nor would she let the rain in his hair, dampening the lock on his brow and glistening on his lashes, move her. "Next time try discovering the truth before you spew out criticism."

"I was angry."

"No kidding. And here I thought you were just being your natural, normal self."

"Sarcasm doesn't suit you, Shanna."

"Tough. It's the way I am." She whirled around, ready to stamp up the hill. Chamomile tea and a good book were what she needed, not this…this…

"Dammit!" He caught her arm. Humor gone, his face hovered inches from hers. His grip while firm, felt oddly safe and protective. "Don't you realize they could have attacked you?"

"Not till later." He had worried. About her. The zing dove straight through her heart.

"Idiot girl. It would've been too late then." He shook her lightly.

"I've never missed a shot yet."

"God." He threw back his head on an explosion of air. "Have you any idea what you do to me?"

Reality settled back. Into place. "*I* do to you? Excuse me, but I don't *do* anything to you. I stay away from you. As much as possible. *You're* the one who continually seeks me out."

"And why do you suppose that is?"

"I haven't a clue." But she did. Oh, how she did. "Maybe you're addicted to squabbling, or you get high goading people. You need to think—"

"Forget thinking."

One neat move and his arms enclosed her. Then she was under his mouth, lost. And home.

Chapter Five

Ah, the feel of his cool, rain-sprinkled mouth!

Running slowly over hers, singing through her head.

Heated wine streaming to her belly.

Her fingers fisted in his jacket. She was weightless. Pliant as melted glass. Amazing, his hewn lips. Soft as the rain she tasted there.

He nosed the hair away from her ear and muttered, "I can't stand it when you smile at another man and not me. I can't stand it when he says your name."

"Michael, this isn't—"

"Yes." He kissed her eyelids shut. "It is."

Desperation closed in and had him holding handfuls of her hair while he took her lips again. His tongue seared as it slipped inside like a mate.

The taste of him. The feel of those long, swift fingers. They looped her neck, slid down her bulky jacket. Up again, to once more slick through her hair.

"I want to feel you," he whispered into her mouth. "Now."

Before she could respond, he glided his hands into her coat and pulled her close. Skimming a palm down her spine. Cupping her buttocks. Lifting her so his sex butted her womb.

"Sweet Shanna. Soft woman. Come to the house with me." Along her neck. Kisses. Words. "Please."

"Michael…"

His name, ravaged by more kissing. He wanted *her*. Ah, but she would live her life remembering this moment—until her last breath, her last heartbeat!

Flesh and bone, curves and angles. Fit to perfection.

No, she thought dizzily. *We don't fit.* Couldn't fit.

Setting her palms against his chest, she drew back. For a moment neither could speak. His eyes stormed with desire, his lungs labored under her fingers. No less, she realized with astonishment, than her own.

"I have to go." She edged out of his embrace.

"Shanna."

"No," she said firmly. "This shouldn't have happened."

His eyes narrowed. "Don't deny it."

"I'm not denying anything. I'm saying we are not doing this again. Ever."

"Why?"

"Because we—we don't fit, jive, dance, you name it."

"Dance?"

"Compatibility, Mike. Admit it. We seldom agree. We live at opposite ends of the social scale. You're my employer, and—" her voice rose on the last reason "—we don't even like each other."

His ridiculously long, rain-dewed lashes blinked.

"You don't like me?"

The hurt in his voice was like Jason's of long ago. Eager for a crumb of Brent's attention. Her throat closed. *Oh,*

Mike. Did your family ever love you? Small sweet-faced boys striving to please their kin. Small pixie-faced girls talking to dolls. Love, for the giving, for the taking. Why had they been missed?

"I like you," she said, her heart sore. "Very much." *Too much.* She wanted to comfort him and take the haunted look from his eyes. She touched the tiny scar on his lip. "What I meant was that we don't get along that well."

One dark brow flew. His boyishness slunk into oblivion. All-American bad-boy sauntered up to home plate. Her tummy spun.

"One quick kiss justifies nothing," she pointed out.

A corner of his handsome mouth buoyed. "Quick?"

She wasn't about to go there. "G'night, Doc." Turning, she trudged up the mud-slicked path toward the cabin.

"Shanna?" His voice wove through the wet night and down her spine. "We will have that dance you're talking about. Very soon."

"Not in this lifetime, Doc," she muttered, glad for the trees and rain that separated them.

On three different occasions, she woke and prowled her darkened rooms. She was so restless her skin itched under the cotton of her nightgown.

We will have that dance. Words to torment her dreams. Have her heart rapping allegro on her ribs.

She had to leave the farm. His attitude and demeanor she understood.

His vow destroyed her.

He would kiss her again. Get his way. Get her into his bed.

The thought terrified her. Tempted her.

She held her middle and stared out the kitchen window. Dawn edged over the hills. A wind wove through the tall tamaracks along the path. Through their branches she saw the dark bulk of the farmhouse—staunch sentry of the land.

He'd grown up in that house; his sister had started her family within its walls. Laughter, voices, arguments, dreams...passion.

She escaped to the bathroom. In a half hour, milking time. She needed to see to the injured Rosebud, tell Oliver to contact the artificial insemination man for two heifers requiring bull semen. She pitied the poor cows, their clinical sex.

She stepped under the shower spray.

Had Michael brought other women to that house on the hill? Classy, disciplined women reared by classy, disciplined parents? R.N. or M.D. garnishing their surnames? *My daddy was a buckle-bunny chaser. And I'm a milkmaid.* But despite Brent, she'd molded her younger brother into a principled young man.

She turned off the tap and reached for her towel.

What, then, was the allure? Her availability? That Jenni had bonded with her? *Jenni.* Lover of flowers and cats and dress-up dolls. Whose guardians were a crippled, aged woman and an aloof, taciturn doctor.

"Dangit, they are not your responsibility." Leaving the towel on the cold bathroom floor, Shanna grabbed up her clothes. Time for work. In the barns, among her big, gentle ladies, she admitted walking away from a child would be the worst mistake.

She decided to stay.

"So, sis, you're milking cows and dunging out barns, huh? Didn't think you'd do it when I showed you that ad."

With a quick grin, her brother crossed his booted feet on her coffee table, stretched his arms along the sofa's back, and wriggled his bony rump down into the cushion. The ritual was one Shanna wouldn't change for the world. Jase was family. Whatever he did—within reason and law—was perfect with her.

"Got a problem with that?"

"Nuh-uh. Long's you're happy."

"I am." *Now you're here.* An hour ago, he had roared up to her door on his flash-fire rebuilt Harley, hollering her name and demanding something good to eat. She wondered what Michael would think when he spotted the long, sleek motorcycle with its chrome pipes and high-backed seat.

Accept it, Doctor. Jason's part of my package.

With a deft slice, she separated their late-night sandwiches and carried the snacks into the sitting area. Legs crossed in a corner of the couch, she put the plate between them.

Her brother shoved half a sandwich into his mouth. "Well," he mumbled around bread, ham and lettuce, "tell me all about it."

"There's nothing to tell. I applied and was hired."

"But why this? It's not something an educated person does."

She shrugged. "People with degrees drive buses."

He wasn't deterred. "What about Unemployment Insurance?"

"And stand in line for hours? No thanks." She smiled. "Anyway, Michael offered more than I'd ever get from UI."

His brows winged up. "You're on a first-name basis with Doctor Rowan?"

"When he's traipsing through cow poop, he's plain old Michael."

Jason laughed. "So, how much does plain old Michael pay for mucking and milking?"

"Enough."

"Hmpf. Like him, do you?"

"He's okay."

"Just okay? Coulda fooled me, Sanny-banany," he sing-songed.

"Don't call me that," she grumped. But a warmth spread from her heart.

"Afraid I might say it in front of your employer?" Jason patted her hand like a tolerant papa. "Don't worry, sis. I wouldn't tell your doctor about how I couldn't say Shanna when I was in diapers, or when you potty-trained me, ban-any meant—"

"Jason!" She laughed, jabbing him in the ribs.

Suddenly, her throat ached. This was her little brother, the love of her life. Palm to his angular jaw, she said, "I'm glad you're here, guy. I missed you."

He ruffled her hair. "Eat," he said. "You're too skinny."

An hour later, she asked, "Have you applied to the University of Washington yet?"

The evening's peace ended. Jason swung his feet to the floor and stood up. "I told you I want to work on engines."

"Jase…"

"Nope, not talking about it, Shan." He picked up the platter, went to the kitchen. "Not going to U Dub."

Shanna followed. "Come on, Jase. I've got money saved. You promised you'd look at going to college this fall."

The plate clanked into the sink. He swung around. "Wrong. *You* did the promising. Your words: 'I promise to get the money; I promise to get you into residence; I promise to pay for food and books.' I told you then and I'll tell you now, I don't need you promising me anything." He whacked on the tap and rinsed the plate. "I can do it on my own, sis."

"I just want what's best for you." *So you don't need years of night school, like me.*

He set the plate onto the drying rack. "I know. But in a couple weeks my luck's changing. I'll be doing what I've

wanted since I was six. If we'd had decent parents you'd
be finished with school by now, probably a CEO of some
big company.''

She took a tea towel to the plate. ''I'd choose the same
road if it meant keeping us together under one roof.''

''You think I don't know that?'' He faced her. ''Shan,
you're the best sister a guy could have. But…I want to get
a place of my own.'' He shook his head. Absolving her
obligations. ''I've been thinking about it for a while now.''

''Oh, hon.''

''I can afford it,'' he said stubbornly.

She looked at the texts, the notebooks—her correspon-
dence courses—stacked at the end of the counter. In the fall,
she'd have her accounting certificate. She could start building a solid career. Categorically not her dream of dreams,
but the bills would be paid regularly without depleting her
savings.

She'd had it all planned for them.

He caught her look and said, ''Just for once see it my
way.''

She stared back, surprised. ''I always do.''

''No, you don't. Most times you want things to go your
way. I'm not saying that's bad because most times you're
right. But, in this—well, I just need to find *my* path. Okay?''

Independence. His wanting it stung a little. Since her
twelfth birthday, she'd strapped the responsibility of her
brother to her heart. Each stage of his life she'd molded
with her hand. Charted with her voice. Designed with her
love.

For years she'd believed Brent and Meredith McKay split
because of her. Because she'd blown out the candles on her
chocolate store-bought cake and nodded eagerly when her
daddy set his cowboy hat on her head and asked, ''Hey,
there, li'l britches, you about ready to rodeo with your old
man?''

Her mother stood up then, went to the bedroom, yanked a scuffed suitcase from the closet, stashed a few clothes in it and walked down the road. Cries from her children and curses from Brent hadn't made her miss a step. Within that bleak hour, Shanna, in the core of her soul, understood why Meredith had left. Just as she understood it was up to her to see to Jason's upbringing. *And safety.* Safety from what might hurt his tender heart.

Her own heart tender for different reasons, she asked, "Was I really that overbearing all these years?"

He took the towel from her hands, hung it up. "Nah. Just mothering."

Mothering. Lovely word. "This job—what is it?"

The eagerness in his eyes shamed her. "It's at Alton's Motorcycles. The owner saw what I did with the Harley and wants me to apprentice for a year in the repair shop." An abashed smile. "I want to open my own shop when I'm thirty, Shan."

Sound dreams. But without a post-secondary education she was afraid. Afraid those dreams would elude him. For years. Like hers. She started the coffee. "It's good to have a goal."

"Yeah." He rubbed his short, buzzed hair. "Um, is somebody planning on painting in here?"

She caught his gaze on the tins beside the door. "I was thinking of asking you."

"Me?"

"Michael's willing to pay well. He wants these quarters spruced up for the sale."

Jason frowned. "What about your headaches?"

"What about them?" She snatched a scrunchy from the counter, plopped back onto the couch, and bound up her short hair.

"Well, for one, the fumes—"

"I'll deal with them."

"How? By holding your breath? You'll get sicker than a colicky horse sleeping in here when it's fresh."

"There's a cot in the barn office. I'll sleep there."

"And in here?"

"I'm not in here that much and when I am I'll keep the windows wide open and tie a tea towel bandit-style over my nose." She smiled and poked him. "Satisfied?"

He snorted. "Right. What's your doctor gonna say when he sees you sleeping with the cows?"

"First off, he's not *my* doctor. Second, I'll tell him I'm on call for one of the pregnant ladies in the birthing barn."

Jason gave her a sideways look.

"It's true. Hat-Girl is due to calve this week."

"Hat-Girl?"

"There's a black hat shape on her left side."

"And if she calves before I'm finished painting?"

"I'll make up some other excuse."

"Why don't you just tell him the real reason, Shan? That the fumes trigger memories of your pregnancy?"

"Because. The last thing I want is Michael thinking I'm susceptible to illnesses." *Or helpless. Or feeble.*

"A migraine isn't a disease, and they aren't contagious. If he doesn't know that, he's a crappy doctor."

Shanna looked away. "The opposite. He's very perceptive."

Jason walked over and sat next to her. "You don't want him to find out about the baby."

"No."

Her brother regarded her. Another perceptive man.

"Or," he said softly, touching her shoulder, "that you were painting your kitchen when Wade—"

"You know too much." She got up and checked the coffee. "When can you start?"

"I have two days off starting Monday."

"Great." Michael she'd deal with later.

They drank their coffee and talked. Summer events, the Lassers, how Jason was coping on his own in their town apartment. At midnight, she stood. ''If you want to crash in the other bedroom, grab some stuff from the linen closet down the hall.''

She slipped into her room and shut the door. In the outer area, the TV came to life in muted sound. *Please, don't ask why I'm sleeping in the barn, Mike,* she thought and remembered his worry for her the night of the dogs. Dread crept around her heart.

Rather than a night of hot sex with him, she invited a biker to her bed. *A biker!* Michael stared at the motorcycle from where he leaned back in the cushioned wicker chair, sandaled feet anchored on the porch railing. His first Sunday off in three weeks and jealousy digested his morning coffee.

Last night his headlights had caught the chrome through the trees. A drowsy niece in his arms, he'd stood beside the Jeep Cherokee studying the cabin's darkened windows.

He'd slept like a man caught in a vice.

Easy to picture her visitor. Long greasy hair tied back with a leather strip. Week-old beard. Studded leather. Colors flying. Boots and chains. In ten years, he'd stitched up more than one injured gang member, thanks to the lake five miles south of town.

A soft, high humming. Jenni. Curled in the corner of the wicker love seat, rocking her doll, singing ''You Are My Sunshine.''

One of his mother's favorites.

Michael wondered when his sister had passed the carefree song on to her daughter. Before this moment, the verse had never crossed the child's lips. Watching his niece, a warmth seeped into his chest. Ringlets framed her pixie face as she bent over the doll, crooning in her sweet girlish voice.

Jen—fragile, vulnerable.

Michael wanted to pull her onto his lap and rock her. "Did Mommy teach you that?" he asked, heart aching to liberate its paternal instincts.

Jen shook her head. "From Shanna. She knows lots of songs."

Shanna. Always Shanna. He took a strong swallow of coffee.

"Do you want to hear 'nother one?" the child asked. Eagerness edged her hazel eyes.

His annoyance dissolved. How could he stay irritated with a woman who coaxed smiles, laughter, song?

He could well imagine her voice. Sweet. A little smoky. Wrapping around lyrics like satin around damp skin…his skin.

"Maybe later, honey."

"She has a guitar, you know," the child continued, weaving a yellow plastic flower into the dull brown hair of the doll. He looked away. "Plays it really, really good. Wanna know her favorite song?"

No, he did not. Favored songs meant discovering a fragment of hidden heartache. Opening its scar.

"It's called…" Jenni's fingers stilled. Her small brows stitched. "'Frozen'!" She beamed a semi-toothed smile. "I 'member 'cause Shanna says to think of ice cream."

"'Frozen,' huh?" He couldn't help but smile.

"Uh-huh. She says My Donna sings it."

"Madonna."

"Uh-huh! Anyway, it's about this person who's frozen and can't see stuff. Isn't that sad?"

He couldn't agree more. *Who was frozen in your life, Shanna?*

"Why'n't you ask her to sing it for you, Uncle M.?"

"We'll see." That he and Shanna shared common ground over an admired Madonna tune unbalanced him. He glanced toward the cabin, then checked his watch. Eight-oh-two.

Forget her tangled in bed with that biker—

"Can I ask her to come over?" Jen persisted, cutting off his image. "She sings really pretty."

"How do you know all this?"

"Because Grammy let me stay with her till real late that time we baked cookies."

Katherine. First, the old woman takes him to task for putting the place up for sale, then offers to repurchase it with a condition Shanna oversee its operation and, before the day was out, lets Jenni spend hours with a woman both of them barely knew.

The cabin door opened. A man stepped out wearing what Michael foresaw: leather and jeans and boots. No colors.

The short hair was a surprise.

Alerted, Jenni rose to her knees. "Who's that?"

"Good question," Michael muttered. He patted the air beside his chair. "Sit down, Jen. It's not polite to stare."

"But who's that man coming out of Shanna's house?"

Michael watched his employee come through the doorway in thready shorts and a pink tank top. She tripped down the steps and flung her arms around the man's shoulders. They spoke nose to nose. She pecked his cheek—another surprise—and stepped back, arms folded around her middle.

Morning sunbeams, warming those bare slender limbs...

Tossing his own advice out the proverbial window, he stared.

Beside her silver pickup, the man kicked the motorcycle awake. A farewell salute and he headed slowly up the graveled drive toward the house. Abreast with the verandah, the rumbling blue beast came to a crawl. From under a standard helmet, he sent Michael a brief nod and Jen a wink.

The little girl giggled behind four fingers.

Mission accomplished, the biker barreled off in a spit of pebbles and dust.

At ten paces, in full sunlight, Michael concluded one

thing. Biker Boy wasn't a day over twenty. What was she doing sleeping with Billy The Kid?

"Shanna!" Jenni rushed down the steps and up the treed path to the woman coming toward them. "See, I braided Octavia's hair!"

"Wow, you've done an excellent job." Shanna examined the doll while Michael's niece skipped at her side.

"Just like you showed me." The child's face tilted up, adoring. "You're a good teacher."

Shanna skimmed a finger down Jen's freckled nose. "You're a fast learner."

"I told Uncle M. you played the guitar."

"Did you?" Shanna raised her eyes to the man lazing in the wicker chair on the verandah deck. Her heart thunked.

He hadn't shaved.

And, what he did to a snowy T-shirt...

Jenni tugged her hand. "Can you play your guitar for us, Shanna?"

"Maybe some other time, honey."

"But Uncle Michael knows the song."

The man on the deck shifted his shoulders. "It's okay, Jen. I can hear it later." He held out his empty mug. "Do me a favor and take this into the kitchen?"

To Shanna the child said, "Don't go yet, 'kay?"

"I won't."

"Promise?"

She smiled and crossed an X on her chest. "Promise."

A dazzling grin and the girl dashed into the house, the screen door clapping behind her.

Shanna came up the steps and sat on the top one. Leaning back, she rested her head against the post. Her eyes found Michael's and clung. Soul cleaving soul. Zooming straight into the most secretive corner that was *her*.

Self-consciously, she tugged at one of the star danglers in her ears. A chipmunk darted from under the Jeep, bounded across the driveway, and scurried up a thick-trunked pine.

"Interesting company you had." That sleepy-eyed look didn't fool her. "What gang does he belong to?"

"Gang? Jason doesn't belong to any gang. He likes motorcycles, that's all."

"Looks like an apprentice biker," Michael grumbled.

First, iron-hawk eyes. Now he pawed the dirt like the stallion in the paddock. She turned away, lips rolled inward. *He's neon-green with jealousy!* Next he'd be flaming fire out his strong, gallant nose. She didn't dare look but, oh, her heart sang a cheery lyric.

Fiddling with Octavia's hair, she debated confessing. It wouldn't do to stray on the wrong side of this man. Michael Rowan was implicitly, potently male. Not someone who'd relish being led down the funny-bone path.

"Actually," she said, "Jason bought the machine from a junkyard three years ago and spent all winter rebuilding it."

"Typical."

"Not when you consider how hard he worked to pay for parts and keep up his grades in the meantime."

"Aah. A fledgling in the making and a smart one to boot."

She smiled. "Are you spoiling for a fight, Doctor?"

He pulled his feet from the railing and braced his bare, tanned arms on wide-spread knees. He speared her with hot eyes. "I'd rather you didn't bring these kind of people onto my land."

Her amusement fled. "Next time I'll be sure to tell *those kind of people* to pick up their tuxes from the cleaners."

"Why didn't you tell me when I kissed you the other night there was a lover backstage?"

"He's not my lover."

Michael made a snorting sound. "Right. You spent the night chatting over milk and cookies."

The man had a one-geared mind. Fine. Let him leap to his damnable deductions. Heck, why not help him shove both feet and a hand in his mouth, as well? "And they were darn tasty."

Disappointment flickered across those gray eyes. Too much, this game. She had hurt him. "I—"

Spent the whole night reliving your kiss and fancying how your mouth would feel all over my body.

Heat shivered over her skin. She set the doll aside and pushed to her feet. "Tell Jenni I'm going for a run."

The issue of Jason would have to wait, when she could think clearly, when her own regret wasn't lodged in her throat.

"Just a minute." He came down the steps and stopped on the last one. "I, uh…" He rubbed the back of his neck and she watched his biceps shift. "I shouldn't have attacked you."

"Don't worry, Doc." She tried a smile. "I have rhino skin."

"Hardly. Come here for a minute."

"I don't think so."

"Please."

A single word and his eyes darkened. Solemn as sheet rain. Deep in hypnosis, she stared back. Such tough-packed demeanor. Such sorrow. She wanted to shield him.

A weighty sigh escaped as he thrust both hands into the hind pockets of his jeans. The gesture limned the solidity of male pecs and a diminutive nipple against his T-shirt.

She looked at her bare, dusty feet.

Michael came off the step and closed the stretch between them until they stood toes-to-sandals.

Amidst thick, dark stubble, the scar near his lip resembled a midget pearl. His eyes questioned. She forced a small laugh. "Rest easy, Doc. I still like you."

"And I still want you. Give him up, Shanna, he's not your type or your age."

Oh, Michael. Without hesitation, she set a palm to his rough cheek. Her thumb stroked the scar. "Jumping to conclusions again, you dear sweet fool? Jason's my brother. Remember I said he would paint the cabin for me?"

Between his eyes the creases deepened, then relaxed. "Why the hell didn't you say?" Cupping her face, he kissed a corner of her lips. "You drove me crazy all morning. *All* night."

"Good." She dove into a sea of shivers and heat. "I didn't sleep a minute, either."

"We could resolve that."

His tongue danced with her lips. Into her mouth.

The screen door squawked.

"Shanna! Look what I made you." Jenni sprinted down the steps and thrust out a sheet of paper.

Shanna stared down at an amazingly mature drawing. No stick people. Jenni had drawn features as fine as dimples and eyelashes, buttons and shoe laces. Done with colored pencils, the picture was bold and vibrant. Jenni had incredible talent.

Shanna identified each character—a woman playing a guitar, a child, an older woman, a doll and cat. In the background stood a double-storied yellow house. On clouds in an azure sky, a pair of teary-eyed angels. Along the bottom of the page, Jenni's rounded print: *Jenni, Mommy, Daddy, Oktvea, Shana, Gran, Sily.*

Michael's absence was like a smudged finger tread on clear glass. Left out as if he didn't exist.

Tears prickled her nose.

Helplessly, she looked up, met his eyes. *Don't pull back into that shell. Please.*

"Do you like it?" Jenni inquired, worrying her bottom lip.

Shanna hugged the child's thin shoulders. "May I hang it on the fridge?"

"Uh-huh." An eager nod. "Can we go to your house right now?"

"Well... I was thinking of putting it in your house. That way both you and Uncle Michael can share in the picture." However possible, she wanted him in this circle of family.

Michael held out a hand. "Mind if I see the picture, Jen?"

He took the drawing. Shanna held her breath. After a pause, he said, "It's very pretty. Shanna's right. It deserves a place in our kitchen where you can see it every day."

"But I want Shanna to see it, too," the child protested.

Crouching on his heels, he met Jenni on her level. "So do I. Why don't we invite her to come see it whenever she wants?"

Shanna wanted to hug him. Tight. "I think that's a super idea," she said brightly. "What do you say, honey?"

The six-year-old backed away. "I don't know. Uncle M.'s never home so why should he have the picture? You're always home and..." she sniffed "...and I like you."

A wrecking ball battering the cheerful morning.

Michael stood up. He handed the paper to Shanna.

"Doc." Her heart broke at the emptiness in his expressive eyes. He was a man of medicine. He healed the ill, the weak, the pained.

And was at a loss when it came to mending the fracture between his sister's child and himself.

Lines ranked his plaintive smile. "It's all right." Gently, he ruffled the little girl's hair. "Go on, Jen. Hang your picture on Shanna's fridge." Turning, he climbed the steps and disappeared into the house.

Shanna wanted to sit in the dirt where she stood and weep.

Chapter Six

Jenni sat cross-legged on the rug next to her bed and looked at Tavia in her dolly rocker. With a squeaky meow, Silly stretched out beside them, purring the way Grammy snored.

Setting her chin in her hands, Jenni waited. What she had to say to Silly and Tavia had to be said right.

"I think," she whispered at last on a big breath, "I did something bad today. And, I think it made Shanna sad."

Tears pushed into her eyes. She swiped them with the back of her hand. Tavia didn't like crying. She always got mad and called Jenni a crybaby just like Marty Olsen did at school.

But sometimes Jenni couldn't help it.

Sometimes her heart felt so big it wanted to bust.

Sometimes she had to bite her lip to keep from crying.

Like now.

Sniffing loudly, she palmed her nose. "I told Uncle M. I wanted Shanna to have my picture instead of him." Her eyes welled as she looked at Silly. "He got this funny look. He gets those a lot when he sees me. 'Specially since Daddy and Mommy…"

Jenni glanced at Octavia and swallowed. Tavia was staring straight into her eyes, same as Mommy used to do when she wanted an honest answer.

Why do you think he gets funny looks? Octavia asked.

Another sigh trembled from Jenni's lips. Tavia would want honest answers, too. "I don't think he likes me."

Do you want him to like you?

Jenni nodded slowly. "He's Mommy's brother and looks a lot like her. Mommy loved Uncle M. and he loved her. Why doesn't he love me? I look like Mommy. Grammy says so."

Tavia didn't answer. Silly kept purring.

"It felt funny when he made my hair messy," Jenni offered.

What felt funny?

"My tummy. It was like a whole bunch of chick'bees were in there flying all over the place."

Tavia smiled. *Were the chick'bees happy or sad?*

"Oh, happy! Uncle Michael never did that before, and it felt just like when Daddy used to mess my hair."

They were silent for a while. Jenni fixed the bow on Tavia's dress. Tavia could never keep the bow tied nicely. She was kind of sloppy that way.

When Jenni was finished, she scratched Silly under the chin to make sure she didn't feel left out. All at once, she stopped, her hand dropping to the rug. She looked at Tavia. Her friend was giving her one of those squinty looks Mommy gave when she knew Jenni had done something she wasn't supposed to.

"Uh-oh," Jenni whispered. "I think I know what the bad thing is now." She bit her lower lip to keep it still. Growling a meow, Silly climbed into Jenni's lap.

Well? Octavia asked in her Mommy voice.

Jenni chewed her lip. "I didn't draw Uncle Michael."

That wasn't nice, was it?

She shook her head. A tear slid down.

You left Uncle Michael out and that hurt him.

Jenni took a long sniff. Bump, bump went the cat's silky head under Jenni's shaky chin.

You hurt Shanna, too, Tavia went on. *That's why she was sad. You know she likes Uncle Michael 'cause of the way she looks at him.* Tavia was silent for a second. *I think they were going to kiss when you came outside.*

Swiping at the nasty tears rolling over her cheeks, Jenni begged in a small voice, "What am I s'pposed to do?"

Tavia kept her mouth shut. She always did with hard questions.

Jenni lay down and snuggled her body around Silly.

She thought of Uncle M. when he looked at the picture.

She remembered Shanna's face when he went into the house.

She wished she could draw the stupid picture over again.

Most of all, she wished Tavia could answer her question.

An orange sun sank behind the hills, sketching long shadows over the landscape.

"So, how many daggers did you toss him, sis?" Jason teased.

"Not enough, it seems," she said, half serious.

With the evening milking done, Shanna sat next to her brother on her stoop, watching the Realtor and his California buyer say goodbye to Michael, who wore reflective sunglasses.

Afraid to let them see your thoughts, Doc? Even in the milking parlor, under synthetic lighting, he'd kept them on.

"You're blowing this a little out of proportion, aren't you?" Jason chided. "It is his farm, after all."

"Maybe," she admitted. "But Jenni needs familiarity. She needs what's left of her parents' memory. He's taking that away."

"Sis. The kid's six, not ninety. In a year's time she'll have forgotten over half what she remembers now." He winced. "Including how her mom and dad looked. Sad, but true."

The way I forgot my mother. By her sixteenth birthday, Shanna'd had to stare long minutes at the picture on her dresser to capture the essence of Meredith McKay. Guilt in those days had been fierce. She hated to think of Jenni shouldering the same emotion.

Jason leaned back, elbows on the step above, and stretched his legs. "Do you expect your doctor to run his practice and a spread this size plus care for the girl all at the same time?" Before she could answer, he continued. "He doesn't have a wife or another sib to unload the kid onto. Sure, you say there's a grandma, but how long can that last? The woman walks with a cane, for Pete's sake. It's him or Child Protective Services. Selling the farm might be his only option for keeping the girl with him."

Sighing, Shanna pushed back her hair. "I hear you. I'm sticking my nose in where it doesn't belong."

"Nah, you've got it bad for the kid, is all."

She grunted.

Jason nudged her. "Look, don't compare her to us. Rowan's not like our old man. He'll see she's looked after properly."

Except Jenni wouldn't be on her own turf and the memories would fade, even with that portrait hanging on a strange wall.

She watched Michael climb into his truck without a glance in their direction and drive off. Not a wave, not a nod. Always aloof, always maintaining distance. *You can't do that with Jenni.* Hugs and kisses and cuddles. That's what little girls needed.

Kate voted for Michael's work ethics. Tending life's miseries with prescribed medication.

But what of the children in the hospital? Did he banter with them to ward off *their* fears? Did he heal their little bodies with empathy? Or with cold medical facts? And when he saw Jenni healthy and alive—after standing by the bedside of a dying child—did he feel blessed?

Shanna shut her eyes and saw the drawing again.

Oh, yes, she thought, *you feel.*

For the hundredth time, she wished she had insisted the child hang the artwork in the main house. Seeing it in her kitchen…it wasn't right.

She understood Michael's apprehension at loving a child.

What she didn't fathom was his emotional rein when it came to a child born of his beloved Leigh.

One glimpse at those tiny hands swishing that frilly yellow dress, and Shanna was lost. In love. Had things been different, her home would have babbled and laughed with a horde of children.

Wade and two dreary relationships put an end to that.

Still, much as she yearned for a child, she wasn't a fool. The father of her next child would anticipate its arrival with joy and wonder. No tracking some far-bound rodeo trail. No accusations of fouling up his life with a pregnancy.

Swallowing the knot in her throat, she pushed to her feet. "I'm going for a run before it gets too dark."

"Yeah, I gotta take off, as well." Jason unfolded off the steps, sauntered to the Harley and took up his helmet. "Don't let them get to you, Shan."

"I won't."

Her brother mock-punched her chin. "See ya tomorrow."

With a wave, she jogged up the path, around the main house, and into the evergreens. Down the lane, the bike rumbled away. Eager for the pungent scent of forest, she climbed the winding route. Deeper and deeper into the woods she went. No longer jogging, but spurring to a blood-pumping sprint. Leaping moss-laden logs. Scrambling over rocky patches. Clambering up weedy inclines. Harder, faster.

Her lungs screamed for air.

Her thighs stung for rest.

She didn't stop. Wouldn't.

She simply ran on, perspiration dripping in her eyes.

At last, the short, shrub-endowed and grassy rise of the summit. An aged pair of ponderosa pines, their roots gnarled and wind-worn, gripped the rock-embedded soil.

Gasping to allay her pillowing lungs, she crouched, hands to knees, under the evergreen boughs and savored the shade and the odor of vanilla seeping from bark. Down the valley, the Harley's hum grew fainter.

Dammit. She knew better. Dreams of babies and fathers. A direct hit to her heart.

She scraped a palm down each cheek and felt the tears. *Damn, damn.* Hadn't she learned yet? Three years since her last flunked relationship. Three years since hope died.

She surveyed the opposite side of the hill where grasses, wildflowers and low shrubs fed off the land. The road to town curved gently, then stretched and faded among several farmsteads. The bike had vanished. By now, Jase was probably home.

Home.

If she was honest, Jason was her home. Just as she was his mother, father, sister, friend. She didn't need dreams. He was her dream, her family. What more did she need?

Lifting a shaky finger, she pressed her right eye where a migraine chewed a thin line to the base of her skull.

Her brother was right. She had permitted Michael Rowan and his niece to creep under her skin.

Trouble was, she wanted to keep them there.

When Michael pulled into the farm's lane, light painted the tiny window of the barn office. Now what? More cow trouble?

Her brother's motorcycle was gone. Her pickup sat in front of the obscured bulk of the employee quarters.

What was she up to?

Unstrapping a sleepy Jenni from the seat, he went into the house. This time he didn't stop to analyze the kiss he brushed over the little girl's forehead before he grabbed up the walkie-talkie and left the bedroom. Instead, he tripped quickly, quietly down the staircase and into the night.

Shanna commanded his mind, his blood.

From the moment he'd stepped into the barns this evening with Cliff and the beachfront buyer, Michael had imagined her thoughts. He could almost verbalize those cut-glass looks of hers, those puppet movements around the cattle: *You're making a mistake. Think of Jenni. Think before you sign on that dotted line.*

Katherine would have been pleased.

And upset. If she'd known about the buyer from Carmel. After stuffing Michael with spaghetti, she'd spent three hours extolling the dubious aftermath of selling Rowan Dairy. Thank heaven Jenni had gone into the family room to watch *The Country Bears*. Michael surmised the old woman had plugged in the video for the purpose of discussing *things* with him.

Through the trees, he saw the outline of a woman behind the office window. Shanna.

He broke into a jog.

Would her eyes flash anger again when she saw him? Or would the onset of night instill dreaminess?

And when she lifted her hips to match his pace...

Wise up, Michael, she's only interested in what happens to this place.

Like Leigh?

Staggering under the thought, he laid a hand to the cold metal surface of the exterior door. Inside, he stood for a moment, breathing the warm pungency of Holstein and barn.

No, not exactly like Leigh.

Ah, sis. Were you ever interested in what I did?

He remembered when Leigh had whispered good-night at his door in those parentless years. Talking of the land ensuring destinies in a way people could not. Except, the land wasn't his destiny. It never had been. The death of their parents cured him of that. All he'd wanted, then, was to escape. All she'd wanted was to cling.

She had not argued his choice. Nor asked why he wanted to become a doctor.

If he enjoyed it.

Felt successful. Happy. Tired.

Lonely.

Of course, he could have been a better brother. He could have shared a beer or two just once with her husband. Gotten to know their little girl. Been part of their family.

Now it was too late. Too late for hellos, for goodbyes and all the time in between.

Ah, but hindsight could be one horrible insight.

Shoving aside the dull ache in his chest, he strode through the sanitized milking parlor, catching the light switches enroute. At the rear entrance he took the stairs two at a time.

Leigh's disregard of him was not the issue. He understood from where it stemmed. At ten, after their parents' funeral, she had chosen the land over love. Driving off with Gramps, buying more feed, checking out new equipment, hanging around the animals, working the fields. Leaving her twin behind, to escape in his own way. And he had. He'd withdrawn from his own world and submerged himself in a world of strangers.

No different than now. He shoved aside the nip.

Yet, Leigh's disregard for all but the cattle, the land and its operation had haunted him, then and now. To her, people had become objects of purpose.

He should have encouraged her to seek help.

He remembered the first time he'd recognized his sister had a serious hangup. Jen was forty-eight hours old. Home a day...

"My daughter will know the value of the land," Leigh told him over the baby's head. *"It'll be her guarantee. She'll never be without."* She studied the little face in her arms. *"Rowan Dairy belongs to Rowan generations."*

He said, "A lame reason for having kids, Leigh."

"Why? Because you've never wanted the farm?"

"Because I don't believe parents should burden their kids with their own dreams."

"Come on, Michael," she cajoled. *"One day you'll meet a nice woman and have your own little rug rats. You'll want the best for them, won't you?"*

"I'm not having kids."

"What kind of talk is that? Sure you will."

He turned, looked out the window at the pastures, the grazing black and white cattle. "I won't subject kids to what you and I had to go through, Leigh. I won't risk it."

"Oh, for crying out loud! That kind of thing rarely happens twice in a family."

But it had.

One stroke of insidious luck and he had Jenni. Passed on from sister to brother, twin to twin, like an heirloom. Like the land. Well, he thought shakily, heading down the small, darkened hallway toward the spill of office light. A farmer he was not.

Instincts for weather, for animals, that was Leigh.

And Shanna.

Shanna—headstrong, opinionated, stubborn, disruptive.

Hardworking and efficient.

Generous and loving with Jen.

Passionate with him.

Hell.

The door stood open. An upbeat country song played a decibel too loud from the radio on the refrigerator. He halted in the doorway. So did his heart.

Humming along to some boogie-woogie thing, she fluffed the pillow and smoothed back the covers on the cot against the opposite wall. What met his eye routed heat under his belt. Sleek, bare calves. Tanned thighs under a pajama shirt of blue kittens.

He grinned. "A woman who enjoys bedtime as much as you should lock her door."

A yelp and she whirled, hand to her throat. "Good grief!" She huffed a breath. "How *many* times have I asked you—"

"Not to sneak up?" He rubbed his jaw, trying to compose the earsplitting grin. "Hm, let's see… Enough to know better?"

She folded her arms, crowding her breasts. Tapped her foot. Glared at him. Finally she shut off the radio.

"What're you doing here?"

"The light was on." He leaned against the jamb, shoved his hands into his slacks pockets. "Have a problem with the colors I chose for the cabin?"

"The colors are fine. The fumes bother me."

His teasing ended. "In what way?"

"They won't let me sleep," she said, but looked away.

Pushing from the door he came closer. Her breathing picked up. He kept his hands cached. "That all?"

"Yes."

"They don't make you nauseated, give you headaches, make the eyes water?"

"No."

"They just bother you."

"Yes."

She had yet to look at him. Okay, he wouldn't push it. The right to privacy and choice of doctor were hers. "Is that why your brother's painting the place?"

She nodded. "He'll be here for a few more days."

"In that case I want you to sleep in the guest room at the main house until he's done."

The announcement whipped her blue-flame gaze to him. "I'm fine here."

He gave in and ran his thumb along the softness under her ear. "I insist."

She stood silent. "Would you have invited Charlie to the house for the same reason?"

"Charlie?"

"Your last milker."

Reluctantly, Michael let his fingers drift from her skin and back to his pocket. "What's he got to do with you staying in the guest room while the cabin's painted?"

"Because *I'm* the hired help now."

"Your point being…?"

"Why do you really want me there, Doc?"

"Ah, you believe I have some calculated motive."

"Don't you?"

"Absolutely not." Right now he didn't. Tomorrow, he might reconsider. "My invitation is only business. I don't want my employees uncomfortable. Once your place is dry and fumeless, you'll move back."

Her eyes narrowed. "Easy as that?"

Easy? He swallowed a laugh. Nothing concerning her was simple. Sleeping in a big double bed on the same floor as him was far from easy. "As that," he conceded.

"All right." She snagged her jeans from the back of the desk chair. "Turn around."

He did, hearing the swish of denim over leg, the snick of zipper over belly.

She brushed past him. "Jenni asleep?"

"Out like a light, as they say."

Without responding, she went ahead, leaving him to switch off the desk lamp and close the office. On the stairs, her summer-meadows scent stamped the musky air.

Without a word they walked under the stars, up the incline, to the back stoop of the farmhouse. A nighthawk screeched somewhere in the darkness above pine and fir. A cow lowed.

Michael hesitated before he pushed open the door. Moonlight lined her cheek against a dark wing of hair. He resisted a touch. "I meant what I said in the barn, Shanna. I want you to know that."

Her smile was wide. "If I didn't trust your word, Doc, I wouldn't be here. I want *you* to know *that*. Shall we go inside?"

What it lacked in space, the guest room made up for in charm. A double bed, a night table, a braided rug, an old wooden rocker. The opposite wall held a large, low window. White eyelet curtains. Across the bed, a matching counterpane.

She eased onto its edge.

Sliding a look toward the door, where Michael watched her from the hallway, she felt the familiar zing. Tie loosened, sleeves rolled on his tan shirt. Not your run-of-the-mill country doctor—or man.

She swept a hand over the smooth surface of the bedding. "This is...lovely. Thank you." In the stillness, her voice sounded soft, hazy.

"You're welcome. What time do you get up?"

"Four. I like a leisurely breakfast. You?"

"Five-thirty. I don't eat breakfast."

"Then I'll see you and Jenni tomorrow at suppertime."

"We'll be eating at Katherine's. I have a hospital board meeting at six-forty-five. I don't know when I'll be home, but the fridge and pantry are stocked so don't wait. Help yourself to whatever you like, whenever you like."

She hid her disappointment. "Fine."

A small silence fell. She sensed he needed something, but not kisses or hugs or more...but simply to watch her sitting on an eyelet counterpane in the shadow of night.

"Well," he said, turning, patting the heel of his hand against the doorjamb. "If there's anything else, I'll be down in the den for a while."

"Okay."

"G'night, then."

"'Night."

A long lingering look and he was gone.

She waited until she heard him descend the stairs, then she crossed the room and closed the door. Against her back, the wood felt cool. Turning, she pressed her right eye against the smoothness of the grain. Three prescription Cafergot after her run and finally the bite of the migraine had abated to a niggle.

Unclenching the fist holding the small plastic bottle within the confines of her sweatshirt, she blessed her one vice—tossing clothing helter-skelter at bedtime. Tonight, the garment had landed in a heap on the office desk, covering her little green painkillers.

She went to the closet, swung it open, and set the bottle in a corner on the top shelf. Away from little fingers. Away from unduly keen eyes.

After folding her clothes on the chair, she cranked open a window panel, slipped under the covers and turned off the lamp. Cushiony and thick, the pillow held a trace of softener. She burrowed down with the nighthawk's lullaby.

At twelve-forty she tossed back the covers. Like a nagging old woman, the headache remained. Two pills in hand, she crept down the hall.

Jenni's door was partially opened and a night-light assuaged the dark. No glow brushed the periphery of the door she assumed was Michael's. *Doctor.* Comfort that chased away pain could be a step and one question away, if she dared. If she were desperate.

She walked on.

In the kitchen she microwaved the milk and sat at the table to swallow her pills.

"Can't sleep?" His voice was deep and quiet as the night. In his house, she had expected him.

He walked to the adjacent chair, curled his fingers over its back. Her heart jumped.

His feet were large, hair-flecked and angular. Male. Dulled navy sweats drooped on his lank hips. The soft fabric gave his sex merit and had her jerking to stare at her mug of milk.

With a grunt of amusement, he swung the chair around, straddled the seat and rested veined, bare forearms atop the back. The maneuver snugged gray cotton across his shoulders.

Closing her eyes, she sipped her milk.

"Don't like what you see?" he chided.

"Au contraire, mon ami. What I see is very enticing." Way too enticing. She'd be smart to leave. Right now.

His eyes were shadowed in the dim stove light, gripping her.

"Seems we're on the same wavelength," he said. "What should we do about it?"

"Nothing. Absolutely nothing. As I've said, we don't dance."

He chuckled softly, a hint of devilry in those silver eyes. She caught her breath at the expression teasing his whiskered cheeks, his straight, tense mouth.

When did you last have fun, Mike? Laugh yourself stupid? Howl at the moon? Paint the town red?

Suddenly, he swung off the chair. "Come on," he said, clasping her hand. "Let's see how well we dance."

"Mike—"

He drew her against him. Close. "Shh. Listen to the music."

"Now you're being silly. The radio isn't even on."

Lazily he began swaying with her wrapped in his arms. "Mmm. It's inside. Here." Gently, he touched fingertips to her brow, where already the pain abated. "And here." A palm above her left breast, heating the skin beneath her nightgown.

"Oh, God," she murmured. This chivalry, this lovely, lovely sweetness in him—she never would have guessed. Immersed in the touch and the scent of rugged, earthy man, she laid her cheek to the soft cottony warmth of his T-shirt. She closed her eyes, dreaming. "I don't do one-nighters, Doc, or casual flings."

"Me, either. Hush, now."

"In a minute. I want to know why we're dancing."

He licked the rim of her ear. "We're dancing," he whispered, "to take away that headache you have."

"How'd you know?"

Silence.

She sighed, resettled her cheek against his warmth. "Dumb question to ask a medicine man."

"Not dumb at all. Have you taken anything besides the milk?"

"Pills."

"What kind?" Circling fingers at her temple. Firm, gentle, hypnotic. She drifted on sensations. "What kind, sweetheart?"

She told him and was disappointed when he quit swaying, though the fingers continued their caress. "How long?"

"This particular champer? Since you left to get Jenni. It's nothing I can't handle, Michael."

Serious eyes. Touching here, there. "How often?"

She shrugged. The shrew of a headache had nearly gone. She wanted his arms to stay forever. He felt wonderful, soothing. Protective. And proudly aroused. "A few a year. Can we dance some more?"

"No. If we do I won't be able to keep my promise."

"Maybe I've changed my mind."

"Well, I haven't and you're going to bed."

"Now you're talking."

"Sorry, babe." Catching her behind the knees, he lifted her and strode from the kitchen. "*You* are going to bed, not me. Geez, you don't weigh more than a peanut. Have you been eating properly?"

"I always eat properly. Look, maybe no one's told you but a headache doesn't affect the feet."

"Shush. Depends how bad it is. Besides, this is an apology for touching without breaking any promises."

"Ah." The feel of his arms, the scent of his skin—touches, promises…night, sheets, pillows… "What were you doing downstairs, anyway?"

"Reviewing a file."

"Patient or farm?"

He gave her a deadpan look. "You don't give up, do you?"

"Nope." She stroked his rough cheek and burrowed her face in his neck. "This place means the world to you."

"Does it now?"

"Yes, you just don't see it yet."

"But you're planning to show me." He took the stairs.

"Uh-uh. It'll show you."

"And how will it do that?"

"I'm not sure, but you'll know when it does. Michael," she whispered, "wait." He had come to the top of the stairs. "Will we wake Jenni if we peek in on her?"

"Nah. She's a typical kid—sleeps totally out of it."

On her feet she felt deserted without the security of his arms. Twenty seconds from kitchen to bedroom, and peace was hers. The headache gone.

Quietly they entered the dimly lit room. Silly raised her head from the small bump of the child's hip and gave them a drowsy-eyed blink. Shadows and sleep veiled Jenni's tiny face on a yellow-encased pillow. A wily ringlet rested at the corner of her mouth. One small hand curled under her cheek.

"Ooh…" Shanna breathed. Visions of Timmy at six slugged her heart.

Tears welling.

A wedge behind her tongue.

"Michael." *I'll die if I never have another baby.*

Clutching him, she hid her face in the warmth of his throat.

Chapter Seven

Vaguely, she was aware of Michael lifting her and shouldering his way into the guest room. Carrying with him her shattered heart. Nine years she'd waged the battle and won over the loneliness, the emptiness.

Until tonight.

Coming to Rowan Dairy was a godsend, she'd thought. A place to hide. No mothers wheeling grocery carts with toddlers here. No school children laughing in the park. No office women talking of families. Here, in the country, among trees and sky and animals, she would find contentment.

She hadn't counted on Jenni.

Or Michael.

She hadn't counted on being needed.

Meredith had walked away. Her daddy sauntered into beer and buckle bunnies. Wade found her useless in the house, lousy in bed. His words. And Jason...Jason, in the throes of independence, was on the way to leaving her behind.

But Michael—if he wasn't so stubborn—and the little one in the next room needed her. *Needed her.*

Gently, he eased onto the bed. With an unfamiliar tenderness, he began tucking her under the covers. When he pushed a strand of hair behind her ear, she caught her lip. Tonight he was at his best.

And, oh, God. She was falling in love with him.

The irony. Over three decades old and for the first time *in love.* With a man star years out of her realm. A man as moody as he was sexy. Intuitive as he was stubborn.

"Want to talk about it?" he asked, sitting next to her hip.

Shanna closed her eyes. No more exposure to her soul. He'd seen enough of her wounds.

He stroked her arm. "What is it, honey?"

Mike. His kindness crumbled the stone fist gripping her heart. "I had a baby once. Timothy. He…he was stillborn." Her throat hurt. "He'd be nine now if he'd lived."

"Aw, babe." Michael leaned forward and cupped her head. His thumbs caressed her temples.

"Sometimes," she supplied a lopsided smile. "Sometimes, it creeps up on me."

Silently, he drew her forward and tucked her beneath his chin. Warm and strong and tender. He was everything Wade hadn't been in the twenty-three months of their marriage.

When her emotions steadied, she continued. "A long time ago I dreamed of having at least four children. I wanted the picket fence routine, the whole enchilada."

"You're young yet, Shanna. You'll get it one day."

"Thanks for the optimism."

Under her cheek, she felt his quiet chuckle. The sting loosened.

"Changing your view of me, Ms. McKay?"

"In this position, how can I not?"

"Indeed."

For several moments she treasured the shelter of his arms. Three times in the span of forty minutes he'd rescued her with comfort and compassion. Three times he'd exhibited a side of the Michael Rowan she thought unreachable. He was not as impervious as he liked her to believe. Simply holding her and offering refuge from the grief gave him away.

Would he let her hold him when he needed it? She had her doubts. There was his pride and those emotional caves. The thought saddened her. Little boy lost.

"I have another dream," she said, wanting the night to close on the positive.

"Tell me."

"To raise mixed Arabians."

"Mixed Arabians?"

"Mmm. Gray-dappled Arabians. Solid stock with fine-boned heads and legs, bred with Morgans."

"To get the strong chest and sturdy back. I like it."

"You do know your horses."

"I've been around a few," he admitted. "We had an old plough horse, Blackie, when I was five. Leigh and I used to ride it together and pretend we were the Duelling Doubles. No one this side of the Mexican border could outshoot, outwrangle or outride the Rowan twins." His smile was imbued with rare fondness.

"Farms are the best."

"Sometimes."

She looked into his eyes. "Oh, Michael," she said softly. "They are. You know they are."

"Yeah, well…" He sighed.

"Don't sell. Let me run the place for you. I can do it. No, don't turn away. Hear me out." Urgently she held his face. "Sell half the cows, two-thirds if you want, but keep the farm. Keep it for Jenni, and for yourself. I can look after it and her, if it's a smaller operation. Kate's getting up in years. It isn't fair to either of you, this running back and forth at all hours from town. Please. Give it a try for a year, at least.''

His lips drew tight. ''Seems you've thought it all out.''

She shook her head. ''Just now.'' Her fingers drifted to his neck. ''Don't you see? It can work if you let it. Jenni can stay where her parents chose to raise her, and you won't have to worry about the farm.'' He made to rise. She grasped his hands. ''Please. Just think about it. This is your home.''

Wariness touched his eyes. ''We've been through this before.''

''Not this. Not about me staying on.''

''Jenni can't take the place of your little boy, honey.''

She blinked. Why hadn't she remembered his directness? ''That's not what I meant,'' she whispered, barely able to push the words past her tongue.

He shifted with discomfort. ''I'm not a marrying man, Shanna. Terrible circumstances I had no control over put Jen into my care, but I'm learning to handle it. I'll raise her the best I can. But I will not be responsible for a wife—or other kids.''

''I wasn't asking you to marry me.''

''Then what? You want to live in some kind of platonic relationship for the next twenty years? Even *you* must know how ludicrous that sounds.''

Harsh words. Clear implication. She saw it in his hot eyes.

She pulled away, drawing the spread over her breasts. ''It's late, Doc. Maybe we should call it a night.''

''Shanna—''

''No. I'll see you tomorrow.''

''Hell.'' He scrubbed back his hair. ''Look, I'm sorry. What I said came out all wrong.''

She forced a smile. ''Forget it. I understand.'' The dusky

corners of the room shadowed his jaw and cheek. She took a supporting breath. "Thanks for the dance. And for listening to…" She turned away her face. *To my woes.*

"Shanna."

"Just go, Michael."

"Dammit, I don't want to leave you like this. Not after—"

"I'm okay." Swallowing hard, she looked at him. "Honest."

He studied her. "How's the headache?" Enough kindness to make her want to cry.

"You put the right moves on it."

Wordlessly, he lowered her onto the pillow. A spurt of anxiety shot into her. He had a demeanor that spoke of swift stubbornness, the type that left little leeway for vulnerability or weakness. She pictured him, lance and laser, in an operating room, disciplining runaway injuries, crushing Goliath diseases—come hell or high water.

He caged her between his hands. His warm breath crossed her lips and throat. Gold and charcoal flecked his irises.

He wanted to kiss her.

She wanted him to and she yearned for the heat, the hunger.

In anticipation, her eyes closed.

The mattress shifted slightly. Breath caught, she languished toward the sensation of his touch, his scent.

His lips caressed her forehead.

"Sweet dreams, little dancer," he whispered.

Unexpected simplicity. Tears pushed to the surface. The pang in her heart threatened to double her over. When she dared look again, the room was dark, and she was alone.

Geoff Garland spun on his right heel, swiped the ball out of Michael's guarded dribble and found the basket in a perfect three-sixty. A slam dunk. Five to four.

"Okay." Michael wiped his face with the hem of his sweat-soaked Tommy Hilfiger T-shirt. "I'll let you win this round."

"Excuse me, buddy." Laughing, Geoff caught the rebounding ball and plunked down on the grassy edge of the driveway where Rochelle had set a small cooler with several sodas. "You didn't let me win anything. I earned it."

Michael grinned. Stretching unused muscles and working up a sweat unrelated to the drama of the O.R. felt good. Oddly, thirty minutes of one-on-one with Geoff relaxed Michael more than his usual run before rounds in the morning.

Sometimes, Roche and Amy joined the game.

Sometimes, seeing the Garlands together stole his breath.

Family was a lure he resisted.

Tonight, however, he and Geoff were alone outside. With Amy already asleep when Roche got home after their hospital meeting, she preferred to stay inside, near her child. Michael wondered whether guilt ate at Roche for those meetings. It did him. He should be home with Jen. Instead, because of the hour and several late nights, she'd sleep at Katherine's tonight.

Ah, remorse, an ugly ghoul that.

Hell. How often did he take time out? He was trying, wasn't he, to juggle work with Jen?

And Shanna's proposition? It would make life easier.

Not for him.

Dropping on the grass beside his friend, he examined the hoop illuminated by the garage lights. "Gimme the ball a sec."

"You'll never make it from this angle," Geoff taunted.

Michael twirled the ball on a finger. "You betting?"

"Nope. Don't bet with losers."

A grunt, a mighty toss. The ball caught the rim, circled, dropped…outside the hoop.

Michael winced. "Damn."

"Looks like you need more practice, buddy." Chuckling, Geoff handed over a Sprite. "You should put up a board at your place."

Michael snapped the tab and let the icy liquid stream down his throat. "Maybe I will." Backhanding his mouth, he contemplated the California buyer who'd decided to bid on a smaller spread near Lynden. "Might add to the property value."

"Still no bites?"

"Nothing worth considering." Lightning flickered across the night. Thunder mumbled. A storm stewed in the northwest. He should get up, go home.

"How's that woman working out?"

Michael took another pull at his soda and eyed the sky. "Fine."

"Well, don't sound too excited," Geoff teased.

Excited? How about hot? Lusty? "She wants me to keep the place. Believes the farm's Jenni's home as well as her inheritance." He didn't add that his lovely-limbed employee included him in the home bit.

"Getting in your face is she?"

In your face. Definitely a packaged vision. What he wouldn't give to be in *her* face, nose to nose, breathing her scent, lips on lips, tasting her skin…

He shifted on the grass and watched lightning sear the dark. Instantaneous. Electric. Vital. The way Shanna affected him.

We don't dance, Doc.

He grunted. Oh, they could dance all right—if she'd ever allow it.

"She's a hard worker," Michael said. "Even if we don't concur on marketing the place."

Geoff shot him a sideways look. "Does she know about Seattle?"

"No, and neither does Katherine or Jen."

They sat in silence for a couple of minutes. Michael felt a fool and a sneak, admitting Katherine wasn't included in his plans. He had no choice. His friend might let Michael's intent slip in front of Amy who would feed the information to Jenni. Smoother to break the news in bits and pieces.

And not think of broken hearts.

A gust of wind rustled in the shrubs along the driveway.

Geoff glanced up at the sky. Black clouds hurried in. "Roche'll miss you, bud." He threw a cocky grin that didn't touch his eyes. "Me, I'll be counting my lucky stars. It's humiliating seeing you weep over a game."

"Yeah." Michael tried a smile but failed. "Same here." He regarded the street. Nothing moved, not even a dust whirl. "I won't get tangled up in the rat race or the chaos, Geoff. My career habits will stay predominantly the same." Brittle convictions. "Seattle is simply a different dot on the map." With a better chance of survival, should the situation arise.

Geoff shrugged. "If it makes you happy, go for it."

"Got that right," Michael agreed. His decision was sound. It mattered not a damn that his world had a fissure down the center.

Last night you put the same one in Shanna's dreams.

He'd hurt her.

What if she'd left?

Oliver arrived at three. The animals would be in good hands.

Anxious, Michael set his empty can on the cooler and got to his feet. "Thanks for the game, man. Gotta run. Looks like we're in for a downpour. Tell Roche I'll see her in the morning."

"No prob." Geoff stood, too. "Hey, we're doing up some burgs on the ol' b-b-q Sunday. Amy'd love to see Jenni again."

Michael loped down the driveway, shaking out his keys. *Hurry. Hurry home.* "Thanks. I'll let you know."

"Heck, bring the woman, too," Geoff called through the thunder-grumbling dark. "She's more than welcome."

Michael climbed into the truck and started the engine. Bring a woman to his best friends' house? That meant she held a special spot in his life. He had no such spot.

Why the rush to get home then?

The headlights caught a patch of white zigzagging through the pasture's thick darkness along the farm's lane.

The sky flared. In its eerie glow he saw her. On a foot chase behind twenty milling Holstein heifers.

Relief. She hadn't packed up and gone.

But she'd put herself at risk. Again. In the middle of a lightning storm. Had another dog pack returned?

Bringing the truck to a stop, Michael leapt from the cab. Thunder clapped and snarled. The storm hovered less than a quarter of a mile away, closer than he anticipated.

"Dammit, woman," he shouted, running toward the fence. "There's a sky full of electricity above you!"

From under the Seahawks ball cap, she threw him a look. Then raced after an obtuse animal. "Help me get these ladies into the free barn!" A whistle pierced the grousing night. Her determination jacked up his distress.

He crawled through the barbed wire, but rather than jogging toward the bawling herd he headed straight for her. "Shanna!"

"Help me, Mike."

"Never mind the animals," he called over an ear-deafening clap of thunder. "It's too dangerous."

"I can't...leave...them." The words caught between gusts of air and he realized she'd been struggling a while over dip and hollow, coaxing his bovine critters toward shelter.

"You're three hundred yards from the barns. It's too far!"

Lightning—bright, white, lethal—speared the inky sky. Thunder smacked. Wind whipped. The Holsteins milled and bawled. And went nowhere.

Michael grabbed her hand. "Leave the damned cows and get in the truck!"

"No, they'll get hit." She tugged free and ran after a frightened beast breaking from the herd.

Michael raced after cow and woman. In ten strides he had her around the waist. "Shanna, listen to me, dammit!" Her stubby ponytail whipped against his mouth. "Better them than you."

Whether his words or the jagged, sizzling bolt at the edge of the woods changed her mind, he wasn't sure. She sprinted for the fence. Within seconds, he yanked apart the wire for her, then crawled through himself. They ran for the truck. Lightning flashed, mean and quick. Sparks scored the night.

Warm and dry inside the cab, she stared out the side window at the frantic, milling cattle. "I shouldn't have left them."

"They'll be okay once the rain comes," Michael assured her. Quarter-size drops clattered on the roof and against the windshield. He set the truck in motion.

Across the cab, her Pacific-blue eyes were laden with worry. "Guess I should thank you for the rescue."

"You're welcome."

She pulled her damp, cotton white top out from her waistband and fanned in some air. The scent of heated skin locked on his nose. He looked ahead and said, "The middle of the night is no time to run after a bunch of crazed cows."

"It's hardly the middle of the night, Michael."

"Check the time." He pointed to the dash clock— 10:18—and shuddered. More than the storm might have hurt her. Those panicked cows stampeding...

"They were confused," she explained as if reading his mind. "Without a leader, heifers just go in circles. Maybe we could put Rosebud with them. Sam Dunham phoned today. Negative on the rabies." She shot a grin at him and slipped off her cap and headband. Bending over her knees, she patted dampness from her face with the hem of her shirt and dragged strands off her neck.

Michael nearly drove into the ditch.

"I heard them bawling." She sat upright and combed fingers through her hair. "I wanted them where they'd feel safe."

"They could have trampled you."

"I knew what I was doing."

"It wouldn't have been a match in a herd of confused, panicked eight-hundred-pound teenyboppers."

She laughed. "Teenyboppers. Cute."

"Nature of the beast." He looked over. "And still no match."

"Yeah, well. I worked four years with Holsteins, remember? I do know something of their behavior."

"And if something *had* happened? We're not exactly in town here. The next farm is a mile and half down the road."

Over her shoulder she peeked into the Cherokee's rear seat. "Jenni staying at Kate's?"

"Work went later than usual." Gripping the steering wheel, he shut his mouth. Easier, the silence, than fighting about lunatic animals in a storm.

She wasn't done. "New style of scrubs these days?" She eyed his shorts.

"I had a game of basketball after the board meeting."

"Fun?"

"Yes."

Out toward the pasture sheet lightning flashed swift and splendid. She wrapped the headband around her wrist and patted her nape. "You have true-blue male legs."

"God, I hope so."

"Long, fast and hairy."

"Sorry," he grumped. "Can't help the hair."

She gave him a grin. "You wouldn't be a man if you did."

The fight went out of him. She liked his legs. They'd be in the house, alone for a whole night.

And she liked his legs.

The rain was coming hard when they pulled up to the house. Wind tore at their heels and moaned through the evergreens as they dashed up the walkway and slammed into the mudroom.

Michael flicked a switch and cursed softly. "Power's off."

Beside him, Shanna ignored the way the humidity of the house provoked his lush, male scent. "Do you have candles?"

"I'll see if I can find some. Stay here." He disappeared into the dark recesses of the house.

Behind the door, she hung her cap on a hook and freed her hair from its band. Rain splattered the windows in gusts. Edgy and hot, she toed off her sneakers and headed into the kitchen where Michael, miniature flashlight in hand, whipped open cupboard doors and drawers.

Lightning winked through the casement windows.

"You'd think she would've kept them in the kitchen," he muttered.

He spoke of Leigh.

"I have two in the cabin," Shanna offered.

He jerked around and paced past her. "You're not going anywhere out there. I'll look in the office." Vanishing, he left her listening to his Nikes squeak across hardwood.

She puffed out her cheeks. Exhaled slowly. Forced herself

to stay calm. Tonight the elements had tossed them together. Alone with the storm outside as turbulent as the one inside.

Thunder exploded above the house. She hurried toward the stairs. *Go to bed and go to sleep.*

Candles she could do without. Because of the charged air, showering was out, as well. *Put on dry pajamas, crawl under the covers, and Go To Sleep.*

A crash on the second floor. The window she'd left open since dawn. *Oh, God. A trillion pieces of glass.*

She flew up the inky staircase. Missing the top step, she flailed for the newel post, caught it and raced down the hallway to her room.

In the wet wind, the window winged helplessly, battering the outside wall. The glass was intact but the bottom hinge and metal rod, which kept the pane ajar on sunny days, had ripped from their wooden frames.

She fought storm and curtains to right the pane. Leaning out as far as she dared, she caught the bottom lip, steadied the precarious glass with her other hand and tugged at the heavy panel. Water puddled on the floor. Sheets of rain washed her arms, face and shirt.

''Here,'' Michael said near her ear over a mighty sky clap. ''Let me do that.'' He pushed her aside, grabbed the frame and hauled it to the sill. ''Keep the hinge and rod free,'' he ordered.

Together they positioned the window into place. He secured it easily.

''Thank you.'' She straightened the drenched curtains. The storm barred once more, the room brimmed with silence.

Michael walked to the dresser and struck a match. Its glow flickered across the walls and ceiling as he set the flame to the hurricane candle he'd brought into the room.

For a moment, he studied her, then closed the shadowy

gap between them. "You're soaked." Removing a strand of hair plastered to her cheek, he said, "You need to get dry."

He stripped off his shirt and laid it around her shoulders. "I'll get a towel."

She stood where he left her. Listening to his movement down the hall. In the bathroom.

His shirt smelled of him. Potent. She rubbed her cheek on its warmth and closed her eyes. *Cross the room, close the door. Lock out what the night will bring.*

She stayed still. And watched him, amber-lit from the candle's glow, return with towel in hand and eyes black as the storm.

"You haven't moved," he said softly.

"No."

Their eyes held. He lifted the terry cloth. The hair on his arms glinted.

Goose bumps rode her flesh.

His hands were gentle—a doctor's hands—stroking through her wet hair. "It has gold streaks," he murmured.

"The sun. Happens every summer. My brother used to call me tiger head."

"I thought it was dyed." He ran a length between his fingers. Caressing, as he would rare silk. "It's beautiful." He watched her. "You're beautiful."

"Too skinny."

"No." He slowed the strokes and massaged her scalp. "You're slim. There's a difference."

"You said I should eat more."

"That was before."

"Before?"

"This. Now." With whispers of touches he dabbed water droplets from her cheeks, chin, throat.

Supple and tanned, his chest blocked the room. She longed to trace her mouth over his skin, feel his silken hair under her lips. "I'm sorry about the window. I shouldn't have left it open when the wind started."

"Forget the window."

She raised her eyes. "Michael…"

"Don't say anything." His voice. Low, thick. "Just let me dry you. Before you get chilled."

The towel caressed her collarbone then slipped to her arms. "I'm not cold," she whispered, staring into his midnight eyes. "I'm burning. Everywhere you touch me, I burn. Since the first day."

Pulling her to him, he took her lips. Hunger. Raw. Primal. The towel slipped to the floor.

His hands swept her spine. Finding the slope of hip, the curve of buttock. A groan as he kneaded there.

Arms locked around his neck, she flattened herself against his lean hard frame, starved for what he could give, eager to replenish the void in their lives.

He touched her breast. Circled its center. She cried out, rising on tiptoes against the rigidity of him.

Fury outside. Fury within.

Dragging himself from her lips, he kissed his way across her cheek, down the angle of her jaw to the area below her ear.

Kisses sprinkling sparks. Urgent need. Power overwhelming her.

This, she thought, dropping back her head, feeling his nip on her flesh. *This is making love* with *a man, not to him.*

No one had ever caught her feelings the way he did. No one. She'd trade her soul for a whole night.

His fingers grasped the soft undersides of her arms. His eyes consumed her. "This could be the mistake of your life."

"Never. Not with you, Doc."

"Especially with me." Voice ragged. "Don't look for more than what's here, Shanna."

"And what's here?"

"Lust."

She shook her head. "Emotion. Harmony."

"You said it yourself—we don't dance."

"And you proved we do."

"Because of the lust."

She smiled. Kissed his jaw. Kept the sharp quick pain at bay. "Because the waltz is harmony."

The candlelight fluttered. Shadows dipped along his cheekbones, deepened the lines around his mouth, and punctuated the tiny scar on his lip. His long, thin nose curved ever so slightly to the right. A masculine nose…and utterly defenseless.

Like him.

Her heart beat its agony at what he meant to her.

She wouldn't think of dreams, hopes, or tomorrows.

Nor would she think of yesterdays and yesteryears.

Tonight was hers. *He* was hers. She held his face, breathed in his warm, earthy scent, and whispered, "Give me this dance, Michael."

Chapter Eight

She didn't need to ask twice.

He gave her slow, wet, mobile kisses that had her toes curling in the braided rug. Had she ever been kissed like this? Maybe in another life.

He gazed down at her and touched his thumb to the corner of her mouth. Tenderness. It pricked her eyes with tears. He asked, "Do you know how hard it was to stay away from you?"

Her heart sang. "You won't have to anymore."

Dark piercing eyes. "One night isn't forever, Shanna."

The song shattered. "I know."

She dragged down his head, seeking his mouth, desperate to patch together the strewn fragments of her joy. And then, it was there. Again. Alongside the need.

His hands sped over her limbs and breasts, then unclasped her bra. He drew her to the bed.

Her palms skimmed his chest. Her fingers pressed against bone and muscle, winnowing through soft, crisp hair.

She found the drawstring of his shorts and released him full and hot in her hands. A guttural sound. His.

In a liquid move, her own shorts were gone, kicked aside with his clothes. Then she was up against him, her legs wrapped around his waist, her hands in his hair.

Pivoting, he twirled them slowly. A dance.

Openmouthed kisses.

Below her private heat, she felt him. "We don't have any—"

"Some in the bathroom."

"There is?"

"Yeah." He pecked her nose and smiled. "Leigh and Bob's."

"Oh." Relief. She cupped her fingers over his ears. "Good." More kisses.

He carried her from the room and into the bathroom. There he set her on the counter, slapped open the medicine cabinet, and hauled out a condom box. In the shadowed light, he paused and said, "Just so you know, my last physical exam was in February. It was all clear. I haven't been with anyone since."

"I've only been with Wade. Ten years ago. There were two others but we didn't… It didn't work out."

His eyes—dark, beautiful. *Intense.*

Her fingers shook with his as they protected him.

In sex she had always stayed focused. With Wade it had been his lead, never hers. She hadn't dared. With Michael she felt bold, wanton, determined to take as well as to give.

"Do it here," she mumbled against his neck, drunk on his skin. "I don't want to wait."

He framed her face, the darkness and his expression swallowing her whole. "When we do it the first time, I want to feel you under me."

As he scooped her off the counter, she swiped up a handful of foiled packages and felt him smile against her lips.

Back in the guest room he knelt on the bed and followed her down, covering her body. He pulled her hands up above her head, scattering the foil, and laced their fingers.

So profound.

For a long moment, he stared down at her in the sputtering candlelight.

"Michael? What is it?"

"No," he said. "Mike. Say Mike."

"But you don't like—"

"I like it when you say it. Only you." With one hand he kept her hands anchored above them and brushed a thumb along her cheek. "Say it, Shanna. Here. Like this."

"Mike."

He kissed her, a butterfly touch of mouths. "Again." One hand traveled down and slipped between her thighs.

"Mike," she breathed. Her own fingers crept along his rough jaw while he worked a marvel below. "Mi-ke."

"Yes, sweetheart." His mouth found the tip of her breast.

"Miiii…"

"I want you, babe. Now."

"Yes. Oooh."

He moved, levering and positioning. His hands sought hers and moved them to the pillow. A slow waltz. Incredible intimacy. Kisses. Savoring. Then he was there, buried to her womb.

Her eyes widened.

"You okay?" His voice was low, torn.

"Yes, I'm—it's…" *Terrific. Perfect.* "Great."

He brushed the hair from her face. "So it is. Wrap your legs… Oh, sweetheart… Just like that. Just…like…that."

Slow, languid. Picking up the pace.

A jog, a sprint. Faster. Harder.

Wild kisses, sexy kisses. Sweat between their bellies.

Desperation, daring. Sheets tangling.

Feeling. Sensation.

She cried his name.

And was lost.

Michael stared at Katherine's file on his desk. Five minutes and she would arrive at the clinic for her semiannual checkup. She was never late. *Review your last notes, fool. Stop dreaming of last night.*

When was the last time he'd had sex like *that?* Never.

Every part of the act, every motion, word, sound—every woman before her...nonexistent.

Give me this dance. God. She'd swing danced and waltzed him clean out of control. Another first. Control in sex was how he liked it. This abandonment, this mindless desire, this *fury,* interspersed with tenderness and feelings scared him silly.

He wanted none of it. Now or ever.

Like hell.

He couldn't wait to touch her again. Her smooth, clear skin.

Be inside her again.

Have her wrapped around him like a downy blanket.

Hear her little sighs.

And, his name—*Mike*—on her lips. Oh, yeah, *that* most of all.

This morning had been a first, too, staying to see dawn in a woman's bed. Yet when he woke with her side empty— the coolness of the sheet telling him she'd been gone a while—an unfamiliar hollowness poured in. He had wanted to watch her eyes flutter open with the first streaks of daybreak.

To kiss her from a dreamy haze.

Make love with her again.

Instead, all he'd done was bury his face in her pillow and inhale her sweet sunshiny-meadows scent.

A knock on the partially open door brought up his head.

"Your grandmother's here, Doctor Rowan," the clinic nurse informed him.

"Thank you, Gerri." Taking the file with him, he rose and followed her down to the examination room where Katherine sat in a chrome-trimmed vinyl chair.

"Gran." Michael closed the door behind him. "Ready for your checkup?"

"No," she snapped. "At my age, who wants an overhaul every six months? It says too much about parts wearing out."

"Now, Grandma. Yours are as intact as they have been for the last thirty years." He pulled down the blood pressure cuff.

Katherine snorted. "That's all you know. I've been having funny aches in my chest for the past month."

He didn't quite believe her. Had she been ill in the slightest, she would have come to see him. Katherine was not someone who left things unattended until the last minute.

Still...

He pegged her with a concerned eye. "What kind of ache?"

"A heavy kind."

"Can you be more specific?" He released the pump and watched for the pulse beat. It began at the normal level.

"Started when I heard you had Rowan Dairy for sale."

"Ah. We're back to that."

"Yes." Her eyes were mulish. "And I'm not letting it go. If I do, this heaviness will never go away. I mean it, Michael. This situation is causing me a lot of sleepless nights. It's not good for my heart."

"Did you come today for medical purposes or is this another bash-Michael day?"

"Hmph! I've never bashed you, young man, and you know it."

Michael sighed. "Not in the physical sense, Gran, but you've never been one to ease into things."

"All I want is what's best for you."

I know. But keeping the farm isn't an option. "Be still for a moment while I check out the heaviness." He set his stethoscope to her chest. Her pulse rate was slightly higher than normal. "Breathe slow and deep. Stop. Breathe again. Slow."

She did as he asked with her back straight and hands in her lap.

After several long moments, the pace slackened. He listened, seeking abnormalities. There were none. Her heart thrummed strong and steady. The matter of the farm *had* agitated her.

"What about downsizing?" Katherine asked as he retrieved the otoscope from the counter and checked her ears. "Maybe if you sold the cows but kept the land for hay and grain. I'm sure this achey feeling would go away then."

He frowned. "Have you been talking to Shanna?"

"What on earth for? She's got nothing to do with the financial aspects of the place. That's between you and me."

Michael shone the ophthalmoscope into the old woman's left eye. "By rights, Gran, the finances have nothing to do with you, either."

She blinked, rapidly. His words cut. *I'm sorry.*

"I'll fight you to the grave, Michael, before I let you sell the place." She pushed his hand away and stood up, clutching her purse to her waist. "I haven't lived seventy-seven years without learning what makes people tick—you, especially. I know that place reminds you of Leigh. I know it reminds you of your mom and dad. I know it holds fears and memories and anxieties you never speak of. But selling is not going to obliterate them, son. Selling will only make you more aware of what it is you're running from. Seeing Jenni every day will be that ghost."

She walked to the door and pulled it open. "I'll reschedule the rest of the checkup for another day. With Rochelle."

Michael wanted to fling the file at the wall.

In the same instant, he nearly called her back to apologize and to give her a hug.

Rant at her pigheadedness.

Hell. Between his grandmother and Shanna, it was like sitting between a stone wall and a brick one.

He was still listening to Katherine's heels click down the hall when Gerri paused in her rush past the exam room. "Can you take a call in your office, Doctor Rowan, or should I tell them you'll phone back?"

"Who is it?"

"A woman. A Ms. McKay."

His heart did a quick leap. "I'll take it."

In his office with the door closed, he picked up the phone. "Hi," he said and felt a goofy grin evolve.

A second's silence, then, "In case you were wondering, none of the cows were struck in the storm last night."

"Good. I'm go—" Dial tone. *What the hell?* Had they been disconnected or had she hung up on him?

Hoping for the former, wanting to say "I missed you this morning, in fact all day," he was about to punch in the farmhouse number when a second call came through. The hospital. A woman in labor and hemorrhaging.

On a soft curse, he hurried from the office.

Dead tired, he got to the farmhouse at seven-forty-five. The birth had been grueling. The woman had lost blood by the pint, but she'd make it. Her and the wee boy.

Jenni scrambled from the truck with a clump of Katherine's brown-eyed Susans clenched in her little fist. The heat and the ride home levied them into a mournful droop.

With eagerness in her hazel eyes, the child raced up the path and burst through the back door.

"Shanna! Shanna, where are you?"

"In here, sweetie."

Rushing through the kitchen, she exclaimed, "Look what Grammy gave me for you."

"Oh, my…!" A quiet sigh. "They're *beautiful*."

When he walked out of the mudroom, the Susans were against her nose, her eyes shut. A smile curved her mouth. A sight he'd remember until he died. This woman he'd made love with. Barefoot in his kitchen. Sexy in a pair of denim cutoffs and one of his blue shirts knotted under her small, round breasts. Her shaggy, sun-striped hair pushed behind her ears, three silver hoops swung in one, dangling dream-catchers in the other.

"Don't sniff the flowers," Jenni advised. "Grammy says they stink."

Shanna opened her eyes. Met his. Her smile faltered. "Well, they're still lovely." She looked down at his niece. "Let's find a vase so we can set them in some water. I think they need it."

Jenni stood on her toes and reached for the sink tap. "Uncle M. said you were living here now."

"Ahh. That's right. You and I haven't seen each other since I moved in, have we?"

"Nuh-uh. You get up too early, and then last night I stayed at Grammy's 'cause of the storm. How long you staying, Shanna?"

In the pine hutch, she found a slender blue vase and filled it under the tap. "Until the cabin gets redone."

"How long will it take?"

"Oh, another couple days." Sorting the flowers on the counter, she nipped off the ragged ends with a knife. Jenni placed each Susan carefully in the water.

Loosening his tie, Michael crossed to the refrigerator. She'd waited for him to come home. The table was set. A fresh romaine salad and grilled salmon sat under plastic wrap. A light supper on a muggy evening. Kinfolk gathered.

And now she arranged flowers in a vase. With a child in desperate need of a mother's touch, a mother's love.

He took out a jug of water and poured a glass. "Add two days for the paint to dry completely and the fumes to go."

Jenni beamed. "You mean it, Uncle Michael? Shanna gets to stay *four* days?"

"Yup. She does, tyke."

He exchanged a look with the woman working the posies. She didn't look pleased. What was bothering her? From the moment he'd come through the door she'd withdrawn.

Jenni's beam faded. "Why does she have to go back to the cabin, anyway?" The girl looked at Shanna. "Why can't you stay here all the time?"

His lover rilled fingers through the child's hair—like she had last night with him. He looked away, but his groin recollected the midnight hours.

"It wouldn't be a good idea, honey," she said. Another stem dipped into blue glass.

"Why not?" As naturally as she had that day in Leigh's bedroom, Jenni wrapped her arms around Shanna's hips. "I like it when you're here. I like coming home and you're in the house. Mommy was always…"

"What, honey?"

Jenni shrugged. "Nuthin'."

Michael knew. *Mommy was always in the barns.*

He'd heard the complaint from Jen last Christmas during the family's festive dinner. Jenni, chattering how she loved Christmas most because it kept Mommy in the house, baking, instead of with the cows. Leigh, laughing it off, ruffling her daughter's hair. *"I'm not down there that much,"* she'd said.

But Bob, gentle man Bob, agreed with his only child, wedging discomfort into the festivities of turkey and gifts.

Shanna offered the vase and its explosion of yellow to Jenni. "Want to set this on the table for me, angel, and then get that bowl by the toaster?"

"What is it?"

"Cottage cheese."

"Eew. I don't like cottage cheese."

"Then you haven't tried mine." She winked at him and he felt a punch to the chest.

They sat and ate the salmon with a brown sugar sauce and the salad, graced with bacon bits and nuts and a tasty homemade dressing Michael could not define. Sliced green onions from the garden, strawberries and cinnamon sugar spiced the cottage cheese. Jenni had second helpings. Dessert was a delicious fruity Jell-O thing he would have sworn came from a deli. Until she told Jenni she'd set it that morning.

For a microwave champ, the meal was a king's charm. At his town house he'd grown used to food on the run— store-bought lasagna, precooked chicken and fish. Because of his schedules and his ravenous stomach when he came through the door, traditional stoves and pots and pans stymied him. With Jen coming into his life the fast-food habit had simply transferred residences.

He watched Shanna across the table. The slow light of evening brushed her skin. Oh, yes, this kind of meal he'd take in a heartbeat day after day, week after week.

For Jenni. For him.

And the nights.

Shanna spooned a wiggly dollop of Jell-O into her mouth. He stared. Shifted in his chair.

Jenni giggled. "Hey, Shanna. Knock-knock."

"Who's there?"

"Boo."

"Boo who?" Another wink his way. His heart floated.

Hunching her thin shoulders to her ears, Jenni snickered. "Whatcha crying for, Shanna?"

Laughter.

His chest tightened. Since Shanna had come into his employ, Jenni had changed into a normal little girl. Laughing, talking a blue streak, reacting impulsively to the world around her.

And the nightmares that had badgered the child after Leigh's death had lessened.

Shanna, of course. Showering Jenni with love.

Possessing him.

Their eyes met. Held for a heartbeat. Then, she focused on his niece again.

Why wasn't she talking with him? Had he come on too strong last night? God forbid—in his craving had he somehow hurt her? Impossible. He carried the half-mooned marks of her nails on his shoulders. She'd taken him clear off the bed once.

Tonight they spoke in circles. To and around the six-year-old between them.

By the time the meal was done, his frustration peaked. It didn't help matters when his arm brushed hers at the dishwasher and his plate and glass found position with a clatter.

At eight-twenty they left the kitchen. Michael escaped to the study. The patient files he'd brought home were waiting. As he settled in the leather chair he heard Jenni ask, "Will you come up and read to me an' Tavia?" Later he heard them on the stairs, giggling quietly.

He felt excluded.

And wondered why that should ache worse than when Leigh had done it to him as a child.

Dressed in Shrek pajamas, Jenni climbed into bed with Octavia under her arm and *The Velveteen Rabbit* in her hand.

"C'mere, Silly," she called to the cat who had followed them in from the bathroom where Shanna had supervised teeth brushing. "You can listen, too."

The calico leapt onto the mattress, her throat-motor revving. Jenni's small body cuddled next to Shanna's shoulder as she settled against the headboard. Shanna kissed the sweet-smelling locks and smiled into happy hazel eyes.

"Comfy?" she asked once the wiggling had stopped and child, doll and cat found the best position for the timeless Margery Williams tale.

"Uh-huh. This is my favorite story. And Tavia's and Silly's."

"Mine, too. Did you know I read it to my little brother when he was your age?"

"You did?"

"Uh-huh. He used to carry it around with him everywhere, so I called him booky-blue."

"Daddy used to call me bunny-bop."

"Your daddy sounds like a nice man."

"Oh, he was the bestest daddy in the whole, wide world."

Shanna took the floppy, worn booklet. Grape juice stained the title. The corners were dog-eared and scratches marred the cover picture of the forlorn, brown velveteen bunny.

A tenderly loved book.

"Mommy must have read this one many times," she said, opening the first page.

"Uh-uh. Daddy read it way more. Me 'n him always read."

Shanna curved an arm around Jenni and cupped her elbow. "Sometimes daddies can make better character noises," she said. "They can growl and grump like bears, squeal like pigs and squeak like mice." Barring rodeo standings, Brent had uttered not a single sound over any written word.

"Uh-huh." Jenni agreed. "Daddy used to make goofy noises and pretend to eat my toes. His moustache tickled."

"I bet you laughed real hard, huh?"

The child nodded, her eyes big, her grin bigger. "Once I peed my pants. But," she added her tone maturing as if the matter was one of extreme importance. "That wasn't when we read bedtime stories. Thank goodness!"

Shanna snuggled the little girl closer and stroked her arm. Warm, soft skin. Precious. Like Timmy's would have been. "Shall we get started?"

They read the book together. And when they were done, Shanna tucked Jenni under the covers and put Octavia in her own bed—a boot box lined with scraps of cloth and bits of lace—on the rug next to the wicker night table. She kissed Jenni good-night. The girl's arms came around her neck in a tight clasp.

"Will you stay, Shanna?" she whispered.

Oh, love, I want nothing more. She sank to the bed and pulled Jenni against her chest. "Of course, peachkins. I'll put the night-light on, too."

"No, I mean stay forever."

"Oh, sweetie."

Serious eyes, serious mouth. All emotion.

How to tell a child, orphaned from her parents mere months ago, that she, too, would leave soon?

"I'll be here for a while yet."

"I don't want Uncle M. to sell the farm," she whispered.

"You know about that?"

"I heard Grammy and Uncle M. talking one night. I was s'pposed to be watching the bears movie, but I seen it a bunch of times so I went to get some juice from the kitchen and then I had to pee and I could hear them talking. They think I don't know. You won't tell, will you, Shanna?"

"I won't tell, darling."

"I wanna live here and I want you to live here with us."
Tears. They hurt Shanna's heart. "Can't you tell him?"

I could if he loved me. "Even when I leave, Jen, I'll always be your friend. We'll visit each other and read together or make suppers together…whatever you like. I'll always be close by."

"Will you?"

"Just a phone call away, honey."

"I can phone you?"

"Absolutely. Anytime, no matter what. Deal?"

The child's chin jerked twice. Her arms sneaked around Shanna's neck again. "I love you."

"And I you." *So much. Far too much.* "Sweet dreams, peachkins. Catch you in the morning."

A giggle erupted. "You'll have to run hard 'cause I'm fast."

"I'm faster." Shanna gave Jenni a little huggy-bear shake. She set a swift kiss on her forehead and stood up. "Want Uncle Michael to say good night?"

Yawning, Jenni rolled to her side. Dark strands of hair flowed on the pillow and lay on her apple cheek.

"Okay. He always checks under my bed and in the closet for the bogeyman."

Shanna smiled. "In that case I'll send him right up."

No moon hung in the night, only stars. Their light cast a gossamer glow across barnyard and trees.

Seated on the rail in the farthest corner of the darkened verandah, her back against the rounded post, Shanna sucked in cool air. Frogs chorused in the mossy pines nearby. Down in the pasture, a cowbell clinked.

She let her mind go blank.

She didn't want to think. Not tonight.

Not when Jenni wanted her to fill the void Leigh had left.

Not when Michael wanted less than she had to give.

The screen creaked. She watched as he stood on the threshold, silhouetted by the lamps inside. Then he stepped outside and closed the door with a quiet snick.

Hands buried in his pockets, he walked to the top of the steps. For several long moments she held her breath as he turned his head and scanned the path between the house and cabin.

She stared her fill. Ivory fabric gleamed on his shoulders. His strong-veined forearms, she knew, were bare, the sleeves flipped back to just below the elbow.

Dollar for your thoughts, Doc.

Was he looking for her? Or storing memories of the quiet, country nights he'd miss?

She hoped both.

One hand came up and clutched his nape. His head lolled back, and he released a long, slow, exhausted sigh. She wanted to hold him and let him rest against her.

Softly she said, "Neck rubs are free in this corner."

He swung toward the sound of her voice. The hand disappeared in his pocket. "Are they?"

He sauntered over and stopped at her knee bent on the rail. His silver eyes locked her in place. "Did you hang up on me today at the clinic?"

She looked down to the paddock. The dark hulk of Soldat D'Anton moved along the lodgepole fence. *Looking for an escape, big fella?* "I assumed you were busy."

"That the only reason?"

Those eyes kept her. Under the shirt she wore—*his shirt*—she tingled. "Is there another?"

"You've been avoiding me since I came home."

She jacked up her chin. "Last night you made it clear that a few hours doesn't chalk up to forever. I wanted to let you know that my making supper tonight wasn't meant to change your opinion."

He searched her face.

"I see. You think because you made supper I might get to liking the idea of coming home and having you barefoot in my kitchen." *Barefoot and pregnant.* He shivered with the image.

Shanna rounded with his child.

No! Yes! Oh, God—

She scowled, bringing him back to earth. "Something like that. I won't be your bed partner."

"Have I asked you to be?"

"No."

"Then, why don't we see where this leads?"

"As in a relationship? Without a stitch of meaning?"

His turn to scowl. "Is that what last night was?"

"You tell me."

"Last night was great. The best I've ever had," he said, wanting to sting because she sought answers he couldn't give.

Her mouth crimped. "And you've had hundreds to compare."

"More than I can count. But," he said, wanting to soothe the hit. "I can't remember a one."

"Quite a line. Use it on all your women, do you?"

"No line." He moved until he was against the leg she'd anchored to the deck. He ran a knuckle down her cheek. "You've destroyed me for all women, Shanna McKay."

"I hardly think so, Doc."

"I know so." And he spoke the truth.

She leaned her cheek into him. "Doesn't matter, anyway."

All day, since dawn, he'd waited for this. This. *And more.* "Oh, but it does." Leaning forward, he sank into her lips. Her lovely, soft lips. His hands threaded into her sun-gilded hair and cupped her head. "I thought one night would end it. I was wrong. It won't." He found the buttons between her breasts. "You're wearing my shirt."

"My clothes are in the—"

He kissed her again, fingers working swiftly downward.

"—cabin and smell like…"

He pushed the cloth off her shoulders, unclasped her bra.

"—paint. Mike…"

Need. For the scent of her skin, her Shanna taste. She caught his shoulders and steadied herself. He pulled her from the rail to strip off her shorts. He drew a foil packet from his pocket.

Now, he thought as he unzipped his slacks. Quickly he covered himself, then hoisted her back onto the railing. *Shanna.*

Legs vising him.

Mouths wild.

In a thrust he was home. Blind with passion. A man drowning in the wine of woman and heat.

Shanna. Her name, a gift, a song, a dance.

She gave.

He took.

In her arms, he was helpless. Helpless to the power of her.

Shanna!

Shivers. Shudders. He pulled her close, waiting for the seduction to end.

He lifted his head, staring. Sweat on her face. Starlight in her hair.

Beautiful woman. His.

Her eyes opened, reeling him into her soul.

Oh, God. Was it possible? *Could* he love her? Was this gut-clenching crazy pang…

Bewildered, he touched her cheek with the pad of his thumb. She kissed his palm. "Love you, Mike."

And there they were. Those words that enfolded a sweetness he hadn't heard since his parents died more than a quarter century ago.

He hung his head, defeated.

Chapter Nine

During the days of his on-call shift, Michael worked late and often through the night. Shanna never saw him. She was gone before he woke and asleep when he returned. When he did get home, he went to his own bed and slept like a wintering bear.

She missed him more than she'd believed possible.

One night, halfway through the week, he slipped into her room, crept naked under the warmth of her covers and, without a word, made love to her. Later, in sleep, he possessed her still—his arms and legs binding her to his body. The poignancy of it hurt.

Jenni's absence was another torture. On-call days meant the girl stayed with Kate.

Late Saturday morning, under wind-scrubbed clouds with a bucket in hand, Shanna checked out the garden's peas. Tonight they would be together, she, Mike and Jenni. *Not a family, a convergence.*

But of what? Friend and family? Lover and family? She shook off the thought. *Plan the meal, Shanna. Do what you're good at.* She decided on a variety of vegetables and greens. Some to freeze, some for the evening meal.

He wants you as a lover, not a loved one.

But her heart smiled. The truth in his surrender was enough. She'd said the words. His silent lovemaking in bed twenty minutes later had brought her to tears.

Still, she remembered his words on marriage.

Remembered who she was.

Farmhands did not revolve in the same orbit as doctors.

But she loved him. Sitting under a cool sky, her hands among the plants, she accepted a second truth: she'd love him as no other. Always.

Hoofbeats caught her attention. Soldat paced the lodgepole fence with his head raised and nostrils flared.

"Smooth ride, you," she murmured, observing the heavy power and undulation of his muscles.

In the corner of the paddock, the stallion stopped, wheeled and paced back. Shanna got to her feet. Since the day she'd moved into the cabin she'd witnessed distress in the animal.

Whistling low, she approached the fence. The horse halted, pin ears batting air. A second whistle.

Soldat whirled and trotted to where she stood. Fifty feet, thirty... Suddenly, his ears flattened. She saw the whites of his eyes.

"Hey, there, big boy," she called softly, stopping six feet from the lodgepole. "That's no way to treat a lady."

The horse breasted the fence. Its lips tightened.

"What's the matter?" she crooned. "No one to play with? Well, old man, this is not how you greet friends. And, I am your friend." *Probably your only friend.*

The animal's ears flicked forward, listening. His intelligent eyes watched. His nostrils inhaled her scent.

She blew gently in his direction, then stepped forward and stretched out a hand. Soldat tossed his head.

Slowly, she stroked the stallion's nose, up toward the star between his keen eyes. "You're some kind of man, know that?" she murmured. "Just like your owner, and I don't mean Leigh."

Abruptly, Soldat's ears leveled and he sidestepped to the left. His lips and nostrils wrinkled tight as he shook his head over the fence at the man crossing rows of plants.

"Seems you've got a watchdog," Oliver Lloyd said. Dressed in barn-cleaning coveralls and rubber boots, the assistant milker stopped beside Shanna and jutted his chin. "He's smitten with you."

"He's unpredictable." She considered the horse.

"Yep. He is that. You're lucky. He hasn't let anyone touch him since Leigh. She was the only one could ride 'im."

"Why did she keep him? He's far too dangerous to be on a dairy farm." *To be near Jenni.* Shanna adored horses. But if one had exhibited any sort of cantankerous behavior within shouting distance of *her* child, the animal would be gone.

Why haven't you sold him, Mike? He should've been first on your list.

Oliver lifted his cap and scratched his balding pate. "Leigh wanted him. What she wanted, she got. It's what killed them, y'know?"

Shanna stared at the old farmhand.

He went on. "She and Bob were heading to an auction to buy another horse." He pulled a face. "As if this 'un wasn't enough. Nope, she wanted a spirited gelding for Bob." Oliver shook his head. "Bob wasn't a cowboy. He was a farmer, plain and simple."

"There was really no reason for them to go?"

"None whatsoever."

Losing interest, the stallion ambled away. Shanna hooked her arms on the fence. So. Mike's demon. An accident that might have been avoided. If Leigh had curbed her self-centered tendencies.

"Tell me something, Oliver. How were they as siblings?"

"Like peas in a pod. Wherever he was, she was. I 'member when they were little coming to church and soon as services were over, they'd be climbing the old oak out by the parking lot. One Sunday they snuck out during services and hid in the branches. When the people came out to their cars, the twins sprayed 'em with water guns." The old man chuckled with the memory. "They weren't always angels." He sighed. "'Course, things changed when the grandparents took over the raising."

"You mean when Michael's—the doctor's parents were killed."

Oliver scraped a boot on the bottom rail. "Huh. Mind you, Katherine and John looked after 'em long before that. The place you're living in? Used to be their home."

Shanna looked back at the squat cabin. Mike had grown up there? In quarters as cramped as Brent's old silver Bolero?

"You mean—"

He nodded. "All four of 'em lived in that little place right till that plane crash took Davey and Trudy."

Oliver hitched up his pants and spat in the dirt. "I shouldn't be gossiping but me and the wife often wondered what woulda happened if Kate and John hadn't hired Trudy Dumas to help with the gardening and housekeeping that summer Davey—that's their son—turned seventeen. She was near six years older and flighty as a three-winged sparrow. Every time you'd turn around she'd be ragging on that young lad to do the dark and dangerous. Went from bear-hunting to skydiving to flying single engine planes. It's a wonder they didn't kill themselves long before it happened.''

''Who's Trudy Dumas?''

He gave her an odd look. ''Michael's mother. She's the one convinced Davey to fly her to Alberta in the middle of a January blizzard. Wanted to ski the Canadian Rockies in Banff.''

Shanna stared at the horse grazing peacefully under cool, quiet skies. ''How—how old was Michael?''

''Ten. That day he changed from a funny little guy to a silent, scared kid dogging Leigh morning, noon and night.''

''I can imagine,'' Shanna murmured, chest aching for that parentless little boy with big, serious gray eyes.

''No, girl, you can't. See, he was sure she'd die on him, too.''

She hadn't seen her father in almost four years. And she'd been expecting him.

Just not today.

Brent McKay, barrel-chested and a grin cracking his leathered face, stood staring at her across the welcome mat at the door of her apartment in town. Meandering aimlessly from town to city, year after year, her homing pigeon father always managed to find his way back into her life at some point. Today was one such point.

''Shanny-girl!'' he shouted. ''Figured that was you who drove up. Been waiting all afternoon.''

''Hi, Brent.'' Years ago, after Meredith's departure, she'd given up calling him Daddy. Daddies did right by their kids. Brent McKay did right by Brent McKay.

She tossed the plastic basket of laundry beside the coat rack and carried the sack of farm produce into the kitchen. Jason sat at the round wooden table made for two.

Her brother home in the middle of a hot afternoon?

''What're you doing here?'' she asked. ''Aren't you supposed to be working?'' When they lived together, she barely saw him from breakfast to supper. Weekends he puttered on his Harley or disappeared with his friends.

He looked away. "I'm visiting."

Oh, Jase, don't get sucked in. She set the bag on the counter and began unloading what she'd picked in the farm's garden a half hour ago. Without a glance his way, she asked, "What do you want, Brent?"

"What? No hello hug for your old man?"

"The last time we hugged was on my twelfth birthday when you wanted me to go on the road. Why break tradition now?"

"Geez, Shan. I thought you'd be glad to see me. Jase, here, and I've been talking up a storm for the best part of an hour. He ain't mad to see his old dad, are you, son?"

Shanna shot her brother a look. Color hued his cheeks as he scrutinized his harness boots.

Darling Jase. Always daddy-hungry. Always needy for what could never be, not in their family. She'd tried. God, she'd tried so hard to make up for it.

But she didn't have what it took to give young sons what fathers—that unique species—could.

Providing they tackled the responsibility.

Providing they loved their children unconditionally.

She said, "It's all right, Jase."

He lifted his head. Gratitude, pure and bright, shone in his eyes. She wanted to cry.

"'Course it's all right," Brent spouted. "Why wouldn't it be? I'm his father. Kid needs to shoot the breeze with his old man once in a while. Doncha boy?" From the sieve she'd put under the tap, he plucked a carrot and bit off its end. "Mm. These are good." Nosing through the sack. "This from that doctor's farm?"

Shanna snatched up the sieve and the bag and set them on the opposite side of the sink. "*This* is for Jason."

Brent finished off the carrot and chucked the greens into the sink. "Think he might have work for a poor ol' cowboy? I could do odd jobs like Jase here's done."

He. Michael. "No."

"No?"

"What part don't you understand, Brent? The *N* or the *O?*"

He slouched against the counter, arms folded, a saucer-sized buckle under his round, soft belly and blue-red veins under his skin. That was her father. Cowboy up on beer, whiskey and rye. Her father, scoring on broncs in the Alkie Hall of Fame. She focused on placing the vegetables in the refrigerator's crisper.

"You're not happy to see me, are you, girl?" His eyes, usually red-rimmed and bleary, were a hard, clear blue. *Had* he quit guzzling? She didn't let the thought sway her.

"Every time you show up it's to ask for money or to crash on the couch for what you claim will be a day or two—but ends up being three weeks to a month. You come empty-handed, you leave without so much as a nod good-bye. And vanish for another three or four years. You play on Jason's feelings simply because you happened to be the guy who sired him. You know he cares. But *you* don't. You don't give a flying ant's burp about either of us, Brent. You never have, you never will." She continued with the lettuce and radishes.

"Well." Brent snorted. "Guess you told me. Or is it your age making you snippy these days?"

"Only thing age does besides make you old is teach you about life. Something," she added as memories bit her heels, "you never learned."

He chuckled. "Now what lessons am I supposed to have learned, little girl?"

Her hands stilled. "For one, I quit being a little girl two

decades ago.'' She looked right at him. ''The hour Mama walked out.'' The hit stung, she could see.

He moved to the end of the counter.

She returned to the garden's yield.

''That wasn't nice.''

''It wasn't meant to be.''

''I didn't expect your mom to leave, y'know.''

''Really? She begged you to settle down. To make a home for us and be a family.''

''I was bringing in the cash, wasn't I?''

''What you brought home,'' Shanna said, voice rising, ''was whiskey on your breath and some floozy's bra in your truck!''

His astonishment egged her on. ''That's right. I know. I heard Mama crying in the bedroom, not once, but twice. I heard you telling her it was nothing. *Nothing!* I hated you for hurting her. How could you do that to her? To *us?* You, a married man with two little kids.''

Tears. Damn the tears. She swung back to the refrigerator and the vegetables. Arranging, rearranging.

''Well,'' he said. ''Least you had a roof over your head and food on the table. Lotta people got it worse.''

She swiped a wrist under her nose, shoved the crisper into place, and faced him. ''A twenty-foot trailer and the ground it stood on wasn't home. You had your electrician's papers. Jase and I could have lived in one town, gone to one school, made friends. Mama would have been able to get a decent job instead of working as a cocktail waitress in every hole in the wall we hit. You could have come home nights instead of—of—'' She punched air. ''We could've been a normal family!''

''Until your mother left we were normal as the next.''

She gaped. The man was her father and had the wits of a candy-greedy five-year-old.

''Of course. You had nothing to do with that. You were

Mr. Big Shot rodeo champ. PRCA, yeehaw. All the ladies' hero.''

Ripe plum spread up his neck. ''Don't knock the Professional Rodeo Cowboys Association, missy. We're talking good, honest work here. A man's profession.'' His shoulders rolled in disgust. ''Know what your brother plans to do with *his* life? Be a mechanic. A *mechanic*. Bah! Grease monkey work.''

''Get out,'' Shanna snapped. ''Now.''

''Sis.'' Jason stood.

''Leave it, Jason. This has been decades too late.''

''You kick me out,'' Brent told her, eyes stabbing his son, ''you'll never see me again. You want that for the boy? Him never seeing his daddy again?''

''He never sees you now as it is.''

Jason moved. ''He didn't mean it, Shan. He didn't mean it about my being a mechanic. Tell her you didn't mean it, Dad.''

'''Course I meant it. Tough, lean kid like you should be out doing man's work.'' He hoisted on his belt. ''Come with me, and I'll introduce you to the best there is. Just say the word, boy, and the money'll be yours.''

Jason shook his head. ''I like working with motors, Dad, I really do. It's exciting and—''

''Exciting? Kid, coming out of a chute on twelve hundred pounds of pure steel is exciting. Sticking your head in a stinking grease bucket all day—''

''Weren't you listening?'' Shanna cried. ''Jason doesn't want to follow that circus of Brahmas and broncs you're so fond of. He's going to be a mechanic and open his own shop one day.''

She looked at her brother. His mouth hung open. *Believe it, honey-child. I've changed my mind. You go for those dreams of yours.*

Brent smirked. ''Always trying to play mama, aren't you,

girl? Well, you're not his mother. Never have been. But I'm his daddy. *Me*." He whacked his chest. "And I damned well know what's best for my kid."

Poleaxed. By her own father. Who'd left them to the wolves. Who'd let her clip coupons. Pick bottles out of ditches. Beg at the Salvation Army for new shoes.

She caught hold of the counter. "Get. Out."

"Shan," Jason whispered.

Brent snatched up his Stetson and jammed it on. "Fine. You want to break up the family, be my guest. I'm outta here." He strode to the door and flung it open. "Have a nice life, kid." The slam shook the glassware in the cupboard.

Silence echoed.

"I'm sorry, Jase."

"It's all right. He's been a bastard all his life."

Her brother. A boy no longer. Her heart stung for what he'd missed. For the father he should've had. "He'll be back."

Jason said nothing. There was no need.

They both knew she was right.

She fixed vegetables and marinated steaks in hickory sauce.

On the radio Alan Jackson sang about a woman and a man and their "little bitty" slices of life.

The back door opened. Jenni, decked in a pansy-yellow jumpsuit with one strap flapping loose, charged into the kitchen. "Shanna! I missed you!" Little arms collided with her waist.

"Hey, peachkins." She crouched and nuzzled the scent of child and sunny day. "Me, too. Missed you like crazy."

"I thought you'd be gone." Hazel eyes shimmered. "I thought you'd be living in the cabin."

"Not till tomorrow." She fixed the child's strap. "Jason

was done a couple days ago. Now I'm waiting for the fumes to leave.''

''But I want you to stay here. In this house.''

''That makes two of us.'' His voice. She looked up.

He waited in the doorway, hands in his pockets, his tie liberated. Fatigue stamped his charcoal eyes and drew lines around his mouth. She thought, *I should go to him. Smooth away the worry, the sadness, that tousled dark lock on his brow.*

Instead, she remained on the floor, the child between them, sipping him in by degrees. *Missed you. Too much.*

''See!'' Jenni patted Shanna's cheeks. ''Uncle M. says it's okay, an' he never goes back on his word.''

Shanna rose and gave Jenni a gentle swat on her rump. ''Go wash up, scamp. We'll talk later. Supper's almost ready.''

When the child skipped down the hall, Michael stepped into the room and swept Shanna's white tank top and blue shorts with one blink. He framed her face in his hands— and kissed her. Long and deep. ''Stay,'' he murmured when she clutched his shirt. ''I need you to stay.''

Need. Not want. A step up the ladder. She felt giddy. A fifty-pound weight floated away before realism dropped in. ''I can't.''

''Please.''

Could she deny him anything when he looked into her heart? ''All right. Until the fumes are completely gone.''

His hands slipped to her bare arms, stroked. ''Thank you.''

''It's not just for you,'' she said.

He thumbed her bottom lip. ''Wouldn't have it any other way. You make Jen happy.''

In ways I can't.

The words slung like tacit stones, as if he'd spoken them aloud.

"Mike."

He bussed her nose. "I'll get those steaks started."

They ate in the backyard, in the quiet, rose-fringed sunset. He'd changed into jeans and a T-shirt that was black and frayed at the hem and cuffs. Her eyes trekked his rangy frame myriad times while he tended and flipped the meat and she sliced tomatoes and pickles.

On the stoop, Jenni fed Octavia tea before the doll's tummy rumbled away. Near the sweet pepperbush, its fragrance heavy in the air, Silly sat on an oblong rock tidying her dainty paws.

Shanna smiled. Flawless vista. Flawless moment. She wished her brother could have joined them. But after Brent slammed out of her apartment, Jason had left to hang out at the motorcycle shop. She knew he'd be safe there. Brent hated motorcycles.

"Hey, Jen," Michael said over his shoulder while giving the foiled corn another turn. "Wanna grab the plates and napkins from the kitchen table?"

"Yay! Hear that, Tavia? We get to eat!" She laid the doll on the step. "You be good, 'kay?" she ordered and scrambled inside.

"Take your time," Michael called. "We don't want to sweep instead of eat." His grin melted his weariness. "Kid's a regular hot wire when she's hungry." His hand reached and caught hers. "C'mere. I'm hungry." His mouth on hers. "Mmm. Starved is more like it."

"Ferocious." Her legs lost strength.

"Sleep with me tonight."

"We shouldn't be discussing—"

"To hell with discussing." The second kiss, tender and bittersweet, caved her stomach and her willpower. "I missed you, Shanna."

Tears stung her eyes. Two kisses, and he showed her everything but his heart. Never his heart.

Sliding out from his arms before they made fools of themselves in front of a six-year-old, she said, "Maybe."

Half an hour later the meal and day were done. They carried in the dishes and stacked them into the dishwasher. Jenni tugged on her hand. "Will you play something on your guitar, Shanna? Uncle Michael's never heard you."

Across the counter her eyes shot to his. She didn't want to play for him. Not yet. Songs hung her soul on the wall. "Not tonight, peach. Besides, my guitar's in the cabin."

Michael strode from the kitchen. "I'll get it."

Jenni raced after him. "I'll show you where she keeps it!"

Shanna sighed. After tonight she'd make it clear. No more family trysts. No more sharing meals. No more yearning looks. No more child's hugs.

No more Cinderella dreams.

The handsome prince would never let her sweep the ashes from his heart.

On the front porch she watched Jenni run through the trees, an elf in yellow with curls bouncing around milky cheeks. Shanna didn't like breaking promises to a child, but she would move back to the cabin tomorrow. Another night like this and—

"Play the frozen one!" Jenni took the steps like a puppy and hopped on the bench. Cross-legged, she patted a spot beside her.

Guitar in hand, Michael followed, a shy, crooked smile under his dark eyes. He handed over the instrument, then hoisted a hip onto the railing across from her. No man looked more savory in spot-worn jeans. For a long beat, their eyes linked.

Do I make you happy, Mike?

On the bench beside Jenni, she bent over the neck of the guitar and picked out a chord. The notes were clear and graceful in the calm evening air. She chose a light melody, easy and uncomplicated, to lift her mood and placate the fire she'd seen in the doc's face.

When the last note queued into the night, Jenni clapped. "That was soooo pretty."

Shanna tweaked her nose. "You liked it?"

"Oh, yeah! Play another!"

"What was it called?" Michael wanted to know.

"'Down In Mary's Land.' It's an oldie by Mary Chapin Carpenter. Ever heard of her?"

He shook his head. "Country-and-western?"

She smiled. "It's just country nowadays."

"I don't listen to it."

"Maybe I'll convert you."

"I think you already have."

She laughed and flowed into several other songs. Madonna, MCC, Faith Hill. The last, "Foolish Games" was a bittersweet number put out by Jewel. Lyrics written for her and Michael.

She closed her eyes, drifting with the moody melody.

When it ended, night converged. Somewhere an owl hooted and in the garden a frog grumped. She looked at the man across the deck. In black, he was power and passion. *Rebecca*'s Max de Winter of the twenty-first century.

"Play one more!" Jenni said, breaking the spell.

Michael came off the rail. "Time for bed, tyke."

"Aw…"

Shanna set the guitar aside and stood. "Come, sweetie, I'll tuck you in."

"'Kay." Her little hand reached out.

Upstairs, burrowing under the covers, Jenni confided, "I wish my mommy had played the guitar like you."

Ho-boy. "Honey, not everyone plays an instrument. I learned because we had an old one sitting around when I was little." In reality, her father had won it on one of his rodeo tours. How he got the battered instrument was any-one's guess. Probably in an all-night poker game where he often lost more than he gained.

"Mommy said I could learn to play the piano one day, 'cept we don't have a piano."

"Maybe Uncle Michael will buy one."

Jenni's arms slid around Shanna's neck. "I don't think so. Uncle M. is awful busy. 'Sides, he doesn't know what kids want 'cause he's not a father." She paused. "I don't think he wants me living here," she whispered. "With him."

Shanna snuggled the little body close to hers. "Sweet-heart, Uncle Michael loves you very much. He cares what happens to you and worries about you. He wants the best for you, Jen."

"He does?"

"More than you know."

"How come he never cuddles with me the way you do? Daddy always did."

"I think he's a little afraid."

Jenni drew back, astonished. "Of me?"

Of his emotions. "In a way. I think he feels you might compare him to your daddy and, well, maybe you won't think he can do things as good."

"But why would I compare him to my daddy? Uncles and daddies are different."

"Yes, but what they feel here," Shanna placed a hand over her heart, "is very much the same."

"Like you and Mommy?"

"Sort of."

For a moment, Jenni puckered her small brows. Crawling into Shanna's lap, she murmured, "I'm glad you're here. You're sorta like Mommy. I miss her, Shanna. Sometimes I wake up in the night and get scared 'cause I think she's standing right by the door. But when I look there's no-

body.'' Her little body shook. ''Can I sleep with you tonight?''

''Oh, peach.'' Childhood horrors. She'd had her own for
years.

''Pleeease.''

''All right. But only tonight.''

''Thanks!'' Jenni bounded up and grabbed her pillow and
doll. ''Come, Silly. Me an' Tavia are sleeping with our *new*
mommy.''

Heart aching, Shanna followed the trio down the hall,
tucked them in and went out to the verandah. She found
Michael sitting on the bench, legs stretched and his hands
behind his head. At the creak of the screen, he sat up and
leaned forward. Setting his elbows on his knees, he studied
her.

''You won't need to go up,'' she said, crossing to stand
at the top of the steps as he had several nights before.
''Jenni's sleeping with me tonight.''

''She afraid again?''

''Yes.'' She regarded him in the darkening light.

''Since the accident…'' He trailed off. ''She has nightmares sometimes.''

''What do you do?''

''I sit with her until she goes back to sleep.''

''Where?''

''Where what?''

''Where do you sit?''

''In the chair by the window.''

Not on the bed. Not close enough to cuddle. No physical
gestures to betray emotion when it was needed.

She rubbed her arms and looked out over the pasture.
Soldat was quiet tonight. She closed her eyes and inhaled
the rich, twilight perfume of animal and grass and barnyard
and fresh-cut hay.

''Do you ever hold her, Mike? Do you ever stroke her

hair when she's frightened?" Shanna looked over her shoulder. Dusk masked the verandah and him.

"She's asleep within minutes. What are you driving at?"

"Nothing."

The bench squeaked as he rose. "Yes, you are." His tread was slow, steady. He stood behind her, big and solid. Tense. It spooled from him. "Look at me," he said, turning her to face him. "Why all the questions? *Those* questions?"

A flag of alarm. "She…she believes you don't want her."

Appalled, he stepped back.

"Do you hug her? Do you ask her about her day at Kate's? Do you know her doll's name?"

He raked a hand through his hair. "She doesn't speak much."

"With me she never quits."

"You're a woman."

Desperate for him, she took his hand. "Oh, Mike. That's the most ridiculous statement I've heard in years. She needs you to look at her, hear her. She's a little girl who's withering for attention. Your attention."

"Katherine spoils her rotten."

"Grandmothers are supposed to. You're all she has left of her mom and dad. Do you know how much you look like Leigh?"

"Don't make more of this than there is, Shanna."

Dropping her hand, she sighed, sad for them both. "You're a good man and no doubt brilliant in your work. But sometimes, Michael, you are downright dim." She moved toward the door, then hesitated. "For once stop loving Jenni from a mile away. She needs you to be there for her, up close—like a father."

"I'm not Bob," he said bluntly. "I never will be Bob."

"No one's asking you to be. A sperm's DNA has nothing to do with a heart's emotion. Don't you know that yet?" She stepped inside and left him with the night.

Chapter Ten

The next morning—his Sunday off—Michael woke moody blue. At seven-thirty he gave up on sleep, dug out a polo shirt and tan shorts then crept downstairs to make coffee.

Sunlight washed the kitchen in cheer and charm. Taking offense to both, he pulled the lacy curtains closed.

Jenni believed she wasn't wanted? God, how could he have not seen *that* coming?

He scrubbed his hands down bristled cheeks. The clinic and hospital consumed him. Selling the dairy ate at him. Worse, he'd been wallowing in grief and self-pity over his sister rather than spending an ounce of emotion over her daughter.

Yes, he looked after the tyke. The same way he looked after his patients. He saw to her welfare and her daily needs. He certified she was progressing and growing as all children should. And he ignored the deep-seated love in his heart by walling it up brick by brick with past fears.

Stupid, he knew, but he couldn't help it, couldn't let it go. Loving a child—*or a woman*—induced susceptibility.

Upstairs, small feet raced along the hardwood. The tyke was awake. Water from the bathroom tap gushed, rattling the pipes.

Yawning, he got a mug from the cupboard and filled it with hot, black coffee. He'd have to remind Jenni not to crank the taps full blast.

An elemental lesson from a real father.

He shut his eyes, breathed the aroma of strong coffee and took a sip from his cup. Feet pattered down the hall again. A door knocked against the wall. Muffled sounds—Jenni's high-pitched voice laced with worry. *What the hell?*

Cup in hand, Michael left the kitchen, climbed the stairs two at a time and strode down the hall to the guest bedroom.

Shanna faced the wall in a fetal position. Jenni, scrunched against the pillows, pressed a dripping face cloth to Shanna's hair above her right temple.

Migraine.

As he entered, the child looked up. "She has a headache, Uncle M.," she whispered. Her face was pale, her eyes cup-sized. "A really, really bad one. Please help her."

"I'll try, Jen." Setting his coffee on the nightstand, he eased onto the bed. Taking Shanna's wrist, he checked her pulse.

A little rapid. "Shanna?"

A grunt. He felt her brow. "Have you taken your pills?"

Another grunt.

"How many?"

"Four."

That told him two factors: the migraine was at least two hours old and the day's dosage of five nearly done.

"Honey, can you turn over? I want to check your eyes."

"Leave me 'lone."

"I will, soon as I see your eyes. Jen, go down to the

fridge and get a cup of crushed ice out of the freezer. And bring a Ziploc bag.''

The child bounded off the bed. Shanna moaned.

Jenni's face pinched. "I'm sorry," she said, her voice mouse tiny. "I didn't mean to jump."

"S'okay," Shanna mumbled, unmoving.

Michael gave the child's shoulder a reassuring squeeze. "Go on, Jen, get the ice."

As soon as she tiptoed from the room, he leaned over Shanna. "Open your eyes for a second, sweetheart."

She did and he checked her pupils. Dilated. Red-rimmed. Bruises under her eyes. Ice-white cheeks. He brushed the hair gently from her face. "Sleep," he said, and kissed her temple.

If she wouldn't let him doctor her, maybe she'd see Rochelle. He'd phone his associate later. "Let the pills work."

"Gotta get up. The garden…"

"Shh. Rest. Jen and I'll take care of the garden."

"The beans…"

"We'll do them." He stroked two fingers along her collarbone where tiny white flowers marched along a rosy cotton neckline.

"I checked Hat-Girl's calf at midnight," she muttered.

"Aw, babe…" She had named every cow and worried about each newborn calf. His palm found the smooth texture of her arm. She was fine-boned, to the point of fragility. A trick of eye and mind when he recalled the dominion of her long legs around his waist and those slim fingers clasping his biceps.

His hand covered hers and, for a second, she clutched his fingertips. This protectiveness in the face of her helplessness was unfamiliar.

It shook him.

Migraines were commonplace and treatable. But imagining her, pained, in her apartment—*in his barns*—left him helpless.

Jenni returned, ice and bag in hand.

Making a small pack, Michael laid it over Shanna's forehead. "Feel good?" he whispered.

Her eyes fluttered.

"Is she gonna be all right?" Jenni asked in his ear.

"I'll be fine, little one," Shanna mumbled. "Go have breakfast with Uncle M. He needs to eat and so do you. I'll be down in a bit." Her eyes drifted closed. "Love you, peach."

"'Kay." The girl offered a careful kiss. "Love you, Shanna."

Not giving a damn about ethics, Michael set his mouth against one of her dark-winged eyebrows. *Me, too.*

He prayed Fate, his old nemesis, wouldn't hear.

A motorcycle grumbled past the house.

Michael—Jenni at his heels—headed out the back door and down the path, to the cabin. The air with its burned-off dew lay tangy as peppermint among the trees.

Jason parked the bike and cut the engine. "Hey, Doc," he called, hanging the helmet on the handlebar.

"Shanna said you'd finished painting a couple days ago."

"Wanted to check for missed spots now it's dry. Hey, short stuff." The young man ruffled Jenni's hair. Easy affection, easy camaraderie. Michael squelched a pinprick of envy.

"I'm not short stuff," Jenni retorted, surprising Michael.

"Sure, you are. See." Grinning, Shanna's brother crouched down. "You're only knee-high to a grasshopper."

"Am not. I'm a big girl now. I made Uncle Michael toast with peanut butter and jam this morning."

Jason laughed. "Definitely big-girl stuff."

"And, I looked after Shanna, didn't I, Uncle Michael?" She craned her head to look up at him.

"You did at that, Jen." His hand stroked her hair. *Easy.* He savored the moment.

Jason's brows knit. "What's wrong with sis?"

"Migraine," Michael told him. "How long has she had them?"

"You asking as a doctor or a friend?"

"Both. I want to help her."

"Does she want your help?"

Michael kept hold of his temper. "Look. She's curled in a ball on her bed right now with an ice pack on her head. Pain like that can cause problems in her work."

Jason squared his shoulders and narrowed his eyes. "I get it. You don't want someone with health problems milking your cows. Well, let me tell you something, Doctor—"

Michael stepped into the young man's space. "The job has nothing to do with my questions or my concern. Being in pain and handling a herd outweighing her by several tons could get *Shanna* hurt." His fingers flexed, itching to strike at something. Anything. *"I don't want her hurt."*

Jason's eyes relaxed. "Well, damn," he said softly. "You *do* care for her." For a long second he studied Michael. "More than normal, I'd say."

Michael remained silent.

Jason stepped back. "Hey, squirt." He pointed to the wooden baskets of geraniums hooked on the verandah railings of the main house. "Pick some of those pretty red flowers over there for when Shanna wakes up, okay?"

"Can I, Uncle M.?"

"You bet. If you put them in some water and leave them on the kitchen table, she'll see them soon as she comes downstairs."

Jenni scampered off, happy in her mission.

Jason eyed him. "It's not my place to tell you, Doc."

"Whatever's said here, stays here. Consider it doctor-patient confidentiality."

Jason shook his head.

"Listen," Michael said, his tolerance ebbing fast. "If there's something I can help her with, tell me."

"I can't."

He spun on his heel, then paced back. "You McKays are the most stubborn people I've ever met."

"Yeah," her brother muttered, "but we come by it honestly."

"Okay." Michael held up a hand. "Let's narrow down the basics, at least. How long do they usually last? A day? Two?"

"Depends. Sometimes a couple hours, sometimes four days."

"How long has she been on the Cafergot?"

"The green pills?"

Michael nodded.

Jason hesitated. "A few years."

"Do you know if she's tried anything stronger? Shots?"

"You'd have to ask her."

"What about her...um, her cycle? Does that trigger them?"

Jason grimaced. "Geez, man. She doesn't tell me *every*-thing. I'm not her gynecologist."

"Okay, forget that. What about stress?"

The young man's eyes flashed. "Guess I didn't make myself clear the first time. Shanna handles stress like a pro."

"I'm not talking work. Do you know if anything other than work causes her worry."

"We all got worries, man. Doesn't mean they cause head-aches. I know you're concerned about my sister. I appreciate that. So I'll tell you this. She's had some bad things happen to her and sometimes she remembers. That's all I can say. Okay?"

The ache left Michael's shoulders. Finally, they were getting somewhere. "Okay," he said. Bad memories he understood.

She was sitting at the kitchen table, dressed in a canary-yellow top, eating toast and jam—Jenni standing at her side—when he entered the house. Fresh from the shower, her shaggy hair surrounded her face in thick, damp waves. Gold gypsy hoops swung at her ears. Above the right one blazed a red geranium. The rest of the flowers stood in a tall, pink glass in the center of the table.

Shanna's blue, blue eyes lifted above the table geraniums and met his. He could feel it coming, the long, hard fall.

"So, Doc." Her smile was warmer than any sunbeam. "Did my bro do a good job?"

What are your bad memories? Can I help?

Michael resumed breathing. "He's done wonders. I'm giving him a bonus."

She arched an eloquent brow and licked a blob of jam from her pinky. "He'll do handstands all the way to Blue Springs."

"How are you feeling?"

"Great. You know your stuff." She gave Jenni a one-armed hug. "Both of you do. The ice pack helped enormously."

Along with four knockout pills, he thought.

She cut a corner of the toast. "Those beans won't stand a chance today."

Scowling, he walked across the room. "Give it a rest, Shanna." Anger churned his breakfast. "Sunday's your day off."

She lifted a shoulder. "Might as well get a head start."

"How about going into town with Jen and me, instead?" Blocking images of her in pain, he smiled at the child curled into Shanna's arm. *Let's do something fun.* ''Want to go to the pool, Jen?''

Her eyes brightened instantly. ''To swim?''

'''Course to swim.'' He grinned. ''Know where your suit is?''

''Yes!'' Grabbing her doll, she bolted from the kitchen.

''Bring a towel,'' Shanna said, tossing a wink in his direction. ''I think you've just made her entire week. It's sweet of you.''

He came around the table, lifted her chin with a knuckle, and studied her face. Clear eyes. No pain. Whoever played the wrong fiddle in her memories would pay the piper *and* his band, if Michael had his way.

''I'm fine, Doc,'' she said.

''I was worried.''

''And very kind.''

''Kindness wasn't in the cards. I want you to see my associate at the clinic.''

She smiled. Lacing her hand around his wrist, she said, ''You don't take praise well, do you?''

And you're ignoring my advice. He let it slide. For now.

A crumb clung to the corner of her mouth. Brushing it away, he thumbed her lower lip. ''Praise doesn't make a doctor.'' He replaced his thumb with his mouth and tasted raspberries.

His hand gravitated down her tanned arm, to her inert fingers curled on her bare thigh below the thready hem of those patched denim shorts he liked so well. He wanted to pick her up, hold her in his lap, shield her from pain and memories, from the grief she tolerated.

I had a little boy once. He was stillborn.

Had she been alone? Had Jason been there? Her mother?

He deepened the kiss, steeped in the earthy instinct to safeguard what was his.

To mend.

When he inched away, her eyes were misty. "Well," she said with a husky note and a smile. "That kind of checkup I can take. Your women patients must be beating down the clinic door."

"Wouldn't let 'em in." *Only you.* He envisioned her eyes decades along. Eyes he'd see upon waking at sixty, seventy—

Small feet thundered into the room. "I'm ready, Uncle Michael!" Jenni bounced to a stop beside them, windmilling her miniature tote. "I have a towel and everything. Even my water wings."

"Good girl." For a second time, he tousled her hair. A half-toothed grin nabbed his heart.

"You swimming, too, Doc?" Shanna inquired.

His mouth twitched. "Only if you do."

"I don't swim."

"Then," he winked at Jenni, "we'll have to teach you."

"Not today. But don't let me stop you."

He wondered if her parents had neglected that life skill in her growing years.

Shanna fixed the clip dragging down Jenni's curls. "Where's Tavia, love?"

"In here." A pat to the tote. "She's sleeping inside the towel."

"Excellent. She won't get sunburned there. Did you pack some sunscreen for yourself?"

"I don't know where it is."

"There's some in the bathroom cabinet," Michael offered.

Shanna stashed her plate in the dishwasher and the geranium from her hair in the table bouquet. "I'll get it. You two head out to the car. Do you have a beach ball, Jen?"

"Uh-uh."

"Then we'll buy one in town."

"Yip*peeee!* Did you hear that, Uncle M.? I get to have a beach ball."

"I heard, Jen." He watched Shanna leave the room. *Oh, man.* He'd tumbled, no, *fallen,* straight down a fifty-foot cliff where he sprawled on his back, wind-knocked and staring up at the sky. He wasn't sure if he'd ever get his breath again. Or wanted to.

Shanna bought the ball at the local Walgreens. As Michael pulled the truck from the curb, she grinned at Jenni and sang, "You are my beach ball, my only beach ball…"

The child laughed, hugged her treasure and sang along, quick to fill in the new words. Done, they exchanged high fives.

Throat tight, Shanna said, "Hey, Jenni-girl, knock-knock."

The girl bounced in her seat. "Who's there?"

"Harry."

"Harry who?"

"Harry up, open this door 'n let me *out.*"

Jenni laughed, clapping her hands above her head.

In the glove box Shanna found a navy marker and sketched a puppy's face onto the beach ball's pink surface: hound-dog eyes, whiskery snout, toothy grin, lolling tongue. "Oh, my goodness," she said and laughed. "We have another Jenni." She held up the ball. "Don't we, Uncle Michael?"

The child squealed and wriggled. "Uh-uh! Nooo!"

Shanna reached back and squeezed Jenni's knees. "I'm going to nickname you Wiggly Willy, the puppy who won't settle down."

More giggles.

An array of emotions chased through Shanna's chest. How could she give up these two people when the time came?

Across the cab—merriment in Michael's gray-sky eyes. The mood altered his face and smoothed the lines. For once, he looked relaxed, happy...free.

Seized by this change, she leaned over and mussed his hair.

"Hey, watch it, lady!" Laughing, he flicked her earring. For a split second, the car rocked in its lane.

Jenni yelled, "More, more!"

They arrived at the kiddie pool, starry-eyed. Because of the hour, few people were in attendance. Shanna took Jenni into the changing room and helped her get ready, then she sat with Michael on a bench at the shallow end. Sunlight roused copper from his burnished hair. He caught her hand, entwined their fingers, and held them on his bare knee. Her throat ached.

"Lookit me, Shanna!" Jenni said, joy peppering each word. "Look, Uncle M.!"

They waved. Laughed. And Jenni—orange water wings on her slender arms—chased the beach ball over the blue surface along with two little boys.

Shanna leaned against Michael. Sunshine, chlorine, his scent—contentment swirled in her veins.

"I missed you last night," he murmured above her ear.

She smiled into his black-ringed irises. Until she remembered why she'd left him alone on the verandah last night.

"Will I see you tonight?"

A quiver ran through her. "I don't know." *I have to start separating myself from you. I can't do that when you look at me this way and say these things.*

He fingered her earrings and stroked her mouth with his gaze. "I want to kiss you," he whispered. "Now. Here. I want to put my hands on you and..." his voice dropped "...touch you all over."

"*Mike.*"

"You make me crazy, Shanna. I've never felt like this."

"What about all those cute nurses you've met?" she asked, to lighten the air, to keep him from seeing inside her heart.

"What about them?"

"Certainly you've dated a few."

"One or two."

She grinned and sent a two-fingered greeting to Jenni. "No craziness there?"

"None."

"What about female doctors?"

"Well, since most are married or twenty years older— What are you driving at?"

That you and I, she thought, recognizing his tone—*are at different ends of the spectrum.* Another wave to Jenni. "It's just small talk."

"Huh. I hate small talk."

So did she. It went nowhere. Neither spoke for several minutes. He continued to hold her hand but some of the sweetness had evaporated from the day.

"You were right," he said when Jenni sent a glint of splashes skyward. "I need to spend more time with Jen. I've been neglecting her because of the sale. I need to get her settled so she'll have a permanent home, instead of this seesawing."

She has a permanent home.

He turned and looked at her. "She'll want to see you once this is over."

And you? Will you want to see me once this is over? "I promised her we'd get together whenever it was possible," she told him. "I won't be far." A few blocks, a few minutes. *A lifetime.*

Regret. She saw it before he looked across the pool where the voices of children echoed in a medley of joy.

* * *

"Hey, all," a cheerful female voice said from behind Shanna.

She and Michael sat on a bench under a leafy maple in Blue Springs Park, finishing ice-cream cones Michael had bought from a nearby store. Jenni squatted on the grass in front of them, her mouth smeared deliciously in chocolate.

A smile tugged Michael's lips. "Out for the daily constitutional, Roche?"

A woman in green spandex shorts and a cream-colored nylon top came around the bench. Her calves were hard, her waist lean. A runner. A tanned, petite runner. The sweat on her face indicated she'd been at the exercise for at least forty minutes.

"Don't knock it, Rowan," she clipped. "Not everyone's got natural abs like you." She set her hands on her hips and bent forward in a stretch. Her sleek, black ponytail fell over one shoulder. "Hi, Jenni."

"Hi, Mrs. Garland."

Straightening, the woman held out a hand and a genuine smile to Shanna. "I'm Rochelle, Michael's associate at the clinic."

Doctor Garland? The associate he had advised her just this morning to see? "Shanna McKay."

"Sorry," Michael interjected. His eyes cut to Shanna, then up to the woman he'd called Roche. "I wasn't thinking. I should have introduced you."

Rochelle chuckled. "I don't doubt you weren't thinking. You men are all alike. Sit with a pair of pretty ladies and your minds go AWOL. Right, Jenni?"

Jenni bobbed her head. "I went swimming today. Shanna bought me a beach ball. This *big*." She spread her arms wide. The ice cream wobbled.

"Wow, maybe you could bring it next Sunday to show Amy."

"Uh-huh, I will," the girl replied and bit into her cone.

Rochelle said to Michael, "You haven't forgotten about the barbecue?"

He stood and tossed his half-eaten treat into the trash. "We'll be there."

"You're invited, too," Rochelle told Shanna.

"Thank you, but I don't—"

"Nonsense. Michael tells me you have Sundays off."

What else did he tell this woman with the sleek hair?

"I'd like you to come," she went on with a wink to Michael. "We women have to stick together."

Sticking together with a woman like Doctor Rochelle Garland? Hardly. Rochelle met every qualification in the book. Smart, professional, pretty. Not to mention athletic. An endless list.

Swallowing the last of her cone, Shanna smiled at Jenni, dug a tissue from her shorts and wiped away the chocolate smudges.

Michael and Rochelle began discussing a case. Tall man, tiny woman. *Doctor to doctor.*

"Good?" Shanna asked the child.

"Mmm-hmm." The end of the cone disappeared into a half-toothed grin.

I love you, little one. How will I live without you?

Standing, she stretched a hand to Jenni. "We'll wait for you in the car," she told Michael.

He glanced over. "Be right there."

"Nice meeting you, Doctor Garland."

The woman waved. "Rochelle, please. And same goes. Be sure you come to the party."

Shanna walked away with Jenni, child of her dreams.

Play and fresh air. Natural Ritalin.

Michael watched a subdued Jenni in the rearview mirror. She stared out the window at the smooth hills and emerald pastures, clutching her doll.

He glanced at Shanna. Silent since they'd left the park. No. Since the pool. Since he spoke of Jen missing her, and his heart had taken its own dive. What he'd wanted to know was if Shanna would remain in Blue Springs. Close enough to see. To visit.

To touch.

Across the cab, he saw her profile. Feminine curve of a cheek. Long, dark lashes. Shaggy brown-blond hair. Not beautiful, but unique.

His kind of unique.

A knob of hurt filled his chest. Shanna.

Her hand lay loosely in her lap. He closed his fingers around hers and held them on his thigh. Their eyes met. *Blue,* he thought. *A matchless blue.* In a few weeks, a memory.

He focused on the road.

At the farmhouse, he parked beside her silver pickup and Katherine's blue Honda. The old woman looked down from the wicker chair, green knitting yarn trailing from a canvas bag at her feet. The calico lounged in a splash of sun on the rail.

Michael hadn't expected his grandmother. Her gaze caught him like a laser through the windshield. *Don't think it, Gran. This is not what it seems, not what you're hoping for.*

"Grammy!" Jenni, tote flapping at her side, clambered from the truck and bounded up the steps, a mini-dynamo of news. "I went swimming with Shanna and Uncle Michael and afterwards we had ice cream in the park."

"Did you now?" Katherine zeroed in on Michael as he came around the hood, then on Shanna as she slipped from the cab and closed the door, knapsack in hand.

"Uh-huh. And Shanna got me a beach ball." Jenni waited while Michael hauled her prize from the back seat. "See?"

"I see, all right." Katherine said, eyes keen on Shanna. "A fine thing to do, young lady. Did you thank her, Jen?"

"Yes, Grammy." The child took the ball from Michael. "Can I play with it in my room?"

"Be careful it doesn't hit anything sharp."

"I will. C'mon, Silly." The cat blinked a lazy eye, twitched its tail, and stayed on the railing.

Michael picked up the feline and set her inside the house.

As the screen creaked closed, Katherine said, "Well, you've done it again, Shanna McKay. You've made my great-granddaughter wildly happy. Something no one has been able to do…in a while."

Shanna crossed to the door. "Please excuse me, Mrs. Rowan. I need a drink of water."

Michael's antennae rose. "You okay?"

"Just thirsty. Would either of you like something to drink?"

The old lady picked up her knitting. "Not for me."

"No thanks. Shanna—"

"Stay and visit with your grandmother," she said and disappeared into the house.

Something was wrong. He'd felt it for a couple hours. He should have kept her in the shade. Better yet, left her alone to the peace of the day, to the quiet of the house. If she hadn't talked about harvesting the garden…

Who was he fooling? He'd wanted her with him. And with Jenni. Shanna filled the gap in the little girl's life. His, too. God, he'd miss her when all was said and done. They'd both miss her. Story of his life. A series of misses.

His parents when he was ten.

His grandfather.

Bob and Leigh.

He reached for the door.

"Has she been ill?" The old lady interrupted his pursuit.

Sighing, he sat on the bench where Shanna had strummed her guitar. "She gets migraines."

Fingers flying with purls and knits, his grandmother said, "It's not a headache that's ailing the girl at the moment."

"What then?"

"Maybe you should ask her. What happened in town?"

"Exactly what Jen told you." *Fibber.*

"That all?"

"That's it."

A long lull elapsed. On the eaves a sparrow chirped. Michael's lungs filled with the scents of pine, barnyard and sunny air. Katherine's needles wove back and forth. *Click-click. Click-click.*

"How was she when you left here?"

"Good. Fine."

Katherine knitted on. "Meet anyone along the way?"

"Just Rochelle jogging through the park."

"How did Shanna react to our lady doctor?"

"Normal. They met and—" he raked a hand through his hair "—Roche and I talked over a case for a minute. A patient who needs a colostomy," he added, like evidence.

"Ahh."

"Look, Gran. Say what's on your mind." Knit one, purl two. He knew the routine. He'd seen it a thousand times growing up.

Katherine set aside her needles and looked him square on. "All right. In case you didn't know, that girl in there cares for my great-granddaughter. Now then. She meets your associate, a woman who's another doctor, and the first thing she does is make a list of comparisons. Know why?"

"I'm sure you'll tell me," Michael said humorlessly.

"She makes them to justify the qualities she lacks so when the two of you part company, she'll be able to tell herself it was all for the best."

"That's ridiculous."

Katherine smiled. "It's a woman thing, son."

"Like I said, it's ridiculous."

"Is it?" Katherine picked up her needles.

Michael strode to the door and jerked it open. "If this is another make-me-feel-bad gimmick to keep the farm from selling, you're barking up the wrong tree." With a clap, the screen shut behind him.

The living room was empty. In the kitchen Shanna's knapsack hung over the back of a chair. He went up the stairs at a gallop. Her room remained silent. Striding into Jen's, he asked, "You seen Shanna, honey?"

"Isn't she with Grammy?"

He should tell her not to bounce balls on the walls, except the light in her eyes was a gift. "No," he answered. "I'm going to look around outside. You stay here with Grammy, okay?"

"Is Shanna sick again?"

"I don't think so, but I want to be sure."

"Can I help look?" She got up, leaving the ball to meander toward the bed. "Maybe she's in the cabin."

Michael crossed to the window. He caught a flash of yellow in the trees. "Keep Gran company on the verandah, Jen. I'll be back in a bit."

Chapter Eleven

Jenni watched her uncle hurry across the grass toward the woods. A path led up the hill somewhere there. She knew about it because her daddy warned her never to wander down it. She had wanted to, but she had always been scared of the dark trees.

She wondered where Uncle Michael was going. Maybe he thought Shanna was lost. Daddy said the woods could make you do that.

That scared Jenni. She didn't want Shanna lost. She didn't want Uncle Michael lost, either.

She stared at the woods. What if they didn't come back? What if something happened…like Mommy and Daddy?

Her chin shook. She crawled onto the bed beside Silly and Tavia. Picking up the doll, Jenni asked, ''Do you think they'll come back from the woods? It looks so dark in there.''

Tavia didn't answer. She stared straight ahead. She wasn't in a talking mood.

Jenni didn't blame her. Sniffing loudly, she looked toward the window. "Please," she whispered, shivering a little. "Please let them come back home. Don't take them away like Mommy and Daddy. I don't want them to be angels." *Or ghosts like Mommy.*

She closed her eyes. She thought about the swimming pool and the park and Shanna and Uncle Michael laughing. Maybe if she thought really hard about nice things, bad ones wouldn't happen.

It took several minutes before he caught her. Spruce and pine towered over them. Sunlight came in specks and splatters. He called her name. "Where you going?" He stuck his hands in the pockets of his shorts.

"For a walk."

"Mind if I come? Jen's with Katherine."

She didn't smile or reach for his hand. "If you want." She started back up the trail.

They hiked in silence. The last time Michael had come this way, he'd been a teenager, yet the route remained unhampered by undergrowth. He wondered when Shanna had found it. Had Leigh wandered it regularly when she was alive? As kids they'd run its quarter mile distance without breaking sweat and played hide-and-seek among the thick-trunked trees and caught spruce beetles in plastic ice-cream buckets.

As a boy, orphaned, he'd come alone to sit in the tall grasses at the top and look down at the world. Sometimes to cry. During his teen years he'd hungered for dreams, but most of all for the peace Mother Nature poured into his lonely soul.

Now, twenty years later, he was climbing the path again—with a woman who had seeped *herself* into his soul.

Nearer the summit, along the barren knob of the hill, she climbed harder, planting her feet firmly and using her arms for momentum. Not once did she look back to see if he followed. *Determination,* he thought, watching her spine sway under each step. Of the qualities he most admired about her—gentleness, sweetness, passion, that unique wit and underlying innocence—her determination captured him time and again. Once, he would have called it stubbornness. When had he changed his opinion?

When you fell in love with her.

He stopped and scraped the heel of a palm over his cheek. *Quit this. It's testosterone, that's all.* A sixteen-year-old's crush. Trouble was, he didn't feel sixteen. Hell, had he ever felt this way at sixteen? He wanted her but not just in bed. He wanted to come home to her, he wanted to grill salmon with her, laugh with her, spend evenings on the verandah, listen to her strum her guitar, sing with her. Share the news on CNN, conversation—Jen.

Share life with her.

Which meant marriage and kids.

She would want kids.

"Giving up, Doc?" She stood on the rounded knoll near the ancient twin pines, a slim female form in an expanse of blue sky.

He sliced the air with his hand and sliced the thoughts from his mind. "Never," he called back and climbed upward.

When he finally stood beside her she ran a lone fingertip down his wet cheek. "You're sweating. And puffing."

"It's been a while." He surveyed the area. "When did you find this spot?"

"A couple weeks ago. I climb up every other day. Come, let's rest." She walked to a grassy spot in the shade of the trees and sat, arms wrapped about her knees.

Michael folded himself down next to her.

"I absolutely adore it here," she remarked. Her lashes cloaked her eyes. Her mouth was lustrous from exertion.

He braced a hand on the grass behind her, ducked his head, and captured those lips in a long, soft kiss.

"Mike," she breathed when they parted.

"What?" he whispered back.

"Nothing. Just…Mike."

He kissed her nose and smiled. They looked out over the valley for several minutes. Green pastures, gold crops. Dark stands of spruce. An ant-sized white pickup, its engine muted by distance, inched toward town. A pair of red hawks circled overhead, their wings floating against high pressure currents.

"The first time I came here," Michael told her, "I was six years old. Leigh carried me up the steepest part because my legs gave out." He smiled at the memory. Even at six, his sister had been big-boned and sturdy. "She was strong. Whipped me in arm-wrestling till I was almost fourteen." He let out a half chuckle. "Surprised the hell out of both of us when I finally beat her."

Shanna's hand slipped into his, weaving their fingers. "Tell me about her."

Tell about Leigh. Where to start? They weren't just twins or siblings, but friends, confidants. Each other's crutch when the days and nights overwhelmed them.

Later, both had changed. And he'd carry that all his life.

"She loved this place. I used to believe it was because of our parents' deaths that she strove so hard to keep it, but I'm slowly realizing there was more to it. She needed the land as much as it needed her."

"How was she with Jenni?"

He shrugged. "Like any mother, I suppose. She loved her."

Beside him, Shanna tugged at a blade of grass. "Not like any mother. Last time I saw my mother I was twelve. She walked out and never came back. Jase was a year old. He's never known her."

Michael's chest tightened. Her quota of heartache seemed endless. "What did your dad do?"

"The usual. Headed for the next rodeo."

"And left you with a baby?" His skin prickled.

"I was twelve, Mike. Kids that age get documents nowadays, qualifying them to look after diaper rash." She tossed aside the grass blade. "Anyway, there was a woman living in the trailer next to ours who kept an eye out for us."

Unbelievable. He was in awe. His own mother had chased after every ludicrous adventure under the sun, dragging his father with her, but she'd never left her kids permanently until she died. And she had loved them. Even Leigh had cared for Jen as much as she knew how.

"C'mere," he said and pulled her against him. They'd been almost the same age when they lost their parents. But he'd had Gran and Gramps and Leigh. Shanna had had no one but an infant.

Resting his cheek on her hair, he blocked out the thought of twelve-year-old stricken eyes.

After a long minute, Shanna asked, "Why did you go into medicine?"

"I always liked science. I was good at it so I figured what better way to use my abilities than by healing people." Although some never healed. He knew that firsthand.

"Was it something you always knew you'd do?"

"Not until I was in eleventh grade. I had one of those defining moments Dr. Phil talks about. Leigh and I were helping Grandpa stack hay bales one fall and he was on top of the stack when he slipped and fell to the ground. He'd broken his ankle. I made a splint out of some bits of wood. The doctor said a chunk of bone had chipped off but the splint had pressed it neatly into place. I walked away wanting to be a doctor."

"Your grandparents must have been proud."

"I suppose they were."

"What did Leigh think?"

"She accepted my choice." A little too readily. But he'd understood his twin's unease about their futures; it had been no less than his own. Left in the care of two elderly people who could, at any moment, leave them vulnerable evoked a never-ending fear they both fought to conceal.

"Well, it was a good one. You're a fantastic doctor."

He smiled against her hair, which was warm with sun and rich in the vanilla aroma of pine bark. "And you're biased because we're sleeping together."

"That has nothing to do with it. News gets around as to who has a terrific bedside manner and knows their stuff."

Ah, the cruelty of irony. "If it wasn't for my stuff, as you put it, she'd still be alive."

"What do you mean?"

For a long time he didn't answer. Couldn't.

"Mike?"

He swallowed back the sour wedge of defeat. "I—I couldn't save her." Compassion, not shock, shadowed her eyes. It gave him courage. "I was on call. It was one-thirty in the morning. She and Bob had gone to an auction in Pullman." His mouth twisted. "To buy another horse she didn't need. They were on their way home when…when a semi lost its brakes on a hill, crossed the center line and… Bob died instantly, but Leigh…Leigh was still alive. Her internal injuries were extensive." *Breathe deep. Hold on.* "I couldn't stop the bleeding. I tried. I *tried*. It just wouldn't—" His voice broke.

The pain. It choked him. He clenched his fists. His fingernails dug into his palms.

"Four miles, that's all. Four miles from home." Abruptly, he wrenched away and buried his face in his hands. *"Dammit."*

He felt Shanna's arms wrap him. "My love." She kissed his hair and rocked him like a child tight against her chest.

He hid in her. "It wouldn't stop, Shan—" His eyes stung. God, he hated himself. "I couldn't make it stop."

"Let it out," she soothed. "I'm here."

"She shouldn't have gone to that auction. She didn't need another horse. She did not damn well *need* it."

The crush of pain. It spewed from him in expletives, in dry, rough sobs. *Leigh! Jen!*

"That's it, let it out," Shanna whispered. She stroked his back, his hair, while his heart fragmented and spilled its grief.

"I knew…" he said when he gained some control. "I knew when I ripped open the buttons of Leigh's shirt and listened with my stethoscope. Her pulse rate was crazy, there was so much chaos…and she…she kept trying to speak. I'd tell her she was going to be fine. It was all lies…."

Again, he heard the pandemonium, the swish of oxygen. Heard himself bark for a chest-tube tray and a 32-French tube to drain her lung. He fought the cold skidding down his spine as he heard his own voice, *"You're gonna be fine, sis. I'll make sure of it."*

Again, he saw her eyelids flutter as he leaned in, his cheek millimeters from her wounded one.

"It wasss…bad…the accident. I…feeelll…it."

"No," he whispered. Not Leigh. Not his strong, twin sister, the one who had been his idol every day of his life. He would defy the force of The Unknown with every breath in his body as well as hers, use every thread of intellect and focus to save her. "Leigh, you've got to hang in there, honey."

Behind his mask his smile faltered. This was not the end. Not like their parents. She had to live, for Jenni—

He lifted her hand—her cold, wooden hand—and kissed it. The wildest horse had felt the touch of this hand—and been calmed. Oh, mercy, that it could do the same for him.

His eyes darted to the IVs, the heart monitor, her blood pressure, the respirator.

Her bruised, tragic eyes watched him.

"I...love...youuu...li'l brooo."

"Me, too, you, sis." *The knot in his throat was unbearable. A tear melted into his mask.*

"Look after...Jenniii, Mich-ael. She...neeeeds youuu."

Sweat ran down his vertebrae. "You'll be looking after her yourself soon. I promise."

Lies.

Anger. So hot it burned his lungs. Hissed through his teeth. Gulps of warm, sunny air.

Shanna kissed his tight lips. "I'm here, Mike. I'm here."

He opened his eyes and looked into her drenched ones.

Her smile. "You're going to be okay."

Yes, he believed so. With her anything was possible. This woman whose mother had abandoned her. This woman who one day would put her child's needs in front of her own.

"Lovely, sweet Shanna. You take my breath." *And my heart.*

She set her forehead to his. "Clichéd as it sounds, you did your best, Mike, your very best. If it wasn't enough then it was because powers higher than yours were involved."

"I don't believe in God."

"You don't have to. But you do need to believe in yourself."

Framing his face, she said, "I'll be blunt. I'm sure you've lost patients before. Leigh happened to be one of them. It doesn't make you a bad doctor or an evil man. It makes you human. It makes you grieve and hurt and stamp your feet just like the rest of us when someone we love is lost."

Her stillborn. The unsurpassable loss, a child of your own body. He traced a finger over her brow. "Your migraine," he said gently, "was it your baby you were remembering?"

She looked away. "Why do you ask?"

"Jason said when you remember certain incidents they cause headaches."

"Jason prattles too much. But no, it wasn't Timmy. Just the paint fumes."

Several days ago, when she wanted to sleep in the barn office, she'd cited the opposite. Fumes bothered her but did not elicit headaches. "How long have you been getting them?"

A shrug.

"Honey?"

"About ten years."

"When your baby died."

"Yes. I...I was..."

He set his mouth against her hair, closed his eyes. "What?" he whispered. "Tell me."

"I was painting our kitchen, Wade's and mine, a light green when he came home. He got mad because he wanted it left white. He said I was trying to change his life. Anyway, he packed a suitcase and left. I haven't seen him since."

First her mother, then her husband.

She emitted a long breath. "Out at the cabin, the paint smell got into my things."

Michael remembered the night on the verandah. What had she said then? Her clothes were in the laundry? And she'd been wearing his shirt. *You should've paid attention to her words instead of her breasts.*

"Yesterday," she went on, "I drove to my apartment to wash some jeans and things."

"There's a washer and dryer at the main house."

"I know, but I had to see Jase. Anyway, our father was there when I walked in. We had a—an argument. It probably triggered the headache. When Wade walked out, my father told me..."

"Yes?" Michael whispered, dreading the man's words.

"He told me to deal with it. I was eight months pregnant at the time. Two days later I lost Timmy."

Michael breathed hard. He ought to hunt down the man and tell him to *deal with it*—after Michael finished breaking every bone in his legs. He ought to hunt down Wade and break his neck.

"If I'd known," he said, the anger in his throat huge, "I wouldn't have bought the paint."

"It's got nothing to do with you, Mike. It's just life."

She would look at it that way. Life, it took you on a white-water ride no matter which raft you used. *Aw, Shanna.* He brought her fingers to his lips and searched her lovely blue eyes where pain still glimmered. He wanted nothing more than to vanquish those memories. Make them both forget, just for a while. For today.

"Shanna," he whispered. Pushing her gently onto the grass, he leaned over her. "Shanna." Her skin was soft as down. "Will you make love with me? Here, on top of this hill, under the sky?"

Her lips curved. "For all of Blue Springs to see?"

"Baby, they'd need superhero eyes. We're three miles out."

"Or a periscope, with this tall grass."

"Mm. Definitely an upside here," he said, freer than he'd felt in decades.

A sultry laugh. "Then let's give 'em a show, cowboy."

Levity fled.

Some matters he failed at, but this—with her—was an art. They assembled a nest of shirts and shorts. He loved her slowly. Skin meeting skin. Open mouths. Her tongue on his. Her beneath him.

Sinking into the force of her. Into the light and glory that was Shanna, that was *life*.

Later, transferring his weight to his arms, he thought: *I*

wanted to lay joined with her forever. Here, in the sun-sprinkled shade.

At last, he rolled aside and gathered her close. Stroking the tangle of her hair, he said, "In all the years of growing up, I never once dreamed I'd come up here and do this."

"Then I'm glad to be the first."

"The only." He kissed her, savoring taste and scent. "I'm sorry for losing it about Leigh."

"You were hurting."

He sighed. "I'm a fool."

"Why? Showing emotion isn't a sin, Mike." She lifted her head to study him. "Nothing you do or say will change the way I feel about you. You're a good man. A *good* doctor."

He averted his eyes. "And when I move away?"

Her face was framed in a tumble of hair and blue sky. How had he thought she wasn't beautiful?

"I'll move back to Blue Springs. By September I'll have my diploma. I've already put out some feelers, got some interest."

"That's good," he said around the stone on his heart. "By next year this time, you'll have your own business."

She reached for her clothes. "Maybe I can do your books."

He waited until she looked at him. *Blue, blue eyes.* He didn't waver. "Not unless you're living in Seattle."

He was leaving Blue Springs and taking Jenni with him.

Hunkered over the pea vines in the garden, Shanna pushed her wrist under her nose. *Plunk.* Another pod hit the bucket. At this rate, she'd be lucky to pick a handful by noon.

Yesterday his angry, dry-eyed grief had ripped her apart. Today her own silent, dry-eyed grief was killing her. *Plunk. Plunk.*

"Why are you moving to Seattle?" she'd asked him, stunned beyond belief at the news.

"Better facilities in case something happens."

"What's going to happen?"

"Maybe nothing. But I want to be prepared, nonetheless. I won't subject Jen to the lack of specialized emergency training that's at Blue Springs General. I'm a small-town doctor here, Shanna. Nothing more. I realized that the night Leigh died."

Guilt and fury edged his words.

Illogical logic. *And he a doctor, believing it.*

Stupid of her to have thought he'd gotten beyond his demons. She should have known better.

"Oh, Mike," she whispered, picturing his face, his solemn gray eyes. "You can't surround your life with what-ifs."

But he had.

And she was at a loss on how to change his mind.

After Katherine left and Jenni was tucked in bed, Shanna and Michael had argued for two hours on the darkened verandah. She'd pointed out the rationale of his fear and reasoned that escaping Blue Springs erased neither past nor memory.

She should know.

Timmy lived with her still—would always live with her.

Did Mike honestly believe Leigh wouldn't follow him?

"You've missed the point," he'd fumed. *"It's not Leigh. It's me."* He'd stormed inside then and gone off to bed. Alone.

A sound brought up her head. Soldat d'Anton paced the far fence, again fretful. *You need company, old man. Your own kind.*

The thought set her on her heels. Was that part of what Michael missed—his own kind? *Was* Seattle the answer?

She refused to believe it.

In the past week, she'd observed the changes. He'd become quieter, less edgy, less restless. Less obsessed with a way out.

A bond was forming between him and Jenni.

Upon their return from the hill, the child had drawn another picture. Mike had been center stage, strong, reliable and protective. His hand held Jenni's while she offered a round, red, three-petaled flower to Shanna…lying in bed. In the background floated Katherine, knitting in a chair. Octavia and Silly were on another bed. The angels, solemn-faced but no longer teary, hung in their respective clouds. Along the bottom: *Uncle M and Jenni making Shanna better.*

The instant she and Mike walked into the kitchen, Jenni shoved the picture into his hand.

Down on one knee, he hugged the little girl.

Ah, the look on his face!

Her heart splintered.

Looking across the sunlit garden now, she saw the horse shake its head and snort. She whistled, low and easy. The stallion became alert, listening.

"You're okay, old man," she called. "You're fine now."

Soldat flicked his ears—and began to crop the grass.

Calm at last.

Somehow, *somehow,* she had to make Mike see that leaving the farm held no guarantees. That here on the land he cursed, a part of his wounded heart, so like her own, could heal.

At his desk in the clinic office on Thursday, Michael returned the phone to its cradle.

Walking down the hall to Rochelle's door, he thought of the call that had finally come through.

Her usual friendly "Come in" answered his knock. Michael liked her voice. He'd heard it comfort the most distraught patients and set them at ease. He would miss it.

Never as much as Shanna's.

God almighty. How would he get through an hour, a day, *a week,* without hearing *her* voice? Without seeing her?

Without feeling her wrapped around him in the night?

Pushing aside the thought, he set a palm to Rochelle's door. "Hey, pard. You up to taking on my slate for a couple days?" he asked. He'd play cheerful and ignore the vise on his chest.

Rochelle looked up. "Did they call?"

He slid into one of two guest chairs. Roche had known about his plans, albeit not his reasons, since his two-day drunk following the funeral. He rubbed his nape. "Five minutes ago. They want me in Seattle tomorrow. I'm meeting with Park and from there…who knows?" He cast her a half smile.

"Shoot, and I was hoping they'd forgotten your résumé."

"Not a chance. Park liked my credentials." The woman, head of the clinic Michael had applied to, seemed bent on surrounding herself with specialists who acquired their degrees from UCLA and University of Washington. Michael's appeal came from the oasis of his experience: small-town doctoring around restraints.

"Why shouldn't she like your curriculum vitae?" Roche tossed her pen onto the thick file spread on the desk. "Considering she'll be getting one of the best doctors in the state."

Michael scowled. "Hardly."

Rochelle linked her fingers over her trim middle. "Have you told Katherine about Seattle yet?"

"I'll tell her closer to the day they want me to start. It'll be a couple months, anyway, maybe more. No point in getting her or Jen upset before then." Or enduring the old woman's bitter criticism and his niece's withdrawal. The first he could take. The latter… After coming so far, he was set to destroy that winsome connection. *Fool!*

A five-second hush fell. Rochelle asked, "You're really sure you want to do this?"

"I'm sure." He looked around the small, tidy office. "It's for the best, Roche. There are educational opportunities in Seattle for Jen this town couldn't dream of attaining in fifty years." He looked back at her. Hoped his eyes didn't lie. "Work will be a challenge again."

She frowned. "You're practically run off your feet as it is. What more of a challenge do you want?" She held up a hand. "Don't answer that. It's your life. Live it the way you see fit."

He stood. "I'll get Gerri to postpone the non-urgent appointments till next week."

"It's all right. I'll look at the schedule later this afternoon and see what she can fit into tomorrow's slate. When are you leaving?"

Michael checked his watch. "Around two. I need to pack an overnight bag. Depending on traffic, I figure it'll take about an hour and a half to get there."

"Well, good luck."

"Thanks. I'll call from Seattle, let you know when I'm returning. Probably Monday morning." He turned from the door. "Damn. I forgot. We won't be able to make your barbecue Sunday."

He could kick himself. Jen was champing to play with Amy. This morning she'd reminded him. *"Can I take my beach ball?"*

"Maybe Katherine can come in your stead," Rochelle offered. "Is Jenni staying with her?"

"I hope so." He had yet to talk to his grandmother.

"Fine, then both she and Jenni will come, and I'll phone out to the farm to make sure Shanna comes, as well."

A warm-water flood of gratitude. He didn't like thinking of Shanna alone, waiting for him. Disappointed in him.

"Thanks, Roche. You're a godsend."

"You owe me, pal." She waved him off and he headed back to his own office with Shanna, not Seattle, on his mind. At the farm, the topic of his relocation had remained closed. In its place was a silent rift. He felt it at night when he slipped into her bed. Despite the passion, she concealed part of herself. Her wild, free abandon now held a reservation.

Dammit, he wanted the old Shanna back.

Can't have it both ways, jerk. At his desk, he shoved his personal thoughts aside to concentrate on his patients.

At noon, he stared at the phone. He needed to contact Katherine and make arrangements for Jenni.

How long could he hold off the old gal's suspicions when they hung over his head like a double-barreled shotgun?

Guilt chewed his gut. Better to lie *this time.* Better for Jenni, for himself, for Shanna.

Tension gripped his shoulders. He detested prevarication. He had never lied in his life. Resigned, he picked up the phone.

Soon, it all would be over.

Soon, he'd be able to get on with his life again.

And let Shanna be a memory.

She would not watch him pack.

She would say goodbye from where she sat on the top step of the porch, then go down to the barns where the Holsteins and Oliver waited for the afternoon milking.

Besides, everything had been said. There was nothing more to add. The deed was done. That she hadn't expected it *this week* was her own fault. She'd expected to matter. For Jenni to matter.

For him to change.

Behind her, the screen door creaked. Michael came across

the deck. Polished leather loafers and the cuff of expensive dress slacks came into her peripheral vision.

Watch the barns below, not him. "Have a safe trip, Doc," she said breezily. *Give him a happy send-off.* She'd learned that from Meredith's leaving. Meredith who never so much as waved goodbye.

"Thank you."

For a heartbeat she thought he might touch her, but he jogged down the steps with his carry-on in hand and strode to his truck. Tears burned behind her eyes. Already he was bent on whatever lay in store in Seattle. Light years from her and this place.

He tossed the bag inside, slammed the door and turned.

The lines cornering his mouth cut his freshly shaven cheeks. In his eyes was sadness. Regret. A muscle bounced under his left eye.

"Shanna..." His deep voice fractured.

Fight it. Don't fling yourself into his arms.

She came slowly down the steps and went to him. Setting a hand to one taut cheek, she said, "I'll be here when you return."

Before he closed his eyes and turned his mouth into her palm, she saw his relief. She nearly cried aloud with joy. He wasn't immune to her, to what they shared. Deep down, she sensed, he hoped for something, *something* to swoop in and rescue him from this path he had chosen.

Raising on her toes, she kissed his cheek. Softly, chastely. "Safe trip," she whispered.

He opened his eyes and, with his emotions shielded once more, looked at her for what felt like an eternity.

Then he rounded the hood of the truck and climbed in. After giving one short wave, he drove down the dirt lane. Seconds later, he was out of sight.

Over the next two days she oscillated between bliss and despondency. For emergency purposes he had given her the number of the Seattle hotel where he was registered. Believing he would call at least once, she waited. But the phone stayed silent.

On the third night she lay in bed, inhaling the lingering scent of him on the pillow, debating if the emotion she'd seen by the truck was a mistake.

One call, she thought, to squash her doubts.

On the other hand, *did* she need a call to prove he wanted her to wait for him? So where did that leave her?

On the corner of Waiting Game Lane and Broken Heart Street.

"Buck up, Shanna. It's time you moved on. The man is an automaton with one gear and one mission."

Hugging her pillow, she let her mind drain.

Six hours later she struggled up a hill. Mike stood at the top looking down at her. As hard as she ran, she couldn't reach him.

The phone dragged her off the hill.

Groaning, she glanced at the clock. Nine-ten. The last time she'd looked it had been three-twenty with dawn's light catching the curtains.

A third shrill. She reached for the receiver. "'Lo."

"Shanna? Rochelle Garland here. I hope I didn't wake you."

"No, it's okay." She pushed up on the pillow. "I was getting up, anyway."

"Oh, poor thing, I did wake you. I'm sorry."

"It's all right," Shanna said, scrubbing back her hair and stifling a yawn. "Something I can help you with, Doctor Garland?"

"Rochelle, and yes. You're still coming to the barbecue this afternoon, aren't you? Katherine's bringing Jenni. We'd love to have you here, as well."

"Um…" Her foggy mind scrambled. *Excuse! Find an excuse.*

"Look," the woman went on pleasantly in her ear, "I'd really like you to come. Besides, I told Michael I'd make sure you did. We're eating at five-thirty. If you came around three that would give us some social time while the kids play."

She sounded friendly. Like a neighbor one had known for years, rather than someone who abided by the Hippocratic oath and diagnosed diseases. Shanna debated. What could it hurt? After today, their crossing paths terminated.

"Jenni will be there?"

Rochelle chuckled. "Or Amy will have my hide."

"All right. What's the address?"

Call complete, Shanna dropped back against the pillows.

Oh joy. Rochelle Garland—paradigm of the super women Mike would work alongside soon—wanted to befriend her. How lucky could she get?

Chapter Twelve

He had no choice but to go where he wouldn't have to rely solely on himself or Roche to save every life that came into his care. Where there was a *convocation* of capable doctors.

Michael followed Allison Park of Park Medical Associates into a low, bricked building on Fourth. The clinic was all he dreamed it would be. Spacious, modern, facilitated with a large, comfortable waiting room. The examination rooms housed high-tech equipment, including a patient database organized and filed by a staff of two clerks and four nurses. Best, the clinic lay a short drive from "Pill Hill" and Providence Hospital where he'd spend half his time.

He met Park's associates, Drs. Paul Johnson and Peter Ackland, and liked them on sight. Each had fifteen years of medical work under the belt to Park's twenty. Michael, with twelve, would be the youngest to join the group.

Mostly, he liked that two days out of five he'd be at one

of the city's busiest hospitals. And one day every three weeks, he'd be on call and working the walk-in.

After spending Thursday at the clinic and most of Friday at Providence, shadowing Park and Ackland on rounds and minor surgeries and meeting other doctors, he spent Saturday and Sunday scouting areas to live.

He found two he liked in older, established areas: Laurelhurst and Queen Anne. Mature maples, elms and pines lined most of the streets from which the houses—both pretentious and elegant depending on the whims of the wealthy—sat well back with manicured lawns and lush gardens.

Although some of the older brick homes, built at the turn of the twentieth century, claimed single-car garages, many of the newer houses hosted up to three-vehicle garages. Often long curving driveways framed by pampered shrubbery and dogwood trees led to expansive homes of wood and cedar shakes.

Laurelhurst offered an elementary school within a five-minute walk of two spacious, wooden houses that piqued Michael's interest. Still, he preferred the design of the smaller, tile-roofed property in Queen Anne better. But then Coe Elementary would be a twenty-minute walk for Jen. He decided to concentrate on Laurelhurst.

Then he pictured Jen entering Bryant Elementary on shaky legs, eyes round, mouth clamping over a sob. Lunch pail clutched against the front of her daisy dress as she stood on the sidewalk, staring at the strange building and strange kids.

Alone.

Her timid little voice floated through his imagination. *"But why, Uncle Michael? Why do I have to go to this school? Can't I live with Grammy and be with my friends?"*

He scraped both hands down his whiskered cheeks and exhaled in frustration.

Hell. It couldn't be that bad, could it? Hundreds—thousands—of kids transferred from one school to the next every year, some moving more than once within a term and despite their angst met other kids and made friends.

Why, then, did he feel like the troll waiting for the littlest goat to trip across the bridge?

"Did you see me throw the ball in the basket?" A breathless Jenni bounced on her toes beside Shanna where they sat at a picnic table under a grand oak in the Garlands' backyard.

"Sure did." Shanna brushed the girl's bangs out of her eyes. "You'll be the next Michael Jordan before you know it."

"Amy threw one, too," Jenni said, eager to keep her friend in the picture.

Shanna winked at the older child hugging a smaller, softer version of the standard basketball to her chest.

"Awesome. You two will be Blue Springs' next champs."

A riot of giggles. The children charged back to the cemented area in front of the detached garage. For several minutes, the adults watched them pepper the hoop. Missing shots, laughing, chasing each other as much as the ball. Across the table, Rochelle said, "Jenni's quite taken with you, Shanna."

Kate grunted. She sat in a cedar-wood Adirondack chair, counting knitted stitches. "Shanna has a way with my great-granddaughter even her own mother couldn't grasp, God rest her restless soul."

Rochelle winked at Shanna. With the pluck of long-standing friendship, she remarked, "Some women have to learn nurturing, Kate. It doesn't necessarily make them bad mothers."

"I know that." The old lady laughed, a little shakily.

"Leigh loved Jenni. She just didn't know how to mother her. Shanna, here, is a natural." She looked up from her knitting. "You should have a house full of wee ones, girl."

Shanna's heart pinched. *I had Timmy and lost him. Now I'm losing Jenni.* Purposely, she focused on the yard. "You have a beautiful garden, Rochelle. Mind if I take a look around?"

"Not at all. Help yourself to some blooms if you want."

"Thanks. I just might."

Shanna headed down the flat stone walkway toward a small, quiet pond tucked in a corner of the yard and bordered by marsh willows, alders and clusters of cattails. She hadn't been prepared for the Garlands' genuine friendliness any more than the home in which they lived.

Surprise struck her in increments. An hour ago, she'd expected to pull alongside an upscale dwelling, trimmed by the well-to-do. Rather, she found a quaint—and a tad shabby—1920s home with a deep, paint-peeled front porch and a narrow two-car garage located in back. Surrounded by wild growth on three sides, both buildings sat on a half acre of land.

The yard took Shanna's breath. In multiple shades, color splashed across the property. Deep, pink roses. White and yellow potentilla. Lavender. Gold rudbeckia. Purple delphiniums.

Jenni ran after Shanna. "Where you going?"

"To look at the garden, peach."

"Can me and Amy come?"

"'Course." The coil around her chest loosened when little fingers slipped around her own.

"There's a koi in the pond, you know." Amy offered, her straight dark pigtails anchoring her shoulders. "Daddy put some baby koi in this spring. They're this big now." She spread her hands apart.

"That big, huh?" Shanna smiled.

The children chattered as they wandered down to the water's edge. A short, newly built wooden pier led a couple yards into the pond. A child on each side, Shanna crouched down as the fish, fins fluttering like butterfly wings, swam toward them.

"Can we have fish?" Jenni asked.

"We'd need a pond first, honey."

"We have a creek. Would they like that?"

"Maybe, but they wouldn't stay then. They'd swim away with the water."

"Oh."

Amy quickly came to the rescue. "You could have fish in a 'quarium. A boy in my class has one and his mom lets him have all kinds in it. Black ones, orange ones, even a rainbow one."

Jenni looked up at Shanna. "Would Uncle Michael let me have a—a 'quarium?"

Maybe in Seattle. But by then, little one, you'll have forgotten this moment and won't want fish or aquariums any more. You may even forget Amy. Will you forget me, too?

"What's the matter?" Jenni asked.

"Nothing, honey. I was thinking about…" *Your future.* "That tomorrow Uncle Michael should be home." Smiling and hugging both girls, she said, "Let's take a look at the flowers. I want to pick a few for our kitchen table."

The children squealed and bounded over the grass toward a weeping willow circled in tiger lilies.

Rochelle approached, hands in the pockets of her white jean cutoffs and her hair pulled into a sleek ponytail. Smiling at the girls the way she was, she might have been a woman in a grocery line, a mother at a park. Not a doctor. Not a lettered woman.

"Amy, love." She tugged her daughter's pigtail. "Why don't you and Jenni get that metal bucket in the basement beside the washing machine? Then ask Daddy to give you the pruners out of the garage. We'll snip a whole batch of flowers for both Shanna and Mrs. Rowan to take home.''

Excitement highlighting their faces, they dashed off.

''What a pair.'' Rochelle watched the girls weave in and out of the trees. ''Amy's going to miss Jenni something fierce.'' She turned to Shanna. ''So are you.''

Shrugging, Shanna moved down the stone pathway, toward the rear of the garden. Silent, Rochelle walked with her.

''You don't agree with what Michael plans, do you?'' the other woman asked at last.

''Jenni is his niece.''

Stopping in front of a climbing jasmine, spilling its white, fragrant blooms across a leftover portion of stone wall, Rochelle said, ''By the way, don't be offended by Kate. She can be outspoken at times. Especially with things dear to her heart.''

The evening lay in sultry folds of shadow and light. In the farthest corner of the garden, they stood in a sunlight wash. ''Does she know why Michael is in Seattle?''

''She believes he's attending an impromptu meeting of surgeons.''

An indirect lie. Shanna said, ''Kate'll survive. It's Jenni I'm worried about. This move might put her back to where she was before.'' *To not speaking.* She turned away. She had no place in the child's life, no right to argue her welfare.

Rochelle said, ''Funny, but our family never knew Jenni until just a few weeks ago. I delivered her, saw her for her immunizations or ear infections, but that's it. She was always a sweet child, shy, timid, not communicative.'' Rochelle glanced toward the house. ''After Leigh died, I wasn't aware it had developed into... Well. I wish Michael had said something. We might've helped her sooner. But he's so damned tight-lipped about his kin.'' She shook her head. "Geez. Listen to me, sounding like the neighborhood fishwife."

"Like a concerned friend." Shanna regarded Kate and Geoff, talking to the girls, voices muted by the distance of the yard. Amy had a silver bucket in hand. "Jenni needs someone like you in her corner."

Only a matter of weeks, and she'd be in a new home with new friends.

She's not yours for the keeping, just like Timmy.

Mild nausea in her belly. Oh, God. Her mind flew to that cusp of seconds nine years ago when, in the delivery room, she stared at the dreadful stillness of her son....

She gulped air to steady herself.

"You okay?" Rochelle asked.

Disoriented, Shanna turned to the woman beside her. She saw again Timmy's pinched eyes, his tiny mouth that uttered not a sound. The obstetrician's concern for her.

"Yes." *Did you know my throat hurts from the screaming?* "I'm fine. Must be the heat."

They moved into the shade. A hummingbird flitted to a nearby delphinium and probed its long, slender beak into a mauve trumpet blossom for several seconds. Closer at hand, a bee tended the nectar of the roses.

Quietly, Rochelle said, "I'm not the one who can change Michael's mind. In the eight years I've known him, he has never looked at a woman quite the way he looks at you."

Embarrassed, Shanna turned away. Here she was talking about the man she loved with a woman she barely knew. Still, the urge to talk to another woman—especially one who understood Michael—was overpowering. "Makes no difference. He won't listen to me."

"There are ways to get a man's attention." Rochelle gave her a direct look. "And I don't mean in bed. Make him realize he can't live without you."

"How?" *Tell me how, please.*

The children were running toward them, shouting, the pruning shears clanging inside the bucket between them.

Rochelle shook her head. "Honestly? I don't know. But you will. You'll know the instant it happens." She smiled ruefully. "Heaven help Michael when it does."

Odd, Shanna thought as she drove home several hours later. On some conscious level she'd always known it would come down to two options. To stay or to pack it in.

"You're home."

Michael looked up from the computer screen at Shanna standing in the doorway of the study. A pang, sharp and mean, drove through his gut. *Home,* he thought. Yes, he was home.

But not without her.

Unable to stop himself, he pushed back the chair and walked over. "I got in a couple hours ago."

Face expressionless, she turned and headed back in to the kitchen. "Did you have a good trip?"

"It was…successful."

"Hungry?"

Hungry? He was ravenous, but not for food, for her. Four days, and all he'd thought of was her. In his dreams. In his daily meetings. Looking for the damned right house. Waiting for the moment he'd see her again. Now, here she was and he couldn't inhale so much as her scent. She kept them rooms apart.

"Shanna?"

"Yes?" Her tone matched the cool air wafting from the refrigerator she'd swung open.

Shutting its door gently, Michael reached for her hand. It was cool, as well. "What's wrong?"

"Nothing. It's been a long day and I'm tired."

He studied the dark stains beneath her eyes. She hadn't

slept any better than him. "Did you go to Rochelle's yesterday?"

"Yes."

"Jen?"

"Amy invited her to sleep over tonight. Rochelle's dropping her off at Kate's in the morning."

He should be grateful she hadn't pulled her hand away. "Look at me," he said quietly.

She did. A chill sped down his spine.

"Something *is* wrong. Another migraine?" If her father had come back…

Her hand slid from his. "I was going to do this tomorrow in writing," she said, her voice flat. "But since we're alone now, I'll simply say it. I'm leaving Rowan Dairy, Mike."

"What?"

She spoke rapidly. "I won't leave you in a lurch, but this is my two weeks' notice. Oliver's willing to fill in for the interim while you find another milker."

"No." He shook his head. "You can't."

For the first time, her eyes lit with anger. Deep, profound anger. "Yes, I can. There's nothing contractually binding me here until you sell."

"It was a verbal agreement," he argued. Fear, sharp and acute, lacerated his gut.

"I won't deny that. But things have changed. We…"

"Started sleeping together." He stepped closer, crowding her space. "So what? It's called natural progression when two people are attracted to one another." He was furious. So furious he could barely keep from shaking her. She couldn't leave him. Not now. Not when he felt the way he did.

And how was that? Why don't you say it? Why don't you tell her how you really feel? Go on, say it.

Before he could open his mouth she struck him in the chest with the heel of her hand, hard enough to hurt. "*So what?* Is that all it meant to you? Just a quick roll in the hay?"

"You know better than that."

"Do I? Not once did the phone ring while you were in Seattle. Didn't you even wonder if the farm was okay? If the barn hadn't burned down? If a cow got sick?"

"I didn't phone because I couldn't!"

At that she laughed. A bitter sound. "You had time to brush your teeth, but not pick up the phone? Good one, Doc."

She spun around. The big, silver pyramids dangling from her ears arced with her hair. Grabbing her denim jacket off the chair, she strode to the door.

"I'll be sleeping in the cabin for the remainder of my employ. In the meantime I think it best if we stay out of each other's way."

"Shanna." In two paces he hauled her around to face him. "I tried to phone. I tried five times but I'd hang up before the call went through." Encouraged by her attention, he struggled on. "I wanted to tell you that I...missed you, that I..." He closed his eyes and swallowed a tide of panic. "I was afraid you wouldn't be here," he said hoarsely when he could look at her again.

Her face, her lovely face, gentled instantly. She covered his hand on her arm. "Oh, Mike. I said I would, didn't I? Don't you know by now I mean what I say."

"Then you'll stay?"

"No."

His hand dropped to his side. "Why not?"

"Because, dammit, I love you and this relationship, it's— it's going nowhere!"

He stared at her. "That's not true." His throat hurt.

Her eyes glistened. "Be honest with yourself. Give me that, at least." She held up a hand. "You're not in this for the long haul. You've told me that enough times. Besides, there's Jenni. She's becoming too dependent on me, and with you moving to Seattle— Look. Before that happens she needs to realize I'm not going to be around.''

He couldn't let her go. "Move with me, then.''

Her jaw dropped. "Say again?''

"Come to Seattle with us.''

In the silence, she blinked slowly.

"Is this a proposal, Mike?'' she asked at last.

Was it? He supposed so, except—could he handle the one criteria she'd want most? She *loved* him. She'd want his children.

Searching her face for some resolution to his dilemma, he found none. She remained stoic. The decision was his. He envisioned her rounded with his child.

Warmth stole around his chest.

Was it possible he could change?

Something of his inner turmoil must have shown on his face. She took a step back. Desperate that she understand, he reached out. "Jen needs you, Shanna.'' *I need you. In more ways than one.*

Except, explanations would mean elucidating those images of her slim body altered with the sweet heaviness of his seed.

She evaded his touch. When she spoke, her voice was stone-hard. "Don't come to me again, Michael. For any reason. Do you understand? Unless you're ready for every single inch of the whole nine yards, this issue is closed forever.''

She turned and fled out the door, into the night.

Something was wrong. Jenni knew it. But what?

Tavia in hand, she climbed onto her bed beside a curled-up Silly. The sleepy cat opened one eye and grumbled a little.

"I'm sorry,'' Jenni said, gently stroking the sleek head.

"I won't bounce again." She tucked Tavia into her lap where the doll liked to be and stared at the tiny pink rose-buds on the wallpaper above her desk. Scrunching her brows, she thought hard.

Since he came back from his trip Uncle Michael didn't smile or tease anymore. Not that he was grumpy or any-thing. He just didn't look happy like he did when Shanna had lived in the house. Jenni knew Shanna had moved back to the cabin. Uncle Michael told her so when he picked her up from Grammy's the other day.

She wished Shanna still slept here. She made Jenni feel as if Mommy hadn't really gone to heaven.

When Shanna was in the house, the dreams didn't come. No one stood in her doorway in the dark, like last night.

She'd been so scared she'd hidden under the covers for a long time. And then she got afraid she wouldn't be able to breathe. That made her sweat. The more she sweated, the more scared she got until finally she threw back the covers and took a big gulp of air. She almost called for Uncle Michael, but thank goodness Mommy had gone away from the door by then.

If only Jenni could talk to Shanna.

Shanna would make the dreams stop.

Shanna wouldn't let anyone sneak into her room.

The last time Jenni talked to her was at Amy's house when they had fun picking flowers. That was Sunday and now Sunday was here again and almost over.

And she hadn't seen Shanna once in between.

She glanced toward the window. The sun was setting fast. Probably because it was going to rain. The wind had chased dark clouds over the hills all day. Right this minute it was making the spruce trees moan like creepy, old witches.

Jenni shivered. She hated the sound. It made her think of her dream and the dark shape in the doorway.

If only she could talk to Shanna. Maybe she should

ask Uncle M. why their friend never came to their house anymore.

She looked down at Tavia. "Do you think they had a fight?" she whispered to the doll.

Tavia didn't answer. She just stared at the pink roses.

Jenni blinked her eyes against two fat tears. She didn't want them fighting. Not like Mommy and Daddy. She wanted Uncle Michael and Shanna laughing and holding hands like the day they'd all gone to the swimming pool.

Suddenly she smiled. "Hey, Tavia, wouldn't it be neat if they got married?"

Tavia grunted, but offered nothing further.

Jenni gazed at the roses again.

Instead of fights and dreams and storms and people not talking, she thought of Uncle Michael in the kitchen with Shanna. She thought of herself drawing a picture at the table, and of Shanna cooking, and of Uncle Michael helping, and the way Shanna would grin at him over her shoulder and the way he would grin back. She thought of how Shanna always called her peachkins, and how Uncle M. sometimes called her tyke.

She scrambled off the bed and went to her desk to get her pencil crayons and drawing book. Maybe if they saw a nice family picture of the three of them, Uncle Michael would start talking again and Shanna would come back. Then the dreams would go away and it wouldn't matter if it stormed outside.

The week passed in a haze.

Shanna moved through her work without thought or emotion. Several times she called Jason in hopes of alleviating the vacuity she felt. But his world was no longer part of hers.

Slowly, over the weeks, the intricacies of camshafts, push

rods, dual carburetors, and other engineware had secured his attention. Her brother had found his niche.

And a girlfriend—a cute, blond cashier at the coffee shop a block from where he worked.

Talking to Jase the last time over the phone nearly broke her down. She'd wanted to spill her guts, cry, scream. God, how she'd wanted to! But Jason was young; the age difference between them yawned like a moon crater. What would he know about comforting a thirty-one-year-old divorcée hung up on a man who refused to believe in himself?

In an effort to relax, she punched her pillow for the fourth time. Outside, the trees muttered in the wind.

An empty, lonely sound.

Like her life.

Until tonight she hadn't realized how Jason's moving on had affected her. She had no close girlfriends. *No man.*

Hand moving over her tummy, she bit her lower lip to stem the surge of heartache. All she could claim was the dusty wake of someone else's forged path.

Well, no more.

Jason could have his motors.

Mike could have Seattle.

She, Shanna McKay, would move on.

About to flop over one final time, she jerked up when the phone rang. The digital clock read twelve-oh-nine. Who would be calling— "Hello?"

"It's me," Mike said needlessly, his voice rough as sand. "Can you come up to the house? Jen's had a nightmare and won't quit crying."

"Be right there."

She leapt out of bed to yank on jeans and shove her nightshirt into her waistband. Rushing through the darkened cabin, her only thought was Jenni. At the door, she rammed her bare feet into a pair of old sneakers, then dashed into the wind-whisked night.

Mike was waiting for her in the mudroom.

Shanna's heart stopped. Like a tiny wood nymph, Jenni clung to his strong, brown neck for all she was worth. Her legs coiled around his waist tight enough to make breathing difficult.

"Peachkins, what is it?" Heart beating again, she reached for the child who went with a loud sniff into her arms.

"The wind made Mommy come again." Jenni choked against Shanna's throat. "She wouldn't go away."

"Are you afraid of Mommy?" Shanna asked, walking into the lit kitchen. She lowered herself to a chair. Jenni continued to cling.

"Only when she comes at night 'cause I know she's not really there."

Shanna watched Mike pour a half glass of milk and take one of the sugar cookies she'd baked last weekend from a glass bear jar on the counter. He brought the goodies to the table and sat down. Their eyes locked. He looked beat. And terribly worried.

Shanna rubbed Jenni's back. "No," she soothed. "Mommy's not really there."

"Then how come I see her?" Obviously feeling comforted enough, the child let go and pulled back to look at Shanna.

"Well…" How to explain ghosts versus imagination? "What you're seeing is a picture you have in here." She tapped Jenni's head. "When you fall asleep and start dreaming, the picture gets really big, so big it can't fit inside here any more."

"How come it doesn't happen in the daytime when I think about her?"

"In the day you're not asleep. Pictures only get really big when you dream. When you see Mommy, what does she look like?"

"Like when she used to check and see if I was sleeping."

"And how was that?"

"She would stand in the doorway, then go away."

"Is that what happens now?"

Jenni nodded. "It's scary."

Shanna hugged her close. "Why's that, honey?"

"'Cause." A tiny whimper. "I think she's coming to get me. 'Cause she might want me in heaven."

Mike winced.

Shanna covered his hand where it lay on the table beside the plate with the cookie and milk. His fingers curled and gripped hers.

"Actually," she said, her voice amazingly calm considering the swell of love exploding inside her. "Mommy doesn't want you there at all."

Jenni eyes went wide. "She doesn't?"

"No. All she wants is to make sure you're all right. Just like she did when she lived here. She wants you to be happy and this is the only way she can see if you are."

"Really?"

Shanna smiled and brushed back downy curls from the pixie face. "Really. It's part of what mommies do."

Jenni thought for a moment. "I guess it's like when I check on Tavia before I go to bed."

"Exactly the same." She cupped Jenni's dear face. "Okay?"

Jenni nodded.

"All right." Shanna shifted so the child faced the table. "Eat your cookie, drink your milk and then it's off to bed."

Chewing the cookie, Jenni asked, "Will you sleep here tonight, Shanna?"

"Peach…" She shot a look at Michael who was waiting as intently as his niece.

"Please," the girl whispered. "The trees are howling."

One more night under the same roof. One more night with the child and the man she loved. One more night like a family—even if Mike, stubbornly riding his fears and hiding from his needs, wouldn't acknowledge it. What could it hurt?

My heart, but what's a few more punctures?

She looked askance at Mike. Resignation hung in his dark eyes. His shoulders slouched. His mouth was tight.

As usual he didn't trust himself to let down his guard or speak on Jenni's behalf. Or his own—damn him.

"All right," Shanna said with an inward sigh. "But you have to promise to go straight to sleep."

She didn't look at Mike again. She didn't have to. Tension toppled off him in chunks and lay at her feet.

Chapter Thirteen

On stocking feet, Michael slipped down the hallway, shadowed with its night-lights, to the guest room. Forty-five minutes ago he had sat in the kitchen, holding his breath, waiting for Shanna to agree to stay the night. When she'd arrived at the door, he had wanted to pull her into his arms, hold her. Kiss her until they both were dizzy. He wanted to tell her everything in his heart. To say, "I was wrong, I'm sorry."

I love you.

Except she hadn't come for him, she'd come for Jenni.

He pinched the bridge of his nose. What a bastard he was, being envious of a dream-frightened six-year-old. Ah, who was he trying to dupe? He wanted Shanna to care about him the way she cared about Jen. *She does, fool.*

He shook his head, speculating on how she handled the situation. She'd eased the little girl's fears. Nurturing her in a way he never could no matter what he did. Sometimes he believed himself emotionally deprived.

But together they made a balance.

She was the other half of his heart. She was the other half of what Jen needed.

He'd watched her lead the tyke upstairs and snuggle that old brown bear into thin, little arms the instant the little girl burrowed under the covers. He'd seen the smile light Jen's sweet elfin face before her chin found soft fur and her eyes drifted closed.

And Shanna. The tenderness, the love. God, she was something. Once she'd given him those emotions.

Now? Caution stilted her approach and in her eyes.

He stopped in front of the guest room door. Lifting a hand to the back of his neck, he took in a weighty breath. Right or wrong, he had to do this. One last time. He had to see her.

In the night. In bed.

He had to fill his soul with her one last time.

Squatting in the garden, Jenni nibbled, squirrel-like, along the split green pod she held between her hands. One by one, tiny pearled peas disappeared.

Shanna grinned. "Better stop eating those."

"But they're tasty."

"Uh-huh. And tummy trouble if you eat too many."

Shanna laid a hand on her own stomach to quell the slight queasiness the morning's eighty-degree heat generated. Thank goodness for wide-brimmed straw hats. As it was, sweat tickled her ribs under her light cotton blouse and her denim shorts stuck to her skin.

Jenni tossed the shell, then yanked at another pod and tore part of the vine. "Can we have a strawberry patch next year? Amy's mom has one in her garden."

Shanna snapped off another handful of long curly beans and dropped them in the plastic pail. One more row and the beans would be history for this year, perhaps forever if the new owners didn't relish gardening.

She glanced at Jenni sitting cross-legged among the pea vines. Dirt streaked the knees of her red pants, a smudge honored one small shoulder and the visor of her yellow ball cap shaded the left quarter of her face. Nearby, in the shade of the foot-tall plants, Silly washed a paw.

Shanna's stomach spun. In a year's time, Jenni and her cat would be elsewhere. The quiet, sunny, blue-sky days of Rowan Dairy would be someone else's memories.

And strawberry patches a lifetime away.

"You'll have to ask Uncle Michael," Shanna replied, wondering indeed how he would answer the question.

Jenni's face drooped. "I guess so. But you won't be here to help pick, will you?"

"No, honey."

"Why can't you stay? I want you to stay." Her voice rose. "I don't want you to leave on Sunday."

Neither do I, Shanna thought and wished back the days since she'd slept in the main house for the last time—when Michael had asked her again...

He'd crept into the guest room and stood over her bed in the darkness. He'd observed her for long minutes before stroking her cheek with a butterfly touch of his finger.

"Shanna," he'd whispered.

"Yes?"

His knees cracked in the quiet, as he crouched beside the bed. Taking her hand, he bent his head and kissed her palm.

"Shanna," he said against her skin.

"Mike, what is it?"

Through the window, a wan, wind-battered moon honed the angles of his cheeks. Above his lip the scar winked.

"Stay. Please."

"You know I can't."

"No, don't say anything now. Just think about it, okay?"

He brushed his mouth over hers, melting her bones. "I want you to stay. I need you to stay." Again he kissed her. "Jen needs you to stay."

"You're hitting below the belt, Doc."

"It's a winner take all situation…"

But not for keeps, she thought now. Not for keeps.

In the end she'd promised him nothing.

Jenni got to her feet. She stepped over two rows of peas to stand in front of Shanna. The bright morning sun shot copper through her curls. "You wouldn't have to leave if you and Uncle Michael got married," she said, her eyes round and earnest.

"Oh, peachkin." Shanna sighed. "Marriage happens when two people love each other very much."

"Don't you love Uncle Michael?"

More than he knows. Looking directly at the child, she contemplated lying. Except her heart hung in tatters from her sleeve. She said, "Yes, but it isn't that easy."

"Why not? If you love Uncle Michael and he loves you, why can't you be married?"

"I'm not sure if he loves me that way, Jenni." *And if wishes were stars she'd have a thousand in her palm.*

Jenni toed a clump of dirt. "Will you come and pick strawberries with me, anyway?"

"I wouldn't miss it for the world." Shanna pulled the little girl into a hug and kissed her brow. "Wherever I am I'll come and pick strawberries with you."

Jenni smiled shyly, then bent and picked up the calico purring against the plastic pail. "C'mon, Silly. Let's get Tavia. I think she wants some peas."

Shanna watched Jenni stroll up the side of the garden toward the house, singing to the cat in her arms.

Abruptly, Shanna imagined herself at some foreign kitchen table, a spinster looking out on a day much like the one at hand, her mind panning video clips of this hour: to the right, Jenni's dark curls hopping on her shoulders…above, a crow flapping against the blue…ahead, August's harvest—

Her pulse tripped. Mike, in cargo shorts and his favorite blue T-shirt, had opened the door and stepped onto the porch.

Jenni climbed the steps with the cat and Shanna watched him crouch to speak to his niece. Laughing, the girl went into the house. Briefly, he turned his head toward the door where she'd disappeared.

Oh, yes. Shanna would always remember.

He stood and rounded on the garden. Across the sunny, fruitful rows their eyes met.

She blinked as a heat wave—or her tears?—hazed that stern jaw, those linear black brows, the slim bumped nose.

Jogging down the steps, he headed toward her, his long legs champing up the ground. Even at sixty yards, the dark fierceness of his look kicked her pulse.

She bowed over her work and swiped her silly, leaky eyes with the back of a wrist.

Two weeks since the night of Jenni's dream. Two weeks since they'd been together.

"Cool hat." His deep voice rained over her. "Red suits you."

She'd been attracted by its full brim, its frivolous white ribbon. "Does the trick." Conscious of his shadow draping her hands, she thought, *The beans, Shanna. Harvest the beans.* And plucked several more vines.

He hunkered across from her, a bottle of water between his fingers. "Want some? I put it in the freezer." He gave her a crooked smile. "Should be nice and cold."

"Thank you." He'd thought of her, up in the house.

Uncapping the bottle, he handed it to her over the plants. His jaw was harsh with stubble and his hair shiny. She yearned to glide her cheek against both, sand and silk.

The icy water cooled her throat. "How's Jen been sleeping?"

"She misses your reading sessions at night." The smile wobbled. "I'm not good at it."

"Don't sell yourself short, Doc. You're a kind and caring—" *father* "—man. Jenni knows that. She'll guide you."

He plucked a couple of string beans and tossed them into the bucket. A yellow butterfly flit by. "This harvesting seems a little pointless, doesn't it?"

Carefully, she set down the bottle, held the delicate stem of a plant, and extracted three pods. "Not if you want to eat."

"Change your mind, Shanna."

She shook down the beans. "Why do you want me to stay, Mike?"

His eyes lifted to her. "I thought I explained that. Jen and I need you."

She climbed to her feet and moved to the next row.

"Can't we at least talk about it?" he urged.

"We're talked out. Besides, I'm packed."

"You're a hardheaded woman, know that?"

She stared at him. "*I'm* hardheaded? Excuse me, but I think you have your wires crossed here. At least I'm honest with myself and not afraid to admit my weaknesses *or* my fears."

"Which are?"

She looked him square on. "That I love you so much it scares the blazes out of me." Squatting, she turned to the plants again.

"I'd never call that a weakness. I'd call it courage."

"Don't patronize my emotions, Mike. It makes me feel cheap, and it makes you look shallow." She brushed a wrist at her bangs. "Look, tomorrow's my last day. Let's make this easier for Jenni by not fighting, okay?"

His gray eyes channeled on a point behind her.

She should've known. The stubborn man wasn't even—

"Oh, my God," he choked. "No! *Jen!*"

Humming a Shanna song, Jenni rocked Tavia in her arms as she wandered down the path toward the garden. Silly hadn't wanted to come so Jenni had left the cat washing herself in that nice, warm sunny patch on the bed.

Uncle M. was down in the garden helping Shanna. That was good because maybe now she would ask him to get married. Jenni wasn't sure if ladies asked men to marry them. Usually the man did the asking. At least that's what Amy said. But Jenni knew Shanna loved Uncle Michael and tomorrow she'd be leaving. If she didn't ask him now she might never get another chance.

Jenni squatted beside an old tree. From here she could see them real clear. Shanna was kneeling in the rows. Uncle Michael squatted in front of her, talking. Far away, his voice always sounded like the truck's engine when he drove up from the main road to the house and parked.

"Do you think he's telling her he loves her?" she whispered hopefully to Tavia.

He could be. Or he might be telling her she picks peas really well.

"Oh, Tavia. He already knows that. Shanna does everything perfect."

Even when she acts like your mommy?

Jenni didn't answer. She didn't want to tell Tavia that in some things Shanna acted better than her mommy.

For one thing, Shanna never said she would read to Jenni after first checking the barns and the stock. For another, Shanna let Jenni sleep with her when Jenni was scared.

If it had been Mommy, she would have said to be strong and brave. Sometimes Jenni didn't want to feel strong and

brave. Sometimes she just wanted to be held and let somebody else worry about all those creepies in the dark.

Uncle M. and Shanna were still talking.

Jenni felt a little ashamed watching them, especially when
they might be discussing private stuff. Eavesdropping
wasn't nice. Even if Amy did it all the time with her mom
and dad. Jenni would never do it on purpose.

She glanced around. Maybe she should take Tavia back
to the house. But…there were some nice, bushy red flowers
in the pasture below the garden. She smiled. Shanna liked
pretty flowers and these ones looked as feathery as those
old paintbrushes her teacher handed out when they did mu-
ral art last year.

Getting to her feet, Jenni took Tavia down the hill path
for a closer look.

"Jenni!" Michael bounded across peas, carrots and potatoes toward the lodgepole fence. *"Jen! Don't move,
honey!"*

The second he'd seen the horse swing into a full trot
toward the tyke, his heart had gone into overdrive.

Oh, God. He had to make it. Make it before the stallion
got to where she knelt forty feet inside the enclosure.

Gripping the top rail, he swung over it. Yelling, shouting.
The devil come to take all and Shanna racing behind him.

Soldat didn't flinch. The beast tacked its ears flat, lowered
its head, and snaked its nose along the ground.

Michael recognized the signal.

Battle mode.

Warning. Leave. Now.

Next would come teeth and hooves.

Michael ripped open his shirt, scattering buttons like
seeds in the wind and yanked the garment off his arms.
Waving it over his head, he shouted, "Go on, get back, you
miserable cur! *Get on back!*"

Ten feet from Jenni the horse stopped and blew a hissing snort. He tossed his graceful head. Those slim, pedigreed ears flicked once.

Michael saw the whites of the horse's malevolent eyes. In another moment the animal would charge.

He leapt between horse and child, slinging the shirt through the air, snapping it like a bullwhip.

"Beat it, you son of a bitch!"

Half rearing on powerful haunches, Soldat flung his big head to the side. His nostrils flared round and red.

Everything seemed to slow, as in the ticking of a grandfather clock. One second—*tick*—Shanna sliding like a baseball player into home plate. Michael flailing the shirt through the air. The next second—*tock*—the stallion wheeling, kicking out a hoof—

Jen tumbling backwards, end over end into Shanna's arms.

Then…Soldat galloping away, across the pasture.

Michael rushed to Shanna's side. "Jenni! Oh, God, is she okay?" He fell to his knees, his hands going to the still child in Shanna's arms.

"Oh, Mike! Omigod. He struck her. Her little arm…I don't know if he…Omigod…!"

Heart in his throat, Michael immediately inspected Jenni's dilated pupils. Thankfully, her eyes hadn't rolled back to show white even though the pain had knocked her out and her arm hung at an odd angle.

"Keep an eye on the horse," he told Shanna, his voice raw as an open wound. He ripped apart Jenni's shirt and swallowed. A semi-concentric bruise was forming on her little biceps. A quick check confirmed what he suspected. The humerus in her upper arm—broken. The question was, how badly?

"He just nicked her, but the damage—"

His heart was on a rampage. *Calm down, calm down.*

Legs trembling, he stood and lifted Jenni from Shanna's arms. "I'm taking her to the hospital," he said, and strode to the small gate down the fence from the garden. Shanna ran ahead and let him through. "My keys are hanging behind the mudroom door," he told her. "Bring the truck down the hill. I'll meet you on the other side of the garden. I don't want to jar her by walking up to the house. I shouldn't even be carrying her." He couldn't believe how rational, how analytical he sounded.

Shanna sprinted up the short incline. In moments they were bound for Blue Springs General. Face foam-white, eyes navy with worry, Shanna gripped the wheel as they headed down the farm's graveled lane. "Tell me…" she said.

He'd been keeping an eye on the child's pulse. "Heart's a bit speedy and her skin's a little clammy."

"Is that…normal?"

"For a horse-kicked child."

Shanna said nothing and he simply held Jenni. He savored her light weight and willed her sweet child smell to compose his banging heart. When they were on the main road, he unhooked his cell from its stand to call the hospital. Then he dialed Rochelle's number.

Jenni's fingers still clutched two bent Indian paintbrush stems from Soldat's pasture.

Rochelle met them at the hospital emergency doors with a stretcher and two nurses. "She'll be okay," Mike's associate said, looking directly at him.

Shanna breathed a prayer of gratitude for the woman who was not only friend and colleague, but someone who understood.

"Let's hope. Right now, she's awake and in pain." He climbed carefully from the truck with Jenni and a pillow

Shanna had brought from the house under the girl's injured arm.

"Poor wee darling. Hi, sweetheart." Rochelle stroked the little girl's hair. "You're going to feel a whole lot better in a few minutes." She hid a syringe at her side while swabbing the girl's healthy biceps. "Just a wee pinch and then—" in went the needle and Jenni's eyes welled "—oops, all done."

"My arm really hurts. Am I going to die?"

Shanna's stomach lurched. She looked at Mike's grim face.

"No, angel," Rochelle told Jenni as the nurses lifted the child onto the stretcher. Within seconds, they were wheeling it down a gleaming corridor smelling of Lysol. "You'll be home real soon. You can even call Amy and tell her all about today."

"Can I?"

Tears welled in Shanna's eyes. Jenni, eager for a morsel of health. Shanna wanted to hug the child and never let go.

"Shanna?" the girl's voice rose, a clear bell.

"Here, peach." She rushed up beside Mike.

"Shanna, you come with me, okay?"

"I'll be right here when you're ready to go home, honey."

"I want you to come." Her eyes ping-ponged from Mike to Rochelle, back to Shanna. "Can she come, Uncle M.? Please?"

"I think, sweetie, you have to let Uncle Michael do his job and that's to get you well first," Shanna told the child. "I can't do that in a hospital. But Uncle Michael and Dr. Garland can. I trust them with all my heart. Will you let them make you well? For me?"

"Okay," the child said, sleepily. "My arm doesn't hurt so much anymore."

"I know, baby."

They approached the examining area. Shanna watched the medical group wheel through the double doors. "See you later, peach," she whispered. The doors closed.

Slowly she walked to the waiting room. She couldn't stop thinking about Jenni's unconscious face. She couldn't stop imagining what lay behind Mike's terrified eyes.

"Want to watch a video, peanut?" Michael asked as he set Jenni on the living room sofa and ran a hand down her silky locks. Whenever he thought of her tiny body under those hooves…

She nodded. *"Scooby-Doo."*

Michael selected the movie from the shelf and shoved it into the VCR. "How about a cookie and some juice?"

"Can I have iced tea instead?" the child asked, hugging her doll with her good arm. Her left arm was in a sling cast and rested on a pillow on Shanna's lap. Thank mercy, the bone hadn't separated.

His pulse slowed to normal. "You bet."

Leaving Shanna with Jen, he went into the kitchen and tried to empty his mind. Fifteen seconds too late and…

No. He would not ruminate over consequences. He'd contact Cliff Barnette, then Seattle. Time to stop hemming and hawing and get on with reality. Up until now he'd been living in a dream world, hoping something would turn around and present a solution to forgoing the sale of the dairy. Well, choices and chances left no odds. The land, the animals—they had to go.

As would the woman he loved. And he did love her. After this morning's scare the door on his feelings stood wide open.

He'd looked inside.

While he wasn't comfortable with what he saw, he wasn't about to turn away. He owed himself that much. To view

the changes in his life for what they were: occurrences far
beyond his control.

Beyond control. Vital words.

Leigh had been beyond control in the O.R.

He leaned over the tray with its iced tea and peanut-butter
cookies and closed his eyes. Soldat. An animal beyond control.

Dammit. Seattle *was* right.

He'd just have to convince Shanna.

Resolutely, he picked up the tray and returned to the liv-
ing room. Jen sat curled into the crook of Shanna's arm.
Color, Michael noted with a boost to his raw emotions,
patched her cheeks. Setting the tray within reach, he said to
Jenni, "Mind if I talk to Shanna outside for a minute, tyke?
I, um, need to ask her something about the garden."

"'Kay."

"You'll be fine for a little bit?"

"Uh-huh."

"Good girl." He mussed her curls and headed out the
door.

In the driveway, he stood, hands plunged deep in his
pockets, and stared across the land. Sap and earth clung to
the air. A crow beat its way toward a distant tree, its raucous
cry chafing the calm. Down in the paddock the stallion
grazed quietly, a paradox to the last three hours.

You're history, horse.

Mentally, Michael cursed. Months ago when Tom Bings
had offered to buy the animal, he should have sold it. But
in those days following Leigh's death...parting with anything bearing Leigh's personal imprint seemed profane. Unlike the dairy, which had been a family venture, Soldat had
been her horse.

First thing Monday he'd give Bings a call.

A sound—gravel underfoot—brought Michael's head

around. Shanna came up beside him, her bluebell eyes solemn and questioning.

For a long moment they stared at each other. He kept his hands secured. Finally, she looked across the garden to the pasture and said, "You were wonderful with her. Calm, collected. You knew what you were doing. She told me you held her hand the whole time, even for the X rays."

"Roche did it all."

She faced him. "No, Mike, you did. Stop selling yourself short. You're a great doctor. I'd put my life in your hands."

Her words sent an arrow to his heart. "Let's hope that's never a possibility." He looked down the slope at the horse. "Do you understand now why this place has to sell?"

"Scary things can happen anywhere. Even on the quietest city street." *Even in Seattle,* her eyes said.

"Farms have one of the highest accident and injury stats going. I want Jen to have a safe childhood."

"No place will guarantee that."

"Still, I want to put the odds in her favor. Getting out of here will improve her chances."

For a moment she was silent. "Is that how you felt when Leigh was raising her? Did you worry about Jenni's safety then?"

Touché. She never did pull punches, this woman. *His woman.*

Shrugging off his frustration he said, "I couldn't very well tell my sister where to raise her child."

"No, but I'd say she was still afraid."

"Afraid?" He laughed. "Not Leigh. She wasn't afraid of a damned thing. She'd face down the orneriest animal—"

"How about her own child?"

He stared. "She loved Jenni." *In her own way.*

"I agree."

"You agree." He snorted.

"Why was it Bob who read her stories, Mike? Why didn't

Leigh tuck her child in at night? Why did she stand in that doorway?''

"Stop dramatizing."

"Stop avoiding the truth." Her eyes flashed anger. "My guess is Leigh had the same fear you do. I think she *drilled* it into both of you when your parents died. Don't love too much because loving means losing. So, she went her way, you went yours."

He took a step back. She'd ripped his heart wide open. "You know nothing about Leigh," he said softly.

"Probably not. But I do know Jenni needs you more than ever. Especially to love her as a parent."

"She's my niece." His jaw hurt. "Not my kid."

"You're wrong. She's your family. *Yours*. Whether you admit it or not you are a father at heart."

His heart felt pulverized. "She's Leigh's daughter." Sweat gathered along his spine, under his arms. Was she right? He focused on the stallion. On danger. It was easier that way.

"She'll always have memories of her mother," Shanna went on as if he weren't drowning in his own stench. "But it's you she sees now. You're flesh, Mike—real. She can touch you."

Touch him? Trouble was, they both touched him. Straight and deep, heart and soul. He was crazy about the tyke, justifiably crazy. And, Shanna...

Don't even go there.

He raked at his hair.

Shanna touched his arm. Her eyes were kind. "Let it go, Doc. Let go and forgive Leigh for dying. Let yourself heal. That little girl needs you. Don't turn away from what's in your heart."

Somewhere deep inside his lifelong vow crumbled like rocks off a cliff. He stiffened, afraid. Terrified. *Damn her.*

Not only had she battered his heart, now she wanted it out in the bright light.

Determined, he reached down for the frayed embitterment he'd nurtured since his parents left him orphaned. He breathed hard. *The stallion's rearing hooves.* What if *he'd* been killed? Where would Jenni be then? He was all she had left. Not a parent. A guardian uncle. But he hadn't guarded her. He hadn't kept his promise to Leigh. Did Shanna not fathom that?

"Don't tell me how I feel," he said coldly. "You know nothing about me. Or Leigh, or Jenni."

Tears in her eyes, she shook her head.

Stubbornly, he continued, "Jen is my responsibility, not yours. I'll do what I deem right, and if that means selling and moving to Seattle for an easier life all around, so be it. You don't have to come along. You don't have to do anything. Go back to Blue Springs, find someone who *can* give you what you want. Leave me be. Leave *us* be."

Her mouth sucked in a hiss of air.

He forged on. Destroying them both. Somehow powerless to stop. "People get hurt. They even die. It happens every minute. Kids get left behind for someone else to raise." His anger and sorrow were tactile enough to scrape. "Your mother was no different." Shanna clamped a fist over her mouth. Still he couldn't stop. "So don't tell me what to do or how to feel. *You*," he pointed a finger, "you of all people should know better."

Chewing her lip, she stood motionless. Damn the woman! Strumming his emotions to her tune.

Singing his weakness.

He stalked back to the house.

Aw, hell, man. She's what makes your sun shine and your heart beat. She's why you whistle as you're shaving and why you race home every night. Admit it. She's your mainline to happiness. To life!

On the porch, he glanced over his shoulder. She hadn't moved. Her gaze branded his soul.

His mouth opened. *Forgive me.* The stubborn words caught behind his tongue—and he knew in those few seconds their relationship was over.

A cooling night wind whipped her coat as she loaded the last box of her personal effects into the bed of the Chevy. It was done, the fantasy. Mike was a man incapable of resolving his bitter fears, of accepting love, of fighting his irrational demons.

She had to believe that or go crazy.

God, she was tired. Tired of crying, of thinking, of her heart hanging battered in her chest.

The farmhouse was dark. He had gone to bed without a second's thought. Just as well. She was terrible at goodbyes.

Climbing into her pickup, she shoved into gear and rolled down Rowan Dairy's lane for the last time—and out of his life.

Chapter Fourteen

An early November sleet fell outside the Lassers' kitchen window. Had the weather been more promising, she might have gone for a walk through the backwoods, but the rain came at dawn and remained until after lunch.

She'd been at her childhood home nearly nine weeks. Hiding. Wallowing in self-pity for the might-have-beens of her life.

Time to get your world back in order, Shanna-girl.

She surveyed the garden where delphiniums, hollyhocks and roses, defeated by frost-filled nights, poked from the earth in brown stalks, while pansies and asters kept their delighted faces to the icy rain. Since she was fifteen, arriving here with her brother in tow—and her father, hat in hand, begging for a job—Shanna had loved Estelle's garden.

Someday, Shanna vowed, she would have blooms cluttering a yard and twining around a white-railed porch. The pain of that thought cut to the quick. White-railed porches, calico cats and sugar cookies.

Sweet memories of one small child.

An overload of regret for one stubborn man.

"Nothing's a hundred percent absolute," the obstetrician had said when Shanna made the appointment after the home test confirmed her suspicions. Well, one thing *was* absolute. She may not have Mike, but she'd have his child. Her private blessing.

She turned from the window. Estelle Lasser—her *real* mother—smoothed brownie batter into a pan.

"You okay, honey?" the older woman asked.

"Just a bit tired."

"In your condition that's to be expected. Sit down and I'll brew us a pot of mint tea. Might even get in a nibble or two before that old man of mine comes in from the barns and starts piggin' out." She pulled a second pan from the oven. "Mmm. Smell that chocolate." Caleb loved his brownies.

Levering herself into a chair at the table, Shanna sighed. "I can't figure it. With Timmy I had so much energy. This one…it's like I've run a marathon twice over in the same day."

"Every baby is different, love." Estelle ran water into the kettle. "Mabel, down the road? Had eight and not a one acted alike in the womb. Psychologists say a kid develops its personality by six. I say it's there before the babe sees day."

Shanna grinned. "You're a wise woman, Mom."

"Not so wise. Just aged." Setting two mugs on the table, she took the chair at a right angle from Shanna and gently stroked her hand. "It's not my place to say anything, honey, seeing's I'm not really your mama but—"

"You're the only mother I have." Shanna laid Estelle's callused palm against her cheek. "The only one."

"Same goes." The old woman's eyes glittered. "You and Jase…my daughter, my son."

They hugged hard. Estelle said, "Okay then. I'll lay my cards on the table." Her eyes were steady. "Honey, it's not good keeping the wee one a secret from its father. Down the road you'll get nothing but grief. Someday the child will want answers you'll have to give and then where will you be? You don't want that baby feeling its father had no rights."

Shanna looked into her cup. "I know," she whispered. "But Mike doesn't want children. I'm not sure he wouldn't hate me for getting pregnant."

"Shanna. Look at me, girl. He had a hand in this, too." Estelle's brows lifted above the rim of her glasses. "Right?"

"But he'd never in a million years expect—"

"What's done is done. How it happened is no longer the issue. That baby," she nodded toward Shanna's stomach, "should have a chance to know its daddy—regardless of how that daddy feels or what he's said in the past."

"I'm not subjecting my baby to rejection, Mom. I know what it's like." *It stings all your life.*

"Oh, honey. You don't know for sure that will happen. I'd bet this farm your doctor will mush out when he hears the news. The man has it in him somewhere, Shan. Otherwise you wouldn't have fallen so hard for him in the first place." Again, the jacked eyebrows and smile. "Am I right?"

Shanna shook her head. "Because of a baby? No thanks. I want him to choose me because he loves me."

"Some men have a hard time admitting what they feel. In the case of your man, it doesn't make him any less in love than you are. Saying those three little words out loud can be scary."

Was it any surprise Estelle pieced Michael together from the fragments she supplied? Years ago, she'd read Brent's self-centeredness with equal astuteness. Later, Wade's arrogance.

Estelle retrieved the whistling kettle and prepared the tea.

Outside the rain thickened to fat, wet flakes.

Shanna rose from the chair to return to the large square window, where she watched the flakes—one by one—shroud the earth. "Mike would never chance it," she murmured.

Estelle slipped an arm around Shanna. Side by side, they watched the snow. Early for a northwestern autumn, and not long to last. The afternoon promised a couple hours of sunshine.

Estelle said, "Give him a chance, dear. The baby—"

"Is mine." Shanna turned and buried her face in Estelle's warm neck. "Mom. She'll have you and Caleb and Jase, as well as me. Four people who'll love her to bits and spoil her rotten." *But not her daddy.*

The thought tore her beat-up heart.

Oh, Mike. What have we done?

Two months she'd been gone.

What made him think he could live without her? That he could come home to this big, empty farmhouse night after night and not find himself looking for a light in the window, a sign she was here waiting for him? That she might be sitting with another clump of Jenni's wilting posies at the table?

As it was, she was there in every room. Smiling at him over toast and jam. Kissing him over grilled steak. Holding a shivering little girl wakened by a nightmare. Hell, sometimes he caught her sunshiny-meadows scent tracking him floor to floor.

Scowling, he stooped to a low cupboard and hauled out a skillet. He was supposed to be making supper, for crying out loud, not losing it over a woman.

He glanced at the table. Jen, dressed in blue—like his mood, *like Shanna's eyes*—sat with her dark head bent over another drawing, fingers working crayons and pastels with furious decisiveness. Since Shanna left, the child hadn't picked up so much as a pencil stub. Tonight, for the first time, she had hauled out her shoe box of supplies. The fact that he'd removed the cast today might have something to do with it.

He wanted to ask, ''How's it feel to have a normal arm again, Jen, instead of the old lumpy one?'' But he was afraid she'd say, ''Nothing's normal without Shanna.''

And, she'd be right.

Their days had fallen into an empty rut: he'd take her to Gran's each day; pick her up at night; throw together a meal; read a bedtime story; tuck her in with a hug and a kiss.

In between, she'd talk to Tavia and Silly, or—while he read the *Journal Of Surgery*—cuddle in his lap, sucking her thumb. Shamelessly, he let her. Her comfort was his. On three occasions he took her for an ice-cream cone after work, but it wasn't the same as it had been the first time, and they both knew it.

Michael looked again at the child. Would tonight be a repeat of the others? Would she wake confused and in tears while he rocked her back to sleep in his arms?

God, it tore him apart, the tyke shaking against him, little arms wrapping around his neck, and her tiny voice sobbing into his collar, ''Wuh-when's Shanna c-coming home, Unc-Uncle M.? Wuh-when? I muh-miss her.''

Once, he'd tried explaining that Shanna had her own life. Jenni simply looked at him and said, ''But she belongs with us. Why's she wanna be someplace else?''

He should have told her then, *''Because I chased her away.''* Instead, he'd kept his mouth shut. He was a coward. King-size.

He dumped egg noodles into the pan and covered them

with water. Somehow, he had to hoist Jenni out of this melancholy.

Find Shanna. Beg her to come back.

After the cruel things he'd said? Fat chance. She'd meet him with a sawed-off shotgun.

Hell.

His life, a balance scale of Yesterdays and Todays.

The Todays, a stream of sad, quiet hours for Jen and himself. The Yesterdays—ah, with Shanna how he'd enjoyed work *and* coming home. Jen had giggled, laughed, chattered. This house, *this home,* had changed under Shanna's touch. Her gift had been packaged with song and flowers, and the belief that maybe, just maybe, they could reach for the stars and be a family.

And he'd let her go.

"What are you making for supper, Uncle M.?"

Jen stared at him warily. Was it a wonder? He held the knife like a scalpel and his lips were slammed together.

He worked up a smile. "Ham casserole."

"The way Shanna makes it?"

For a second, air staggered in his lungs. "You bet."

"She puts onions and red peppers in it."

The grin came naturally now. "And mushrooms." He remembered.

Jen nodded, thumping against the chair leg with one untied sneaker. A long lace dragged and clicked on the floor. "You gonna make a salad with tons of those little orange slices?"

"I'll give it my best shot, tyke. But I'm not good at making salads." That had been Shanna's domain.

"S'okay," Jen said, her long-lashed eyes serious. "I like your cooking, too."

Her words pinched his heart.

Michael diced the last of the meat. By Christmas they'd

be settled in a new place. She'd have a fistful of new friends and Shanna would be a blurry memory.

Right.

Face it, Rowan. You don't want Seattle anymore.

Maybe he never had. Shipping Soldat to Tom Bings two days after the stallion broke Jen's arm was a necessary solution to a drastic situation. Marketing the farm had been Michael's compensation. For Leigh.

Except, nothing could compensate for his sister.

She was forever gone.

But her daughter lived. Jen, sweet little Jen, breathed, smiled, told jokes.

Here. In this house. On this land.

Jen, with her courage, hadn't needed to escape or relocate. She advanced day by day, braving nightmares, sorrow, and loneliness. She anticipated each morning and moved forward.

Like Shanna who, at twelve, faced the world for her brother.

Not unlike Leigh when they were kids.

His pulse rate kicked hard and fast. Moving forward. An excursion of the soul.

He looked around the cozy kitchen, familiar to him all his life: the ancient pine cupboards, the scarred wooden spice rack, the herb plants in the greenhouse window. And then he visualized a kitchen with cold-swept architectural lines.

Where Jen would cry for Amy, for Katherine, for Shanna.

Where *she* would never cook or sing or shoot him sweet, snuggle-with-me glances.

Where, out back, a rising stand of evergreens with its hidden path to a certain knoll wouldn't exist....

Michael jerked away from the window. If he lived to be a hundred he'd never take that trail again. Not without her.

The whispering swish of pencil tugged his attention.

Jenni, head bent, tongue peeking from the corner of her mouth, shaded cerulean around a slim white cloud. His throat hurt. *"She's your family,"* Shanna had said. *"You are a father at heart."*

Six words that shook his soul. And leaked from his eyes. *Aw, Shanna. You were right. I was blind.*

He laid down the knife. The meat could wait. His beloved little girl needed him now. He went to the table and squatted at the child's chair. "How was school today?" She'd been thrilled to begin second grade.

"Fine."

"Just fine?" He fought the urge to reach out and hug her. "Nothing important happened?"

"No."

"Mm. What're you drawing?"

"A picture."

"Of what?"

"Us."

"Yeah?" He craned his head for a better glimpse. Man, woman, child. "Want to tell me about it?"

Jen shook her head.

Michael edged closer and stroked her hair. "Why not, peanut?"

"'Cause." She swiped her nose. "It's not true, anyway."

"How so?"

"Shanna's not here."

He rotated the paper in his direction. "This her?" he asked, pointing to the figure with scruffy brown hair sitting on what appeared to be the verandah steps, guitar in her lap.

Jen nodded.

For several moments they looked, lost in the drawing. A man—him, presumably—sat next to Shanna with his arm around her shoulders. The child, Jen, crouched at their feet, rocking a doll. On the railing sat bright red flowers and a mottled colored cat, licking its paw. The house took up most of the background. In the upper right corner were two slim clouds with angel faces peeping out.

As in previous drawings, this one depicted an astounding talent. His pride skyrocketed while he studied details such as ears, fingers, leaves and petals.

Jenni touched the Shanna figure. "Why doesn't Shanna love us no more, Uncle M.?"

Love us.

"Why, Uncle Michael?" Her eyes swam. "I miss her. When can I see her again?"

He couldn't take it. Rising, he picked Jenni up off the chair and cradled her in his lap. "Soon, honey," he murmured against her soft, lemon-scented curls. Her tiny hands cradled his neck. He closed his eyes and swallowed hard. "You're going to see Shanna real soon. I promise."

If it meant pleading, begging—*praying.* He'd get her back.

Back where she belonged.

Where they all belonged, dammit.

Here. *Back home.*

Jen's damp face crowded into his neck. In a tiny, teary voice, she said, "Knock-knock, Uncle M."

His own eyes filled. "Who's there, sweetheart?"

"Canoe."

"Canoe who?"

"Canoe guess how much I love you?"

Sunset rays spearing off black gloss caught her eye and had her looking toward the lane where a Jeep Cherokee emerged.

Mike. A thousand memories.

He'd found her.

What did he want? Had he heard of the pregnancy? Had Estelle—against her wishes—called him? Had Caleb? And how was she to deal with his anger and rejection when they came?

The truck curved in front of the house and stopped beside her tired pickup. Max, the Lassers' border collie, let out a couple of yaps and ran toward the vehicle.

In the open doors of the birthing barn Shanna moved around the rump of the pregnant, doe-eyed Holstein she was checking and stepped into the corridor, shutting the gate behind her.

Michael climbed from the truck. The door slammed like a gunshot. Her heart slowed; her breath thickened. She could feel those gray eyes pinning and seizing her across the distance of the dusk-shadowed yard. Then, he strode toward her.

Should she duck among the cattle? Hide behind the milk tanks? She should have gone with Estelle and Caleb into town. Wiping her hands on her cords, she stood rooted beside the free stall. Waiting for his approach in an unfamiliar brown leather bomber and gray fleece.

She tried not to think of how incongruent they were—as usual. Her, tired and grungy in a flannel work shirt flapping at her hips with her hair in a haphazard ponytail. Him...chic, classy...incredibly dear.

He stopped within arm's reach. "Hi."

Hearing his deep, very-missed voice she nearly buckled.

"Mike." Slowly, with a synthetic indifference, she tucked her wind-roughened hands beneath her arms. She hoped the movement would lessen the chance of reaching out and touching him. "A little out of your neck of the woods, aren't you?" At least another twenty-five miles *farther* from Seattle.

"Jason told me you were here."

"Well, then. I'll have to whip his butt, won't I?"

A corner of his mouth went up. "No need. I threatened to dismantle his Harley."

She bit off a smile. This closeness brought the scent of leather and fresh-shaved skin into her space. Those eyes, dark as a winter's night, bored into her soul. "What is it you want?"

"We need to talk."

A sudden fear. "Is it Jenni? Has something happened to her?"

"Jen's fine. She's with Katherine. Look, Shanna—" She saw his unsteady fingers before he rubbed his neck. "I...I came to ask you back—to the farm. I'm not selling. And I've given up the offer in Seattle. Roche and I are scouting for a third doctor, another surgeon. We've already got a couple applications." A step and he was there, hands on her upper arms. "I want you in my life. Both Jen and I do. We need you. I'm sorry," he whispered. "So damned sorry for what I said. It was cruel and it hurt you, and I'll never forgive myself for that, but, please, let me make it up to you. Give me a year, five, sixty. Doesn't matter. I'll do anything. Just come back. Please."

For five long seconds she stared at him. She stepped out of his hold and hugged her waist. Where the baby lay.

"What are you really asking, Mike?"

"That I want to marry you, make a home for us, raise Jen like our daughter."

A home. Jen as her own, *their* own. So perfect, so right. He hadn't said he loved her.

Would he ever? And could she live with that kind of emotional dissonance? Lover but not beloved? Her marriage to Wade had ended because he'd scuttled under sheets besides hers. Lust not love.

From his coat pocket, Michael withdrew a sheet of paper. It trembled between his fingers. "This...is for you from Jen. It's how she sees us."

Shanna unfolded the drawing. *My New Family*. Jenni's printing. In the picture, Shanna saw herself gathered under

Mike's arm on the front steps of the Rowan farmhouse, strumming her guitar. Jenni cuddling Octavia on the bench. Silly, eyes shut, washing a clawed paw. Kate knitted in the rocker. Flowers and vegetables grew up the sides of the steps, across the railing of the verandah.

Shanna's vision fogged. Angels, Bob and Leigh, slept at last. Peacefully in the clouds. *Oh, Jenni. Your wish is mine. But I won't go into a marriage again without love.*

She handed back the sketch. "Tell Jenni, thank you, but I can't accept this."

She turned into the barn. The cows needed a clean bed of straw.

Michael caught her hand. "What do you mean you can't accept? I'm asking you to build a future with me, to raise Jen with me. The Holsteins are gone, Shanna. The barn's being renovated into a riding arena." His palm was warm on her cheek…so warm. "Tom Bings took Soldat and is willing to exchange five fillies for him. Not Arabians, but Appaloosa lineage. All you need to do is pick them. You'll have your horses, honey, to train and show and whatever else. I'm keeping the farm, hear? I want us to live on it, raise horses and a little girl who needs you like crazy." His mouth wavered into a smile. "Let's go miles past those nine yards."

Tears burned her eyes. He was offering her her lifelong dreams on a platter. The country house, the horses, the child. Him. All of it, down to the cat on the railing. She thought of the baby in her womb. Under her heart. If he knew, what then?

"What about other children, Mike?"

"If they happen I'll love them like Jen." His thumb touched her chin. "I hope they happen," he whispered.

She pressed the slight round of her stomach. "One has."

Silence. In the stall, the Holstein groaned as she lay down. Michael stared at Shanna's middle. "You're pregnant?"

"Yes." One word. A commitment for life. She watched his Adam's apple bob.

"You—" He cleared his throat. "You weren't going to tell me, were you? Not before—"

"No."

His eyes went black. "Guess I had that coming."

Her chin hiked. "You didn't want children. Ever."

She hadn't believed silence could ring.

"God." A gut-deep breath. A lingering look at her waist. He trailed up, searching her face. "How far along?"

"Two months, three weeks." Clinical gestational analysis. "Under the tree on the hill."

Where heartache and heartbreak had melded.

Where they hadn't used a condom.

He stood very still, shock in his eyes. His gaze shifted again to her midsection as if he could divine the life they'd created. She watched that tough chin yield, that handsome mouth bow a delayed smile. "Our...*baby?*"

"Yes."

One step and he had her wrapped in his arms. "Shanna." Against her forehead his throat worked. "Will you forgive me?"

His scent. It made her drunk. Escaping his hold, she searched his face. "There was never anything to forgive, Mike. But I still can't go with you."

"Why not?"

"Because marriage isn't just about making a home or having kids."

"I know that. It's a lifelong commitment."

She took a shovel from a hook. "I have work to do."

Say the words. Just, please, say the words.

"Shanna, wait."

She shook her head.

Say the words. A mantra. Hoping he could read her mind. She understood his past. She understood the reasons and his fear. All of it, she understood. And forgave. Still, she needed to hear the words if they were to venture into the unknown together.

She watched his mouth grow grim, and a part of her died. *Say the words.*

"If you think I'll let you raise my baby alone," air huffed from his nose, "you better do a double take. I won't allow it."

"You have no choice, Doc."

"Don't do this, Shanna. Let's talk this out."

"Everything's been said. Please. Just go."

"Babe, be reasonable."

Pinching her eyes shut, she dropped the shovel and covered her ears. *"Go!"*

He did.

Inside the dim, warm barn she wept and shook with cold.

Damn stubborn woman!

Five hundred yards down the road, Michael banged the steering wheel. How? *How* could she not believe he meant what he said? A thousand light years into the future and his decision would remain. His commitment was to her, to their child. Simple as that. He loved her. She loved him. Her ocean eyes said it in every look. Her hands in every touch. Her voice around his name.

So why her refusal?

For the tenth time, he clicked verbatim through their conversation. What had he said wrong? What had he missed?

Nothing.

Not nothing. Something. He felt it. But what?

Dammit, he hated all this mystery. If she'd been a man, he would've known right where he took a wrong turn. Women! What the hell was he supposed to do—read her mind?

Again he thought of the drawing, that precise moment

when she withdrew. Was it Jenni's dream? Her hope at becoming a family? That they loved her?

Love you, peach.

I love you, too, Shanna.

Me too, he thought that morning when she lay under the scourge of the migraine.

He slapped his forehead with the heel of his hand. *Idiot!* He'd never spoken the words.

But I thought them, Shanna. I thought them a thousand times while you waited for me to open my mouth.

Not good enough, fool. You missed the mark.

Jamming the brakes, he skidded the truck to a halt. In the time it took to turn the vehicle around, a full forty-five seconds in mud and gravel, he was grinning ear to ear. He wasn't leaving without her. She was his family.

She and Jen and the baby.

His baby.

Their baby.

Damned if he'd let three little words get in the way.

A pickup approached fast, its headlights swaying in the ruts. Michael recognized her battle-scarred Chevy. Pulling to the right, he stopped and jumped from the cab the instant she opened her door. Wiping a hand over his mouth, he erased the grin.

Halfway between the vehicles they met. Halfway was how it should be. Marriage, a meeting of two halves. Two halves making a family whole. He and Jenni; Shanna and the baby.

Mud clinging to his boots, he looked down at her. "I was a toddler when people smoked pot and called it flower power," he said, drowning in her Pacific eyes. "I never smoked, but there is power in flowers." Smiling, he curved a shaggy clump of hair behind her ear, where the dream-catchers swung. "Jen put one in your hair and I fell in love."

She blinked. "You did?"

"Yep. Got worse as the summer passed."

"Worse?" A little breathless. He liked that.

"Yeah. Got so bad I could barely sleep, never mind think. You had me hooked. Every second, every minute." He held her face between his hands. "When you left…"

Looking at her hurt.

She kissed his mouth and he pulled her close, nuzzling her mist-damp hair. "Ah, babe, I missed you so damn much. Work suffered. Jen suffered. Our lives… I felt I'd died. Do you have any idea how much I love you? Never, never leave me again, Shanna."

"Mike…"

"Shh." He kissed her cheeks where her tears lay. Kissed her mouth and lingered. When he lifted his head, her eyes were closed, her lips dreamy. He liked that, too. "Were you coming after me just now?" he asked against her forehead.

"Maybe. All right, yes." She laughed a little. "I was chasing you. I couldn't resist those mares you offered."

"That all?"

"Well, no." Her arms tightened around his neck. She kissed him again. Long and deep. When it was done, her face was the light in a dark tunnel. "Fact is I'm unequivocally and totally loopy over you."

It was easy to grin now. "That so? I know a place where we can get unequivocally and totally loopy together."

"Where?"

Slipping a hand between them, he laid his palm across her tummy. "Where this one was created," he whispered. "Home."

The joy in her blue eyes banished the last of his fears.

*   *   *   *   *

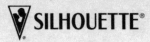

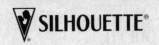
♥ SILHOUETTE®

0506/23b

SPECIAL EDITION™

ALL HE EVER WANTED
by Allison Leigh

Montana

When young Erik fell down a mine shaft, he was saved by brave and beautiful Faith Taylor. Faith was amazed by the feelings Erik's handsome father, Cameron, awoke. But was Cam ready to find a new happiness?

PLAYING WITH FIRE by Arlene James

Lucky in Love

Struggling hairstylist Valerie Blunt had a lot on her mind —well, mainly the infuriatingly attractive Fire Marshal Ian Keene. Ian set Valerie alight whenever he was near…

BECAUSE A HUSBAND IS FOREVER
by Marie Ferrarella

The Cameo

Talk show host Dakota Delaney agreed to allow bodyguard Ian Russell to shadow her. But she hadn't counted on the constant battling or that he would want to take hold of her safety—and her heart.

Don't miss out!
On sale from 19th May 2006

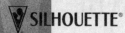

FREE

4 BOOKS AND A SURPRISE GIFT!

We would like to take this opportunity to thank you for reading this Silhouette® book by offering you the chance to take FOUR more specially selected titles from the Special Edition™ series absolutely FREE! We're also making this offer to introduce you to the benefits of the Reader Service™—

- ★ **FREE home delivery**
- ★ **FREE gifts and competitions**
- ★ **FREE monthly Newsletter**
- ★ **Books available before they're in the shops**
- ★ **Exclusive Reader Service offers**

Accepting these FREE books and gift places you under no obligation to buy; you may cancel at any time, even after receiving your free shipment. Simply complete your details below and return the entire page to the address below. You don't even need a stamp!

YES! Please send me 4 free Special Edition books and a surprise gift. I understand that unless you hear from me, I will receive 6 superb new titles every month for just £3.10 each, postage and packing free. I am under no obligation to purchase any books and may cancel my subscription at any time. The free books and gift will be mine to keep in any case.

E6ZEE

Ms/Mrs/Miss/Mr...Initials ....
BLOCK CAPITALS PLEASE

Surname ....

Address ....

....

....Postcode ....

Send this whole page to:

The Reader Service, FREEPOST CN81, Croydon, CR9 3WZ